To Love a Cowboy

Justice

RHIANNE AILE

Published by
Dreamspinner Press
4760 Preston Road
Suite 244-149
Frisco, TX 75034
http://www.dreamspinnerpress.com/

This is a work of fiction. Names, characters, places and incidents either are the product of the authors' imagination or are used fictitiously, and any resemblance to actual persons, living or dead, business establishments, events or locales is entirely coincidental.

ISBN: 978-0-9795048-8-4

Printed in the United States of America
First Edition
August, 2007

eBook edition available
eBook ISBN: 978-0-9795048-9-1

Acknowledgements

I have to start at the place where we all start – my mother. She taught me that I could do anything and to follow my dreams, however they might look.

My husband and children love me unconditionally, put up with my endless hours in front of the computer screen and late nights clacking away at the keyboard. I thank them for leaving me be and pulling me away. I need some of both.

Like any author, I had a turning point. I wrote something, put it out, expecting no one to read it, and held my breath. A wonderful woman responded, encouraged and became my writing partner as I matured into an author capable and willing to stand on my own. Without her wisdom, love and support, I'd never have written another word. Thank you, Jean.

Thank you to Mara and Stacy for giving *To Love a Cowboy* breath and bringing my cowboys to life. Our friendship means more to me than you could ever imagine. The original 'Cowboys at Sunset' picture was taken and graciously shared by Cameron Chapman.

For crossing my t's and dotting my i's, I owe many thanks to my comma goddesses, Donna 'Al', Jess and Renee, who saw me through multiple revisions and never once sent me a book on proper comma usage.

Last, but certainly not least, I owe an amazing debt to the group that screens my stories and keeps me sane, providing feedback, constructive criticism and general cheerleading. It has given me some of the best friends I have ever known.

So, Nancy, where to now?

To Love a Cowboy

Chapter One

PATRICK LASSITER rolled his shoulders, trying to dispel the tension that had been building in them all day. He was getting too old for this shit. The same work he'd done in his twenties without batting an eye was going to make him sore for days. Today, he'd been pulling barbed wire because one of his wranglers hadn't shown up. Striding into the barn, he skidded to a halt at the wanton sight that greeted him. A young man was leaning back on a stack of hay bales, shirt open, jeans around his knees. His eyes were closed, his fingers wound tightly into the hair of Patrick's missing wrangler.

Patrick's eyes slid from the long, dark, tousled curls over the well-defined olive chest and lower. All he could think was, 'Shit, Roan's back.'

Roan.

Roan Bucklin had shadowed his every step as a boy, turning into the young man who had haunted his every thought. Seven years ago, he'd left for college and Patrick had finally found some peace – peace that had just been shattered. Roan's soft panting competed with the wet smack of Adam's mouth as the younger man's cock slid between the wrangler's lips.

The foreman mentally shook himself. "What in the fucking hell do you two think you're doing?" Patrick yelled, snatching Adam up by the scruff of the neck and tossing him away from a disgruntled Roan.

Roan glared at the older cowboy. "I think I'm getting a blowjob, and it's really none of your busin—"

"It *is* my business because I pay that man to work." Patrick pointed at the lanky cowboy sprawled in the dirt. "Not to pleasure the boss's son. I'm the foreman of this ranch, not some uptown pimp, so pull your damn pants up and skedaddle, *kid*."

Dismissing the pouting brunette, he turned to Adam, matter-of-factly stating, "You! You're fired. Clear your gear out of the bunk house. If you're gone by sundown, you can come get your paycheck on Friday."

The wrangler glowered, but he didn't say anything. The first lesson you learned on the Bucklin Ranch was that you didn't argue with Patrick Lassiter. Adam was a full head taller than Patrick and had at least thirty pounds on him, but the foreman had thrown him around like a hay bale. Standing up with as much dignity as he could muster, he brushed the dust off his jeans, skipping the knees, which was too degrading, and headed for the door.

Patrick turned his back on the still half-naked vision of temptation, leaning sullenly in the exact same position he'd been found in, and marched towards his office. Biting the inside of his cheek – hard – he tried to regain some control of his rampaging libido. Fuck, the image of Roan sprawled on those hay bales could have been plucked from one of dozens of his fantasies, only it was always him pleasuring the younger man until he came completely undone screaming Patrick's name.

Like his thoughts had conjured Roan's voice, an angry shout came from behind the foreman. "Patrick!" The older man's steps faltered at the timing. "Wait just a fucking minute!"

Grabbing Patrick's arm, Roan tried to spin the foreman to a stop. "What in the hell do you think you're doing? You can't just waltz in here, throw Adam in the dirt, and then fire him. I'm not eighteen anymore. I was a perfectly willing participant."

Patrick clenched his teeth. He didn't need to be reminded that Roan was old enough to have as many lovers as he damn well pleased, and he *really* didn't need to be reminded of what had happened when Roan was eighteen. Just the thought of anyone else's hands on Roan was enough to make him see red. "That was obvious from the moaning," he snapped. "However, I can and *did* fire Adam. He works for me and, call me old-fashioned, I like my men to actually *work* while I'm paying them." Patrick started towards his office again.

Roan ran to get in front of him, placing a hand on the middle of Patrick's chest. His shirt was still unfastened down the front, completely baring his smooth, tan chest. He'd pulled his jeans up, but hadn't taken the time to fasten them. The open buttons displayed most of the narrow, dark trail of hair leading down from his navel, exposing the Thunderbird tattoo decorating his left hip and leaving no doubt that he was wearing nothing under the worn denim. "That's not fair. He gets fired when it was my idea."

Roan's confidence wavered under Patrick's intense stare. Growling, Patrick leaned towards the subject of his dreams and nightmares. "I can't fire *you!*"

Patrick stalked forward, causing Roan to retreat instinctively until his back collided with one of the horse stalls. They were about the same height, but something about Patrick's age and muscular build made him seem bigger... stronger... definitely more intimidating. Frankly, it was making Roan hard again. He'd had a crush on Patrick from the time he'd turned fourteen. He thought he'd gotten over it, grown up, moved on. Obviously he hadn't.

Patrick braced an arm against the stall to Roan's right. The younger man couldn't help but run his eyes up from the sun-bleached hair covering the defined forearm to the bicep and shoulder stretching the worn cotton shirt taut. He licked his lips unconsciously. A hitch in Patrick's breathing caused Roan's eyes to jump to the foreman's face. Raw lust burned so brightly in the ice blue eyes that a shiver traveled up Roan's spine. He blinked and the look was gone. Patrick's eyes were completely expressionless.

Shoving away from the wall, Patrick cursed, "Damn it to hell. Trust me, I wish I could." Spinning on his heel in the well-packed dirt, he was gone.

Roan slumped against the wall, his heart racing like a cornered rabbit. *Fuck!*

PATRICK purposefully worked through dinner, drawing out the weekly feed and supply order for a ridiculously long period of time. He also planned on taking it into town himself at the crack of dawn. If he were lucky, he'd manage to waste the whole day in town and miss dinner tomorrow night, too.

Exiting the barn, he glanced at the main house, seeing only two bedroom windows still illuminated. It made the dark house look eerily like a jack-o'-lantern. Scuffing his boots in the dirt, he shuffled his way across the yard to his log cabin, automatically avoiding the creaky first step of his porch by taking the steps two at a time.

He was just pulling the screen door open when he heard a low voice from the shadows at the far end of the porch. "I brought you some leftovers."

Patrick hung his head as his boss and best friend Finn Bucklin's voice dug at his conscience. "You didn't have to do that. If I was hungry, I'd've come up to the house."

"Bullshit. I couldn't have dragged you up to the house with a lasso and our best ropin' horse tonight. You plan on starving until he leaves or ya gonna take up cookin'?"

Patrick realized he was still standing half in and half out of his front door, hand on the knob. "Come on in. I'll pour us a drink."

The shadows shifted and a tall copper-haired man appeared in the beam coming from the yard light. Patrick hadn't left any lights on in the house, not expecting to return after dark. He waited until Finn grabbed hold of the screen. Turning the crystal knob, he entered the house, kicking lightly at the bottom corner of the door. It always stuck when the humidity was high.

"You should plane that out," Finn suggested, stepping onto the worn braided rug that covered the soft pine floor.

"I'll add it to the list," Patrick answered out of habit. They had exchanged the same words dozens of times before. The ritual was comforting. He used the cactus-shaped bootjack by the door to pull off his well-worn Ropers and left them sitting on a rubber mat inside the coat closet. Silently, he crossed to the buffet and poured two tumblers of scotch. He handed one to Finn, who had already seated himself in Patrick's favorite chair, before sitting in the corner of the large leather couch. Propping his feet on the low oak table, he rested the glass on his stomach and stared into the empty stone fireplace.

"Why didn't you tell me he was coming home?" Patrick finally asked.

Finn took a sip of his scotch, pursing his lips like he was thinking about how to answer. "Wasn't any sense getting you all worked up over it, and quite frankly, I was afraid you'd consider leaving. It was time for him to come home, Patrick. He's finished his degree, played foreman at that city slicker dude ranch down in Galveston and left a swath of broken hearts across the Southwest, big even by Texas standards. He needs to settle down, and he can only do that here."

"I know you're happy to see him."

"And I know deep inside you are, too," Finn replied.

Patrick reflected on that for a moment. Was he happy that Roan was home? The young man had been the bane of his existence from the moment he came to live on the ranch when he was ten. At first, he was like a curious puppy, dogging his every step, an accident waiting to happen, but the kid had caught on fast.

A natural rider, he had a way with all the animals and wasn't afraid of hard work.

Somewhere around fifteen, Roan had actually become an asset to the ranch. When he wasn't at school, he worked with Finn and Patrick from sunup to sundown. Smiling at the memory, Patrick nodded slowly. "Yeah, I'm happy to have him home. He belongs here. It's his home, too. I'm just not sure we can *both* live here, Finn," Patrick admitted honestly.

Finn owned Bucklin Ranch and was Roan's father, but he was also Patrick's best friend. He knew every detail of the history between Patrick and Roan, except for this afternoon's episode, but that was only because Patrick hadn't seen him before now.

"Patrick, you are so full of shit. You and I started this ranch, side by side. The only difference between us was the inheritance that allowed me to buy this patch of dust. Now, I've given up arguing with you about the ridiculous habit you have of referring to yourself as foreman and calling me 'boss', but I draw the line at you leaving for any reason, including my son. You own forty-five percent of this ranch, and ironically, the only reason you don't own fifty is because you gave five percent to Roan as a graduation gift." Finn leaned forward, setting his empty glass on the table.

Patrick chuckled. "Yeah, that was one of my better ideas."

"You think so?" Finn scoffed. "I'd say it was right up there with swapping with Conner when he pulled Deadly Diego up in Cheyenne. Bulls never were your strongest event."

Patrick shrugged. He'd spent eight weeks in the hospital and several more sweating through physical therapy after that stunt.

"Patrick, I didn't know I'd left a son back in London until Susan wrote me three months before he showed up. You and Roan are the only two people on this Earth who matter to me. I've been your friend - your brother - for more years than I've known he was alive. Don't make me choose between you. It would break my heart."

Patrick looked directly into the washed out, blue-green eyes of the only family he had. "I promise, Finn. I'm not going anywhere. We'll work this out." Silently he added, 'I'm not sure how, but we'll work this out.'

The older man nodded solemnly, knowing Patrick's word was stronger than any legal contract. He stood slowly, placing a fist in his lower back to push out the kinks and reminding both of them that he wasn't as young as he used to be. "I'll see you at dinner tomorrow," he said in a tone that brooked no argument. "And heat up that plate." He pointed to the foil-wrapped circle on the table.

Patrick shook his head in resignation. One of these days he'd win an argument with the crafty old Irishman, but it would probably be after Finn was dead and buried; although, if he could figure out how, he'd argue back from the grave. He walked Finn to the door before picking up the plate and putting it in the refrigerator next to the six pack of beer, bottle of ketchup, and jar of pickles. Heading upstairs, he showered and fell into bed. First light came earlier every year.

THE sun was clearing the tops of the trees when Patrick pulled into Fredericksburg. He was running a good two hours behind his planned schedule. He'd slept past sunup by a good hour, something he hadn't done in twenty years. It might've had something to do with not falling asleep until almost four.

He had quickly checked to make sure the horses had all been turned out before grabbing the checkbook from the safe and heading into town. Given his late arrival at the barn this morning, he avoided the teasing from his hands as much a chance meeting with Roan. Patrick did his best to convince the men who worked for him that he was one step beneath God. They wouldn't miss a chance to rib him for oversleeping.

Slamming the door of the pickup, he gave it an additional shove with his hip to get it to close completely. Like all the doors in his life, this one could use a little work. If he were the superstitious sort, he'd be wondering what that meant. Raising a hand in greeting, he hollered across the street to the chess-and-checkers contingent already solving the world's problems in front of Harold's General Store. "Hey, boys! Wives chase you out of the house already?"

There was a barrage of lewd retorts that Patrick acknowledged with a grin and a salute as he headed into the feed store. The cool air felt good. Today was shaping up to be a real scorcher. If they didn't get some rain soon, they were going to have to supplement with hay this summer, which would put them low for next winter. He made a mental note to call Jeb Riley. Jeb always baled more than he needed and usually had some to sell and, with a new baby on the way, could probably use the cash.

George walked out from the back of the store at the sound of the bell. "Patrick, what brings you to town?" The man looked genuinely shocked.

"Hell, George, I *do* come to town occasionally," Patrick defended.

George grinned and reached out his hand to clasp Patrick's. "Not unless you have to. What can I do for you today?"

Patrick ruefully admitted the truth to that statement; most of what he needed was right there on the ranch. Right this second, though, there was someone there he needed so much it had sent him scurrying to town. "I brought in next month's order. I needed to get some other things, so I thought I'd save Finn the trip."

George accepted the offered form, laying it next to the register. "Good, so whatcha need today?"

Shit. This is why I don't lie, Patrick thought. One always leads to another. "Well, I need some leather to repair a set of reins and could probably use a new set of hardware, too." He'd noticed the last time he went over Roan's tack that there were a couple of places nearly worn through. Hadn't been any reason to repair them at the time, since Roan wasn't around, but having Finn's son take a fall because his tack failed when Patrick could have prevented it wasn't 'getting along', and he had promised.

George nodded and moved about the store to collect the random objects Patrick requested.

His purchase was tallied and he was writing the check when George's daughter, Stacy, flew into the room. Coming to a sliding halt, she pushed back her hair and tried to appear calm. "Patrick! Surprise, surprise. Gwen said she thought she saw your truck."

Patrick looked at the girl suspiciously. As he recalled, she had been in the class behind Roan and had never taken an interest in the foreman's whereabouts before. "And here I am," he responded drolly, waiting for the true reason for her interest to be revealed.

"So some folks at The Red Dog last night were talking about Roan being back home. Any truth to that?" she asked, attempting to sound casual and failing miserably.

George rolled his eyes at Patrick, and the two older men shared a knowing smile. Patrick handed the check over to the storekeeper. "Roan got back day before yesterday. I'm sure it won't be long before he'll be out dancing at The Red Dog. You could always call up to the house. I'm sure he'd be delighted to renew his old friendships."

The young girl blushed a charming shade of pink, and Patrick almost felt like he should warn her – 'You know he's into men, right?' – but he kept his mouth shut. Roan's social life was not his problem.

"Tell Roan I asked after him," she requested.

Patrick nodded. Gathering up his purchases, he pushed his way into the sunshine, giving his eyes a minute to adjust to the light as he looked left and right, wondering where he could go to extend his trip. Nobody would begrudge him a day off. He could just jump in his truck and head out to the lake for a day of fishing, but that smacked just a little too much of hiding, and he wasn't about to give Roan the satisfaction. What he needed was a couple more errands that could reasonably be construed as 'necessary'.

His eye caught on a rotating red and white pole. "Haircut," he announced to the empty sidewalk, starting across the street. He dropped his parcels in the back of the truck as he passed and jogged slightly to clear the road when Johnny beeped at him from the mail truck.

This door made an electronic chime as he pushed it open. Six pairs of eyes turned to watch his entrance. Greetings ranging from "Patrick!" to "Hear Finn's boy is back" filled the room. Maybe being in town wasn't such a good idea after all, if he was going to have to spend the day fielding questions about Roan.

After two stores and the diner, Patrick'd had enough. You'd think that Roan's return was front-page news. Glancing up from the sidewalk, he spotted Henry eyeing him hungrily from the front window of the newspaper office. Hell, maybe it was. Reaching in his open window to grab the lever to open the pickup's door, Patrick pretended not to hear the older man hailing him as he slipped onto the seat and cranked the ignition. The rumbling of the engine concealed any further shouts as he backed up and headed out of town.

Even taking the long way home, he pulled into the yard just slightly after three. Still a lot of daylight hours left before he could retreat to his cabin. Snagging the tops of the bags out of the back, he headed into the barn, habitually checking the paddock for horses to know which of the men were working away and who would be around. Both of the horses Roan preferred to use were on the far side of the field, munching on the longer grass by the fence. A quick glance towards the main house told him Roan's truck was parked under the sycamore. Damn.

Putting up his purchases as he went, Patrick entered his office, kicking the door closed behind him. The door swung about halfway and stuck. With a curse, he kicked at it again, wedging it firmly against the uneven floor. Fuck, that's what he got trying to close a door that hadn't been shut in at least ten years. Leaving it jammed, he sat behind his desk, pouring out the tools he needed to fix Roan's tack. Working with his hands always calmed him down.

SEVERAL hours later, Patrick pulled off his leather gloves and sucked on his sore thumb. Preoccupied men should not be allowed to work with sharp objects, he decided. A sound from the main barn caused him to sweep his project into a box and kick it underneath his desk. Glancing at the clock, he realized it was dinnertime and the men would be heading in.

The not-so-subtle clearing of a throat raised his eyes to the half-open door. Roan leaned his shoulder against the doorframe, cockily hooking his thumb in his front belt loop, pulling his obscenely low-riding leather pants even lower. There was a large strip of sun-kissed skin visible between the tight, almost see-through T-shirt and the pants. One black boot was planted in the dirt and the other scuffed back and forth, causing small swirls of dust. "I'm headed to town to meet Adam. It's Friday. I thought I'd take him his check… save him a trip."

Patrick scowled but flipped the book he'd been pretending to write in closed. Sliding open the top drawer, he pulled out a white envelope. Laying it on the polished wood, he flicked it towards Roan, who folded it in half and slid it into his back pocket, the pressure causing the pants to dip dangerously lower.

"He's promised to make it up to me… our aborted encounter," Roan explained unnecessarily. Patrick wasn't likely to forget anytime soon.

"Hmm…," he answered noncommittally, hoping that Roan would just disappear before he did something he couldn't take back.

Pushing away from the door, Roan prowled towards the desk, walking around to the side Patrick was on and propping his hip against the edge. "I'm horny as hell. I've been walking around half-hard for the last day and a half, and it's all your fault."

Patrick's mind raced. Did Roan mean that Patrick made him hard, or that he'd been hard because Patrick had interrupted him and Adam before he'd come? Either way, it was a dangerous line of thinking. There was no way to keep his cool while thinking about Roan being hard… making Roan hard… or better yet, making him come. Patrick pressed his eyes shut and groaned, silently praying that Roan would be gone when he opened his eyes.

No such luck. Patrick raised his eyelids to find Roan's eyes sparkling brightly and entirely too close. "Uhm… don't you need to go? Wouldn't want to keep your date waiting."

"He's not a date. I've heard that he's a good fuck, and I…." Roan shrugged.

Patrick snorted, "Who told you that?"

"Well…," Roan hedged.

Standing, Patrick pinned the younger man with his gaze. "Roan, tell me Adam didn't tell you that himself." A crimson blush stained Roan's cheeks, answering the question for him. "Fucking hell, Roan. How naïve are you?"

"Well I—"

"Do you believe every cowboy trying to get into your pants?" Patrick looked down with a leer. "Not that there's room for anything in those pants but you. I'm not even sure there's room for you."

Roan shoved against Patrick's chest, stepping between him and the desk. "Hey! I happen to like these pants, and I think I look good in them. Just because you're a prude—"

"A prude?" Patrick leaned forward, pinning Roan back, a hand on either side, trapping him. His eyes darkened to stormy gray as his face drew nearer. He'd restrained almost every sexual impulse he'd had around Roan since the kid hit puberty, ignoring innuendos and ducking advances. A prude. A man could only take so much taunting and temptation without wanting to strike back – to reach out and take what was being offered.

Although pushing Patrick's buttons was one of his favorite pastimes, maybe, just maybe, it was possible to push Patrick too far, the younger man thought. Roan's voice cracked slightly, betraying his nervousness. "Yeah… uh… I'm confident in my sexuality, and I'm not afraid to show it in the way I dress."

Patrick shook his head slowly, his eyes locked on Roan's like a bobcat staring down a rabbit. He leaned forward, causing Roan to lean back at an awkward angle and feel physically as well as emotionally off-balance. "You're confused. The cock that parades through the chicken yard, chest puffed out and feathers ruffled, is the one that's trying to attract mates because he has none. A real man knows exactly what he can do and doesn't need to show off."

Patrick's eyes scanned down Roan's lithe body, pausing slightly to watch his lower stomach quiver like his gaze was a physical touch. "I can make you hard just by looking at you," he rasped.

Roan didn't bother to argue. The proof of Patrick's words was straining against the leather, and they could both see it.

Patrick drew closer, his lips a breath away from a kiss, a kiss he would never take. He'd held Roan in his arms and stroked him to completion, once before, but their lips had never touched. Patrick knew with certainty that he'd never survive the touch of Roan's lips under his.

Roan's eyes drifted closed, his lips parting to receive Patrick's instinctively.

For a second, the older man wavered, his lips drifting so close he could feel the wet warmth of Roan's breath. Roan swayed toward him and Patrick shifted, his lips riding the aura of Roan's body around to his ear. "I could make you come with just the right words."

Roan shivered, knowing without a doubt it was true.

"With every touch of my hand, you'd beg for more until you wouldn't even know what you were begging for... but I'd know. I'd know exactly where to touch you... how to touch you... how to love you." Patrick's lips grazed the sensitive skin of Roan's neck, and the young man whimpered.

Patrick straightened, keeping his body suspended over Roan's but not touching, the electricity pulsing between them. "*That* is sexual confidence, knowing that my touch could undo you in a way no other man's could. A man with that kind of confidence dresses in a regular shirt and blue jeans because he doesn't need sexy clothes."

Roan's eyes blinked open, trying to focus as he felt Patrick's presence retreat. The foreman was across the room, standing by the door. "I want…" Roan stuttered.

Patrick smiled. "I know, but I only said I could, not that I would. You enjoy your evening with Adam."

Roan's curses and the crashing sound of something being thrown followed Patrick out of the barn. He smiled smugly. Whatever Roan had broken was worth it. For the first time since the whelp had gotten home, Patrick felt like himself again.

Chapter Two

PATRICK combed his hair. Ruffling a hand through the still damp curls on his chest to dry them, he stared at the six shirts that hung in his closet. Bah, since when did he primp for a Saturday night at The Red Dog? Grabbing a medium blue chambray button-up, he swung it around his shoulders, fastening it quickly and shoving it into the tops of his best pair of jeans. He'd even taken the time after dinner to buff the dust off his boots. If he checked the sky, he was sure he'd find pigs circlin' in and out of the clouds, but he didn't want to examine his motivation too closely. Grabbing his hat and truck keys, he headed out the door. Enough beers to make him forget this week was exactly what he needed.

The beer had done the trick. Patrick had actually had a great time tonight, laughing and joking with everyone. He'd even taken Miss Rose for a spin around the dance floor before returning her to her 'girls'. Of course, every one of them had seen their eightieth birthday, but they were still girls. He'd actually felt like himself for the last – he checked his watch – damn, four hours. Rubbing the back of his neck, he rolled his shoulders, encouraging the last of the tension in his muscles to release and realizing how much he found himself doing that lately. Lifting his mug, he drained the last of the beer before heading out.

His eyes drifted towards the empty corridor leading to the men's room and then to the front door. Fuckin' luck. Roan strode through the door, looking like an ad for Wrangler western wear. It really ought to be illegal to look that good in clothes, Patrick thought. Of course, he looked even better out of them. Raising a hand to his suddenly aching head, he groaned, tipping up his beer and finding it empty. He turned back towards the bar, signaling Randy for another.

Roan plopped himself nonchalantly onto the bar stool next to Patrick with a pleased grin. "I found you! I thought you turned into a pumpkin if you stayed out past midnight. Aren't you usually in bed by ten every night?"

Not making eye contact, Patrick replied, "Not every night, no."

Roan ordered his own beer when Patrick's was delivered. Then he proceeded to steal a long draught off Patrick's before the foreman could even touch it.

Patrick warned himself not to look, but he couldn't seem to keep his eyes from following Roan's throat, moving up and down as he swallowed. Fu-uck, he needed out of here.

"Thanks, I was parched." The younger man grinned, setting the beer back on the bar, half gone.

Suddenly, a strong hand gripped Patrick's elbow. He smiled in relief without even turning around. "You can finish it," he offered, getting to his feet.

Roan looked between Patrick and the rugged blond man who had appeared at Patrick's side. He was roughly the same build and age as the foreman.

"You ready to go?" the blond asked, his voice like spun silk.

Patrick smiled, tipping his hat to Roan. "I reckon." Enjoying the stunned expression that had replaced the younger man's normally cocky visage, Patrick made the introduction, "Ty – Roan. Roan – Tyler."

Tyler smiled and placed a finger on the brim of his black Stetson. "Nice to meet you. You're old man Bucklin's kid."

Roan nodded, still unable to find his voice.

"Well, see you 'round." Tyler's hand slipped from Patrick's arm to hook around his waist as they walked across the saloon.

Roan gaped as they disappeared through the door.

Once they were out of earshot, Tyler leaned close to his date. "So that was Roan, was it?" His voice dripped with amusement.

"Yes," Patrick said, his voice clipped.

"Damn, the tension was so thick when I walked up, you coulda cut it with a knife. Nice ass though. You sure you wanna come home with me?" Tyler joked.

Patrick punched playfully at Tyler's shoulder. "Fucker. You've got a hell of an ass yourself, you know?"

Tyler shook his head ruefully. "Yeah, but it ain't nothin' like that one... and those eyes. Shit, Patrick, I don't know how you— "

"I know. I know," Patrick interrupted. "Just take me home and fuck me, Tyler. I'm not much in the mood for talking tonight."

Tyler grinned, stopping at the side of his truck and curling a hand around Patrick's neck, pulling him closer for a passionate kiss. "If you insist. Oh, the things I endure for you!"

The two men climbed up in Tyler's pickup. Patrick had left his truck at Tyler's, having every intention of drinking – possibly to excess. Neither man noticed the figure in the shadows of the eaves, watching them go.

Patrick laid his head back on the seat, watching the trees roll by. One of the things he loved about Tyler was his comfort with silence. Patrick only believed in talking when there was something to say, but some people found his long silences uncomfortable.

Tyler pulled into his driveway, parking next to Patrick's pickup. Walking side by side into the dark house, Tyler flipped on a lamp next to the couch. Looking back at Patrick still hovering in the foyer, he nodded towards the sliding glass doors. "Why don't you go out on the deck? I'll grab us a couple of beers."

Patrick hadn't even been aware that he was holding his breath until it rushed out in a relieved sigh. For the first time since he'd met the sexy blond, a part of him hadn't wanted to rush straight to the nearest bed. Walking into the still-cool evening air of late spring, Patrick leaned his hip against the railing and looked up at the dark sky. The stars weren't nearly as visible here as they were from his own front porch. Even a town as small as this one produced its share of light pollution. A cold bottle nudged his arm and he reached for it, smiling his thanks.

Tyler sat in one of the chairs and propped his legs on the chair opposite, stretched out and crossed at the ankles. "So, wanna talk about it?"

"Not really."

"There's obviously more going on, Patrick. The boy you described was an irritating kid, confused about his sexuality. The man I saw tonight was just that— a man— and he didn't look the least bit confused about what he wanted." Tyler raised the dark bottle to his lips and tipped his head back. When Patrick stayed silent, he continued, "You were right to stay away from him, let him grow up and explore, but he's come back. Have you asked him why?"

Patrick looked over at him, surprised. "No. I just assumed he'd come back 'cause it was home."

Tyler shrugged. "Not everyone comes back home. In fact, I'd say the vast majority stay away. Based on what I saw in Roan's face tonight, I'd say he's back because of you."

Patrick's gut tightened at the idea that Roan had come home for him. "If he came back for me, he has a funny way of showing it. The first sight I had of him, his cock was halfway down Adam's throat," he growled.

Tyler barked out a laugh at the possessive tone in Patrick's voice. "Well, it got your attention, didn't it?"

Patrick rolled his eyes. "He's still a baby. I'm a challenge, nothing more."

"If I was to believe that, and I don't, what would be the problem with bedding the kid? I certainly wouldn't throw a piece of ass like that out of my bed."

Eyes narrowed in a fierce glare, Patrick kicked Tyler's boots out of his chair and sat down. "Fuck you."

"Well, that *had* been the plan, but I'm thinking your mind is on someone else, and I don't feel like having you both in my bed tonight," Tyler mused. "So what would be the problem with sleeping the kid out of your system?"

"I can't... I'm just not... casual just wouldn't work," Patrick finally mumbled, staring at the beer in his hands.

"You and I have done casual for almost two years, so I guess it's just Roan you can't do casual with."

Patrick looked closely at Tyler's face, but didn't see a trace of hurt or anger. "You know what you mean to me, Ty."

"Yeah, I do, but soul mates we're not. Explosive sex and best friends— I've had worse relationships. In fact, I've married for less. Three times." The blond laughed. "But you don't have my track record. You've never tried for the happily ever after, and after seeing the way the two of you looked at each other tonight, I'd say it's because you've been waiting for your Prince Charming to grow up."

Patrick simply stared at his friend and lover, stunned at the words coming out of his mouth.

"I'm just calling it like I see it," Tyler offered, casually propping his legs in Patrick's lap as he took another pull off his beer.

Patrick swatted the boots out of his lap with a soft, "Fucker."

"Not tonight, I'm afraid. Go home, Patrick. Work this out. If something comes of it, I want to be best man at your wedding. If not, I'll be happy to go back to our *arrangement*." Tyler leaned forward and reached out, running his fingers down Patrick's chiseled cheek. "Give love a chance. I know I'm the poster boy for the triumph of hope over experience, but if you've got a chance at the fairy tale, you've got to go for it." Softly, he pressed his lips against Patrick's, pulling back almost immediately. "You okay to drive?"

Patrick nodded, standing. When Tyler got to his feet, he pulled him into a tight embrace, whispering into his neck, "I do love you, you know."

"Yeah, I do, but you have no idea what being 'in love' means. It can bring you to your knees and send you flying to the stars. We are entirely too comfortable to be 'in love'." Tyler kissed him again gently and pushed him towards the door.

PATRICK sat in the large bay window watching the first tendrils of pink tint the sky. Sleep had completely eluded him. He blew over the top of his most recent cup of coffee and wondered if the caffeine would get him through the day.

He should have been just stirring in Tyler's bed, thinking about whether to indulge in a little morning sex before starting his day, not sitting sore and stiff from watching the moon cross the sky. Tyler would have made him coffee, all the while complaining about his aversion to mornings. Patrick would have growled in return. Tyler was a morning person by nature. He was a morning person by necessity, but that didn't mean he had to like it. That was what was familiar, not this anxious knot that had taken up residence in his stomach. He didn't know if it was excitement or dread.

Tyler's words had raised some conflicted feelings in Patrick. It had been easy to discount Roan when he thought the younger man's motivation was making Patrick a conquest, taking revenge for the indiscretion that happened when he was eighteen. If there was even a possibility that Roan had true feelings for him, as Tyler seemed to think, that was a completely different problem, one that Patrick had been thinking about all night.

It didn't help that the spot that normally held Roan's truck had been empty when Patrick arrived home… and was still empty. Patrick didn't want to consider what Roan's reaction to his little show with Tyler might have been. If the boy had responded true to form, there were plenty of cowboys in that bar that would have been happy to take him home.

Shit.

Unbending his legs, he carried his mug to the sink. He'd be the first one in the barn today. Maybe he'd gain some insight if he got to work, preferably hard physical labor. Putting his back into a familiar task often let his mind work unhindered. Some of his best ideas had come while mucking out stalls. He chuckled to himself as he grabbed his hat off the hook by the door. 'Which is why Finn is always telling me my ideas are horse shit.'

PATRICK had been the first person in the barn that morning and the last one that evening to leave. He'd lost count of the number of times he'd glanced towards the sycamore, searching for Roan's truck. Where the fuck was the kid?

He paused slightly, trying to decide if it was too late to go up to the main house and rummage up some food. His stomach grumbled at the thought. Hell, he'd promised Finn that he wouldn't leave the ranch. He wouldn't last long if he kept skipping meals 'cause he was afraid of who he'd find in the kitchen. With a determined stride, he headed for the house.

He was standing next to the stove, sipping his umpteenth cup of coffee while his stew heated when Finn wandered in. "I wondered when your stomach would finally send you up here," he commented drolly.

Patrick ignored the taunt. "Think we'll get any rain out of the front headin' this way?"

Finn grinned, pulling a chair out from the table and settling in to keep Patrick company while he ate. "Only God knows. If He had intended me to be a weatherman, He'd've made me prettier."

Patrick snorted at the familiar line. Dishing up a bowl of stew, he took the seat across from the older man and started eating.

The silence stretched as Finn watched Patrick eat. "You gonna ask where he is?"

"Hadn't planned on it," Patrick mumbled around a mouthful of food.

"Well, that's good, 'cause I have no clue. Thought maybe you might know," the redhead suggested.

"Me? Why would I know?"

"Well, he got all spiffed up last night and said something about going out to find you." Finn looked pointedly at Patrick, an expectant look on his face.

Patrick took another bite. "He found me. I was at The Red Dog." He paused. "With Tyler."

"Ahh…." Finn sighed like a secret of the universe had been revealed to him. "How'd he take it?"

"Don't rightly know. We were leaving as he showed up. Maybe I ought to drive out there and talk to Randy. See if he knows anything," Patrick wondered out loud.

"Roan's a grown man."

"Yeah, but sometimes The Red Dog draws a rough element." Patrick got up and rinsed his bowl in the sink, propping it in the drainer to dry. With several efficient movements, he cleaned up everything he had used to prepare the food.

Finn watched him speculatively, realizing that Patrick had already made up his mind. "Fine with me, but if you find him, don't go tellin' him I sent you."

"Is it such a crime to be worried when someone disappears for twenty-four hours?"

"It is when you're a grown man and shouldn't need to account for your whereabouts to your dad." Finn stood, straightening the chairs around the table.

Patrick grunted, pulling his truck keys out of his pocket. Finn's soft voice stopped him as he reached the door. "If you find him, call me. Just 'cause I shouldn't worry, doesn't mean I don't," he explained sheepishly.

PATRICK pulled into The Red Dog parking lot, which was considerably emptier on a Sunday night than it had been the night before. Sitting in his truck, staring at the front door, he tried to talk himself out of going inside. "Just turn around, go home, and go to bed. This is none of your business."

"Fuck," he swore, turning off the truck and swinging his legs out of the door. He had just started to stand when the door to the saloon swung open and a familiar lanky shape came through it… draped all over a tall, well-muscled cowboy.

Patrick sat back down in the truck, pulling the door shut to kill the interior light. He tried telling himself again to go home. Roan was obviously just fine, and Patrick was a fool for worrying about him, but he couldn't force his eyes away from the stumbling pair, weaving their way across the parking lot. Their meandering path seemed to be caused more by the way they had their bodies wound around each other than the amount of alcohol they'd consumed.

Roan reached his truck under the canopy of trees at the edge of the parking lot. Leaning back against it, he pulled the tall, dark, and bulging body against him. Patrick made a sound suspiciously like a growl when their lips met and then cursed in the dark cab. He couldn't see where the guys hands were, but Roan's had made their way to the denim-clad ass currently grinding into him.

Patrick cursed again and was out of the truck and striding across the parking lot before he made a conscious decision to move. One hand circled the guy's bicep, swinging him around and away from Roan. The other hit the man squarely in the jaw before he even had a chance to catch his balance. If you followed the rodeo circuit, you learned how to fight or you spent a lot of time in the dust. Patrick prided himself that the only time he'd been knocked to the dust was by a bronc or a bull.

The guy looked up, shaking his head, his hand moving his jaw to see if it still worked. "I didn't break it," Patrick growled, "but I can if you'd like to try and get up. Since I turned forty, my lower back doesn't like it when I lift dead weight." As he spoke, he advanced menacingly. The guy scuttled backwards like a crab, finally getting to his feet and running for his truck, shooting Patrick anxious looks over his shoulder.

The 4x4 took off in a spray of gravel. Patrick watched it go, pleased with himself. It was nice to know he could still make a twenty-something cowboy turn tail and run.

"Bloody hell, Patrick, you've gotta quit riding to my rescue like a knight in shining armor! In case you haven't noticed, I'm trying very hard to get laid. I'm not a damsel in distress; although, I admit I'm in a good deal of distress right now. So grab your club and go play caveman somewhere else. I'm going to call my friend back here so we can finish what we started."

Something inside Patrick snapped. Spinning, he snatched Roan's phone out of his hand, sending it crashing into the side of his truck. "No, you fucking aren't," he ground out coolly, smashing his lips against Roan's brutally. Violently, he fucked Roan's mouth with his tongue, claiming him, attempting to wipe every trace of the stranger's kiss from his mind.

Roan whimpered softly, and Patrick clasped his hips with strong hands and pulled them together forcibly. Guiding Roan back and forth with his hands, Patrick brushed their enflamed cocks together until he was panting and Roan was crying out softly with each stroke.

Patrick snarled at the man trembling in his arms. "This is so fucked up."

Roan just looked him straight in the eye. "You're the one that has to have it this way. I want you. I'll admit it. I'd love for you to lay me down in your bed and make gentle love to me all night long, but I have to fucking piss you off to even get you to acknowledge me. The only three emotions you seem capable of are rage, jealousy, and lust."

Patrick's hands dropped limply to his sides. Roan was right. He couldn't do this in anger. Not again. Silently, he walked to his truck and drove into the dark night.

Roan sank to the ground, wrapped his arms around his bent legs, lowered his head to his knees, and slammed his fist into the gravel in frustration. "That was so *not* the reaction I was looking for," he muttered into the denim.

Pulling himself together, he got in his own truck and drove home. Standing on the steps to the house, he paused for a long time to stare at the log cabin. Maybe he should just go inside, strip down naked, and crawl into Patrick's bed. Force his hand, make him acknowledge that there was something powerful between them... always had been.

An amused voice broke the stillness. "Planning on standing in the yard all night? He stormed in about fifteen minutes ago. I doubt he's asleep if you have something to say to him."

Roan turned around and smiled guiltily. "Sorry, Dad. You don't still wait up for me, do you?"

"Nah, just up reading and came down to the kitchen for some water. I saw you standing out here, lookin' a little lost. Wanna talk about it?" Finn offered. He'd never been one to push, but if the two hardheaded fools weren't going to work this out on their own, he was gonna have an aneurysm. He'd always hated hospitals.

"Actually, I was wondering why Patrick built the cabin after years of living with you in the house."

"Ah, well, come inside and let's put some tea on. Some discussions go down easier with tea," Finn explained, taking Roan's arm gently with his large hand and steering him towards the house.

Both men remained silent as Finn efficiently put the kettle on. When the steaming mugs rested securely in their hands, he began, "You know your mother and I were only married a little over a year."

Roan nodded.

"I had no idea when we divorced and I moved out of the country that she was pregnant. Neither did she, to be fair. The first I heard of you was a letter that arrived here about three months before you arrived. It had been forwarded through a complicated series of hands to finally find me. I had pretty much severed all my ties with my family when I left Britain."

Roan nodded again. He had heard all this before, but didn't want to interrupt the flow of his dad's thoughts.

"Anyway, Patrick and I had established ourselves pretty well. Taking on another mouth to feed was no big deal, but the idea of being a parent scared the shit out of me." Finn grimaced at the admission. "I felt like I had no idea how to raise a son, so I decided to find me a wife. It seemed like the perfect solution. I'd have a wife to help me raise you, and you'd have a mother."

Roan chuckled softly at that. He could see his father expecting all the puzzle pieces to fall neatly into place, but life was never neat.

Finn continued, "Patrick tried to talk me out of it. Said we could raise you just fine and that I should marry for love, not some twisted sense of what made a family. I was never much good at listening, though. I'm much more of a figure it out by myself kind of person, so I started dating my way through Fredericksburg's eligible female population like a 'to do' list. It took me three weeks to find Amanda and four to marry her. Well, you know how that turned out."

"What exactly does this have to do with Patrick's cabin?" Roan asked, gently prodding his dad in the direction of his question.

"Well, Amanda moved in about a month before you arrived and started immediately in on me to move Patrick out. It didn't fit her idea of what a 'family' looked like. She thought we should have the house to ourselves. I wasn't about to do that. Patrick built every inch of this place beside me and had as much right to the house as I did, and I told her as much. Unfortunately when I said 'no', she turned to Patrick. He wasn't about to stay when he wasn't wanted."

Finn took a sip of his tea and chuckled, his eyes soft and unfocused, obviously lost in the memory. "I got her back though. We built Patrick the cabin, and I made sure it had every modern convenience this place doesn't. The master bath even has a Jacuzzi tub." He looked at Roan and smiled. "Yeah, that was probably the beginning of the end for me and Amanda."

Roan gathered the cups from the table, rinsing them in the sink. Cleaning up after himself was second nature. Everyone pulled their own weight or they didn't last on the ranch. Finn had put the milk and sugar away by the time he was done.

Wrapping his arms around his dad, Roan hugged him hard. Somewhere during his teens, their hugs had become squeezing competitions. It was tradition. Tonight after the pressure eased, Roan stayed put, enjoying the warmth of his dad's embrace. It had been a long time since he'd just been held. "Love you, Dad," he whispered against the cotton shirt.

"Love you, too. Now get to bed. You've got a day's worth of chores to catch up on in the morning."

Roan groaned but smiled all the way up the stairs. It was comforting to know that there were some things you could always count on.

Chapter Three

ONE of those things you could always count on was that the sun managed to rise at least an hour before you were ready to get up. Roan squinted at the golden light streaming in through the white lace curtains, a holdover from Amanda's time on the ranch. With a groan, he swung his legs out from under the warm quilt, hissing as his feet hit the cold wood floor. Getting up was like removing a Band-Aid— best done in one quick movement.

Wrapping his arms around his bare chest, he wished that he'd gone to bed in more than his boxers. Deciding against trying to find a shirt clean enough to put on, Roan made a mad dash for the bathroom and a hot, steaming shower.

Less than fifteen minutes later, he was standing in the kitchen pouring a cup of coffee. He'd found clean jeans and snagged a shirt from his dad's closet, but he was going to have to face the laundry room later that night.

"That shirt looks familiar," Finn drawled, walking in from outside.

"Yeah, well, it looks better than anything I could have found in my room this morning," Roan replied, pouring his father a cup of coffee and adding in three spoonfuls of sugar before passing it to him.

Finn shook his head. "You never did like laundry."

"I'd rather muck stalls," Roan agreed.

"Well, it's time to muck something, that's for sure," Finn stated seriously.

Roan looked at his dad's expression and pulled a chair out from the table. Finn joined him, staring down into his mug as he collected his thoughts. "Roan, you know I try and respect your privacy, stay out of your business."

"I respect your opinion, Dad. If you have something to say, just say it."

"Patrick is a good man. We've stood side by side through more storms than I can count. It isn't easy being gay on the rodeo circuit, let me tell you. Cost me more than a few black eyes being his friend. Plus a date or two." Finn grinned, trying to lighten the mood a little. "But at the end of the day, people could see the good in his heart, and they came around. Well… if they were worth a shit, they did. I don't want to see him hurt by my own son after watching his back all these years."

Finn looked steadily into Roan's eyes. "I've never had a problem with you being gay. You can thank Patrick for that. I got over any hang-ups I had about homosexuality long before you donned your first rainbow bracelet."

Roan unconsciously fiddled with the braided yarn around his wrist.

"You could do a hell of a lot worse than Patrick, that's for sure, but he's not like the men you've been hanging out with since you left home. He doesn't do casual. In the almost two decades I've known him, he's had three relationships. You've been with more men in the week you've been home." Finn raised a hand as Roan started to protest. "There's nothing wrong with that. Hell, when I was your age…. But I watched him come home last night and then I watched you. You two have to come to some sort of agreement. Lovers or friends, I don't much care. I just can't stand to watch you hurt each other." Finn reached out and covered Roan's hand with a squeeze.

"I take it you've had this conversation with him, too?"

"More or less," Finn admitted.

"I can only promise to try, Dad. He has to meet me halfway."

"That's all I can ask. Now get your butt out to the barn before you get the reputation of a pampered prodigal son," he ordered playfully.

Roan paused in the doorway. Looking back at his dad sitting at the table, he was struck with how much older he appeared. "I want him, Dad, and not just for a fling. I've loved him forever. He's the one being stubborn."

Finn grinned at his son. "He is that. How else would he have put up with me for all these years? Convince him, lad. There isn't anyone, man nor woman, capable of resisting the Bucklin charm."

Roan laughed. Carrying his coffee mug with him, he made his way to the barn. Patrick was talking to a cowboy Roan didn't know in front of Marigold's stall. She was due to foal any day now, and Patrick was keeping a close eye on her. She'd lost a foal last spring, and Roan knew Patrick didn't want a repeat. Walking up to Jeff, one of the men that had been with the ranch for as long as he could remember, Roan nodded in Patrick's direction. "Who's the new guy?"

Jeff laughed. "You're the new guy, sprout. That's Reece, and he's been here... goin' on four years."

Roan chuckled, shaking his head. "Yeah, I guess I am at that. It feels weird as shit to be in the most familiar place on Earth and not be familiar with it."

Jeff patted his shoulder, then hoisted a bag of feed and headed for the shed. "Don't worry, sprout. You'll catch up. Patrick'll need help with Taranis in a few minutes."

Roan nodded, accepting that the hands who knew him would assume he'd be working with Patrick. Since he'd learned to ride and wield a hammer, he'd dogged the foreman's every footstep. He wasn't convinced that Patrick would want his help, though, not after the last few days. Sitting back on a bale of hay and sipping his coffee, he waited for Patrick to finish with Reece.

Taranis was the stallion they used to 'walk the path', a test to tell which mares were in heat. They'd tie the mares out and walk Taranis behind them. Mares in heat or just about ready would 'show' in the presence of a stallion, physically trying to entice the stallion with scent and action. Most stallions were damn near uncontrollable in the presence of a showing mare, but Taranis remained docile, at least if Patrick's hands were on the reins. Before he left, Roan had been getting good at working with Taranis. Patrick had even said that it might be time to let Roan try 'the walk'. He wondered how long it would take him to get back up to speed and no longer be the odd man out at his own ranch.

"You here to help, or are you planning on anchoring that hay to the floor all day?"

Patrick's sarcasm cut through Roan's musing. Hopping up, he brushed the seat of his jeans. "Where do you want me this morning?" he asked.

Patrick bit his cheek. Was the boy incapable of a conversation that didn't involve sexual innuendo? Roan came to a stop right in front of him, innocent expression on his face. Patrick slapped himself mentally. It had been a straightforward question, and his mind was spinning it into more. He'd spent all last night convincing himself that if they were going to live and work side by side, they were going to have to start somewhere. "Help me walk Taranis and then we'll ride out and check on the yearlings in the north quadrant." The invitation was as close as he could come to an apology for his behavior the night before.

Roan nodded. "Are the mares already out?"

"Yeah, I had the guys take 'em out earlier. Go bridle Taranis and throw a saddle on him. I'll ride him out later." Patrick pulled a clipboard off the wall and stared unseeingly down at the record of mares' cycles, waiting for Roan to go do what he told him to do. It was impossible to focus, standing this close to him.

Roan hesitated. He had so much he wanted to say to Patrick, but couldn't form the words to start. It was a like a crowd trying to push through a door, everyone trying to come out at once and no one getting through.

"You *do* remember how to saddle a horse?" Patrick asked, raising one eyebrow.

Several sharp retorts sprang to Roan's lips, but he bit his tongue and headed for the tack room. Patrick had actually suggested they work together for the rest of the day. He wasn't going to burn an olive branch like that.

Roan saddled Taranis and stuck his head in the door to Patrick's office to let him know they were ready. The walk went well. Taranis was a perfect gentleman, and two mares were placed on the schedule for the next morning. Patrick and Roan would bring the high strung stallion, Galahad, from one of the outer paddocks on their way back. He was too unpredictable to be kept closer to the mares. Last spring he'd kicked out four fences and impregnated three mares that Patrick had intended to breed with a different stallion.

Patrick tossed some tools and basic veterinary supplies into a saddlebag and glanced over at Roan with grudging admiration. For a boy – man, he corrected himself – who had been away for years, he picked the routine right up. Every time Patrick had needed him, Roan had been at his elbow. In most cases, the younger man had anticipated what Patrick wanted and was doing it before Patrick could even ask. During times Patrick hadn't needed him, he'd pitched in and helped Jeff and Finn with their projects.

Initiative. Roan had it in spades and always had. It was one of the things Patrick most admired about him. He was certain that both ranches Roan had worked on since graduating from Texas A&M had been sorry to see him go. It was one thing to find a good hand who did as he was told. It was exponentially more valuable to find someone who did something *before* he was told.

Patrick glanced at his watch. "I'm not hungry yet, but I sure as hell will be by the time we get done. Why don't you throw together a bag of sandwiches while I get us packed up, and we'll take 'em with us?" he tossed out.

There was a flash of something through Roan's eyes that was gone before Patrick could identify it. Lifting the leather flap, he dug through the pouch, making sure he had everything he needed.

A picnic? Roan tried to tame his frolicking thoughts all the way to the house. No, idiot— *lunch*. We'll probably eat while we ride, he told himself, but his mind refused to surrender its image of Patrick stretched out on his side on a blanket under the willow by the pond. Most of Roan's favorite Patrick fantasies involved the pond. Throwing together several roast beef sandwiches, Roan quickly packed a Tupperware bowl of fruit and stuck some of the M & M's from the freezer next to the ice pack. Patrick had a major sweet tooth, and Roan wasn't above exploiting it.

Patrick was already mounted when Roan got back to the barn. Securing the cooler behind Bonniebelle's saddle, Roan swung up and clucked her into motion as Patrick took the lead. For as well behaved as Taranis was, he wasn't much of a follower. He'd tolerate them riding side by side once the path widened out.

Patrick looked up at the forget-me-not blue sky and took a deep breath. The air didn't have the oppressive weight of summer heat yet. The grass and leaves were still green, but by far the most beautiful sight was the young man he'd occasionally catch glimpses of riding behind him. Damn, Roan looked good on a horse. Actually he looked good just about anywhere, he admitted. On a horse... sitting on the fence... laughing at Finn over the dinner table... stretched out in Patrick's bed. The older man swallowed the tightness that had gripped his throat. That was a sight he hadn't seen but would love to judge.

Just like he was reading Patrick's mind, Roan piped up, tapping Bonniebelle's sides to bring them even, "God, I'm so sleepy, I could drift off in the saddle." The second the words were out of his mouth, he frantically wished them back. Brilliant ploy, idiot, he cursed himself. You're finally getting along, so you bring up something to mess it all up.

Surprisingly, Patrick didn't respond the way Roan expected. "I'm a mite tired myself. If we get the herd checked over quick, maybe there'll be time for a quick nap by the pond on the way home."

Roan's heart leapt into his throat as his earlier fantasies of Patrick by the pond flooded his brain, and his jeans suddenly seemed a little too tight. "That'd be nice," he managed to choke out. "Maybe we can eat under the willow to get out of the heat."

Patrick turned and looked at Roan speculatively. If Roan was up to something, he couldn't read it in his face. "Sounds good to me. Let's get to work," he said, pulling up beside the gate and unlooping the chain. He backed Taranis several feet so Roan could pass through before going through himself and securing the gate. "You herd them my way, and I'll check 'em over."

Roan nodded, taking off at an easy canter across the field.

TWO hours later, Roan dismounted next to the pond. Patrick was already off Taranis and loosening his cinch. Dropping the reins over Bonniebelle's head to the ground, Roan rummaged for the food he'd packed. Sticking the thermos under an arm, he walked around the horse to find Patrick spreading a blanket under the willow. He froze for a second watching the play of muscles under Patrick's thin T-shirt as he leaned over to wash his hands in the pond. The older man had shed his outer shirt in deference to the heat, but rarely went shirtless, much to Roan's frustration.

Stepping onto the blanket, Patrick toed off his boots and sat down with a sigh. Between the shade and the spring-fed pond, this was the coolest place on the ranch. Looking up, he spied Roan staring at him. "You gonna bring that food over here, or do I have to come get it?"

Roan grinned slightly at the thought of daring Patrick to try and catch him and taking off. Deciding that their truce was still a little too new to withstand a stunt like that, he walked over and sat on the edge of the blanket. "Sorry, surprised you thought to bring a blanket, is all."

Patrick felt himself flush a little. It did sort of look like the set up for a seduction scene. "I… It always pays to pack for any emergency when riding out this far. I've slept several nights wrapped in this blanket when I couldn't get back to the house for one reason or another."

Roan seemed to accept his explanation, doing a quick wash up himself before tucking into a sandwich, pausing to lift pieces of melon and strawberries to his mouth with his fingers. Patrick watched him eat for a few minutes until his own stomach reminded him he was holding an untouched sandwich.

The edge taken off his hunger, Roan lay back on his elbows and watched dappled light from the willow branches play over Patrick's face. "So what's left on our 'to do' list?" he asked.

Popping a piece of watermelon in his mouth, Patrick replied, "Not much, actually. I've got a desk full of paperwork waiting on me, I'm afraid. Finn said something about some repairs at the house that he'd like you to work on when you got a minute."

"Ahhh… *now* I understand." Roan grinned.

"Understand what?" Patrick looked confused.

"Why you told me to bring food and why we're sitting here enjoying a picnic instead of eating it on our way back to the barn. You hate paperwork," Roan stated knowingly.

Patrick looked down a little sheepishly. If he hadn't spent the last few nights obsessing over Roan, the work would be done. He started to gather the leftovers of their meal. "I guess we should head back. Sooner I start, the sooner I finish."

Roan laughed, tugging Patrick back to the blanket. "In a minute. Dessert first."

Patrick's stomach flipped, and his cock jumped at the playful suggestion in Roan's command. Patrick knew exactly what he wanted for dessert.

If Roan had been looking, he probably would have said to hell with the chocolate and drowned in the look of abject desire on Patrick's face, but by the time he turned back around, Patrick had schooled his features into simple curiosity.

"Chocolate," Roan announced, holding up the bag of colorful candies with a grin.

Patrick groaned, reaching for the bag. "You're evil, you know that, right?"

Roan held his hand up high, out of Patrick's reach. "You have *noooo* idea." Batting at the grabbing hands, he held a candy to Patrick's lips.

It was a bad idea. Patrick knew it, but his lips parted anyway. The cold chocolate and the tip of a rough finger pushed into his mouth. His tongue reached out to scoop up the M&M, stroking the fingertip and causing Roan's eyes to flutter and his breath to catch. Patrick swallowed. The duel sensations of the melting chocolate on his tongue and the way his touch obviously affected Roan played havoc with his control.

Roan reached out to feed him another candy. Patrick caught his wrist. "This isn't a good idea, Roh."

Roan hesitated at the sound of the unfamiliar nickname, the jagged rasp of Patrick's voice dancing along every nerve leading to his cock. "Why?"

"We don't do…" Patrick gestured between them with his hand, "…this well."

"How do you know?" Roan asked, scooting closer on the blanket and lifting the candy melting in his fingers to his own mouth. Eyes never leaving Patrick's, he licked at the color staining his fingers and then sucked them into his mouth, watching the older man's eyes dilate with desire. "We've never tried this… getting to know each other as adults… actually exploring the electricity between us. I'm not a kid anymore, Patrick. Give this – give me – a chance." He held out another candy.

Patrick groaned softly in surrender and parted his lips. His eyes drifted closed as Roan pushed the candy into his mouth, his thumb lingering to stroke his bottom lip. Catching Roan's wrist again, he kept him from retreating this time, pressing a kiss into his open palm and whispering, "How do we do that?"

"Just like this. Nothing big. No commitment or grand promises. Just quit running from me."

"I guess I can do that."

Roan's face broke into a smile that made Patrick willing to promise just about anything to see it again. "We'll take it slow, yeah?"

Patrick nodded, his pulse racing. He hadn't felt this scared since drawing his first bronc on the circuit. What exactly did this mean? Were they dating? Fuck, he was too old for this nonsense.

Warning himself not to push, Roan popped the last candy into his mouth and got to his feet, suggesting, "Let's get you back to your paperwork."

Reluctantly, Patrick reached for his boots, standing and folding the blanket as Roan repacked the remains of their lunch.

"I feel like I'm standing too close to a raging fire. You're going to incinerate me," Patrick murmured as he watched Roan mount.

"GODDAMNED, cursed piece of shit!" Roan swore, kicking the side of the washing machine as it thumped and rattled. He struggled with the lid, managing to lift one side an inch or two. "Let go! Give me back my clothes!"

A deep chuckle made him spin around. Patrick was leaning up against the doorframe, laughing at him.

"Quit laughing!" Roan fumed. "Damn possessed machine is trying to walk across the room, and it won't let me open it to try and fix it."

"You know Matilda May runs a really good Wash-n-Fold in Fredericksburg," Patrick teased.

"I don't need a bloody laundry. I need a machine that works." That was obvious, since Roan was wearing worn boxers loose and low on his hips – and nothing else.

"Six men manage to clean their clothes in this machine just fine, Roh. I think it's your delivery. You've hurt her feelings." Patrick walked over to the machine, petting the enameled top and pushing a button. He lifted the lid easily, rearranged the sopping clothes, closed the lid, and pushed another button. A gentle whirring filled the room.

"Fucker," Roan mumbled, glaring at Patrick through a veil of dark eyelashes.

"It's just a washing machine. It's not out to get you," Patrick snickered.

"That's easy for you to say. You've haven't been in here fighting it for the last three hours."

"Poor baby." Patrick's tone was teasing, but he reached for Roan to comfort him with a squeeze around his shoulders anyway. He was obviously tired and agitated. At the last instant, Roan turned, changing the slightly sideways squeeze into a full frontal contact embrace.

Patrick's breath caught, and Roan moaned, tilting his head up and nudging at Patrick's chin in a silent plea for a kiss. Patrick's arms tightened reflexively, pulling Roan tight against his body, his mouth claiming the one already open and waiting for him. It felt like cresting the first hill of a rollercoaster: excitement, fear, and anticipation all rolled into one moment, but also the sinking feeling of *I want off, but it's too late.* He could have handled a hug for comfort, but having his walking fantasy melt in his arms shattered his illusions of being able to take anything with Roan Bucklin slow.

Patrick's tongue pushed into Roan's mouth, tasting, possessing. Roan melted against him, slipping slightly in his arms as his knees gave way. Patrick stepped forward, pinning him against the washing machine and shifting slightly so that his thigh pressed between Roan's legs.

Roan mewled as delicious jolts of pleasure shot from his groin to his brain. He hooked a bare foot around Patrick's knee, attempting to pull him closer and succeeding in positioning him in the cradle of his legs, their cocks sliding against each other. He moaned again, trying to tell Patrick he wanted more, but unwilling to release the older man's lips for even an instant.

A feral growl rumbled from deep inside Patrick's chest. Roan shivered. It was the kind of sound that would have had him reaching for his gun if he'd been outside. Strong hands grasped his sides, lifting him up until he was sitting on the washing machine. Roan murmured his approval into the kiss, wrapping his legs around Patrick's hips and rocking against the hard ridge in his jeans. "Fuck... need," he gasped, breaking his mouth away, his fingers scrabbling at Patrick's jeans.

"Shhh... baby," Patrick soothed, his lips buried in Roan's curls. "Gonna take care of you." He could do this. He could funnel his need into pleasing Roan and maybe, at least, keep himself from carrying the younger man upstairs and fucking him senseless.

Roan's head fell forward onto Patrick's shoulder. Rough hands skimmed up his sides, causing him to shiver and then moan as the thumbs found his nipples. He turned into Patrick's neck, sucking at the hollow above his collarbone.

Patrick made another primal noise, twisting one of the large, dark nipples with his fingers.

"Fuck, yeah!" Roan cried, his hips jerking forward to match the feeling with some friction on his cock.

Patrick leaned in to suck at the sensitive nub, worrying it gently with his teeth. Roan leaned back, bracing himself with his arms to grant greater access. The front of his boxers were damp and tented obscenely, but Patrick made no move to touch him. Roan had promised that they could take things slow, but if Patrick didn't touch him soon, he was going to lose his mind. Threading his fingers into the sandy hair, he tried to encourage the foreman to move lower.

Patrick felt the not-so-subtle guidance and chuckled. It was a pleased, masculine sound that skipped across Roan's skin, making him whimper with need.

"I don't suppose I could convince you to fuck me?" Roan asked plaintively.

Patrick shook his head, his lips brushing one wet, swollen nipple repeatedly. "You have an interesting definition of slow," he rasped, knowing even as he said it that he wasn't sticking to their agreement either.

"So fuck me slow. I want you inside me," Roan declared.

Patrick stopped, pulling Roan close and resting their foreheads together. "I want you, too, but I'm not going to rush this. Too much at stake."

"But...!"

"Shhh... I promised to take care of you," Patrick reminded, his lips skimming down Roan's abdomen, the muscles twitching and jumping under his ghosting touch.

Roan hissed as a warm hand finally cupped his erection, cradled it and then gently squeezed. His hips lifted completely off the washing machine, seeking firmer contact. Patrick used the freedom to slip the offensive garment off, baring Roan to his gaze.

Roan was about to protest the length of time without contact when glorious wet heat surrounded the head of his cock. He thrust up with a cry. Patrick's tongue danced in erotic patterns, unerringly hitting all his most sensitive spots. Roan lost himself in sensation overload as his erection was pulled in deep and then released slowly with just the barest hint of teeth scraping up the length. His hips followed, instinctively trying to maintain contact.

Patrick pulled back slightly and, looking up, caught Roan's eyes. Holding the stare, he moved his tongue in slow circles, up and over the sensitive slit. His lips curved into a predatory smile as he swallowed the entire length again.

"Fuck!" Roan screeched.

Patrick sucked harder, causing Roan's hips to buck violently. He could feel Roan's thighs trembling under his hands. Lifting one of his legs until the foot rested flat on the top of the washer, Patrick's hand slipped between them, cupping his balls and squeezing lightly as he began to rhythmically suck. His finger flicked lower, pressing against the tight entrance.

"Oh, please," Roan whimpered, trying to push up into Patrick's mouth and back on his finger simultaneously.

The finger slipped inside, deeper and deeper with each thrust until it rubbed firmly over Roan's prostate. Stars exploded behind Roan's eyelids. His fingers contracted in Patrick's hair. "Oh fucking hell... oh fuck, Patrick!" he screamed as his cock convulsed in Patrick's mouth.

Patrick swallowed, hummed and licked, coaxing Roan through multiple aftershocks before allowing him to slip, sated and limp, from his mouth. Roan swayed, collapsing forward onto Patrick.

"It's done," Patrick said softly, still cradling Roan in his arms.

"Yeah, done," Roan murmured sleepily against his shoulder. "Completely done in."

"Your laundry, Roh. It's done." Patrick nudged him.

Roan just burrowed deeper against Patrick's chest and wished they were lying in a bed. He was so sleepy. Firm hands were gripping his shoulders, sitting him up. "What?" he protested.

Patrick kissed him, a slow lingering kiss that drove some of the fog from his mind, replacing it with renewed desire.

"Ummm... nice." Roan licked at his lips, savoring his lover's taste.

"Change your laundry and go to bed," Patrick instructed gently. He stepped away, missing the warm body in his arms immediately. He wanted to help Roan to bed, but he knew he'd never be able to leave him. "I'll see you in the morning, baby. Sweet dreams."

Roan grinned, still dazed. When Patrick was gone, he collapsed back against the wall, his head hitting with a thump. The pain helped wake him up and snap him out of his post-orgasmic cloud. "Fuck," he cursed. "That makes two times Patrick's brought me off, and I haven't even touched him in return. The first time I might have been too young to know better, but no more," Roan vowed. Patrick Lassiter was due for a serious seduction, and Roan wasn't taking 'no' for an answer.

Hopping off the washing machine, he laughed joyfully. "Maybe laundry isn't so bad after all," he chortled, petting the old appliance and sweeping his boxers off the floor. "I could easily grow attached to spending time in here."

Chapter Four

ROAN flew into the barn the next morning, six inches off the ground. He immediately looked for Patrick, not with the sense of dread from yesterday, but with anticipation. Spotting him talking with Johnny from the livestock auction house, he hung back in the shadows, admiring the way Patrick's jeans clung to his thighs. Watching those muscles gripping the sides of a horse had spawned many a wet dream as a teenager.

Patrick's hands were traveling over the flanks of a horse Roan didn't recognize, pulling up each hoof in turn as he made his way around the animal. A shiver traveled up his spine as he thought about those rough hands stroking him the same way, the slight catch of calluses on smooth skin. Pressing the heel of his hand down the zipper of his jeans, he adjusted his growing interest.

Johnny laughed at something Patrick said, and, with a friendly punch to the foreman's shoulder, walked back to his truck. He was pulling an empty horse trailer, so Roan assumed he'd been delivering, not picking up.

Giving Patrick a minute to lead the new horse into a stall and secure the latch, Roan hurtled across the barn, his body slamming into Patrick's, pushing him back into his office and sealing their mouths together. Patrick reacted automatically, returning the kiss and cupping Roan's ass to lift him closer.

"I suppose it's too early to suggest we go back to the cabin so I can ride you until you scream," the younger man suggested throatily.

Patrick groaned, stepping sideways so there was more room between them. He'd noticed lately that his brain function seemed to decrease proportionally to how close Roan was standing. "You'd be right."

"I guess I'll just have to settle for making out in your office then." Roan shrugged and reached for the older man.

Patrick avoided the touch, moving to put the desk between them. "That would be a really *bad* idea, Roh. What if someone saw us?"

Roan liked the sound of the new nickname, since it seemed to appear when they'd been touching. He tilted his head with a puzzled frown. "You think a kiss is going to threaten your authority with the men? They already know you're gay and that I am, too, for that matter."

"It's just not right. I can't do the same thing I just fired Adam for," Patrick explained. "With the same man, I might add."

Roan's eyes narrowed suspiciously. He was still too high from last night to be truly mad at Patrick. "Okay, so will you meet me for lunch?" he asked with a saucy wink.

"Finn and I are supposed to go to town. We'll probably grab lunch at the diner so he can flirt with Nancy."

Propping a hip on the side of the desk, Roan frowned. "Are you regretting our decision already?"

"No," Patrick denied, though a part of him realized he was. It was hard to simply give in to a feeling you'd been fighting for almost ten years.

"I don't want to hide this," Roan insisted. "If we're really going to try to get to know each other, people are going to have to see us together."

"I know," Patrick agreed. "I just want to keep to that slow pace you promised. Get used to being with you before I have to share you with others." Silently, he added, 'When it doesn't work, it'll hurt less if I don't have to deal with everyone's pitying stares.'

"Okay," Roan said, his tone still not convinced. "Dinner? Just you and me? I'll even cook."

"You cook?" One eyebrow rose incredulously.

"I've been on my own for seven years, Patrick. During college, I pretty much lived on fast food and pizza, but it gets old after a while."

"Dinner," Patrick agreed. "Now, I've got to go find your dad. Can you help Jeff with the breeding this morning?"

"Sure," Roan agreed, hooking Patrick's arm as he moved towards the door and spinning him behind it, against the wall. He used momentum and body weight to pin the older man. "One kiss to get me through the day?" he begged.

Patrick sighed in mock exasperation. Honestly, Roan's attention made him feel desired and damn good. Cradling Roan's face with his hands, he pressed their lips together. He'd intended only a brief taste, but Roan caught his lower lip and sucked. Patrick moaned, dropping a hand to Roan's hip and pulling him in firmly, his tongue pushing past the yielding lips.

Roan melted against him, one thigh insinuating itself between Patrick's legs and pressing into his swelling arousal. Small noises of encouragement sounded from his throat. Fingers hooked in Patrick's belt loops for stability, he held on for the ride.

A discreet cough brought Patrick crashing back to reality. He tensed and pushed Roan away abruptly. Roan, recognizing the sound, refused to release his hold, keeping Patrick between him and the wall, his head resting on his lover's shoulder. "Dad, sometimes your timing sucks," he complained without turning around.

"Oh, I don't know. If I hadn't arrived when I did, you two might have been caught doing something considerably more embarrassing," Finn chuckled, amused. "I hate to break things up, but if we don't get to town, we'll… well, we'll be late," he directed to Patrick.

Patrick placed a quick kiss on Roan's cheek, whispering in his ear, "Yeah, late for Nancy's shift at the diner."

Roan laughed and hugged him one more time before relinquishing his hold. "Tonight," he promised, turning to lean against the wall, looking flushed and slightly ravished.

It took all of Patrick's willpower to follow Finn out of the barn.

PATRICK walked into the cabin, inhaling the unfamiliar scent of cooking food and, judging from the aroma, damn good food. Following the smell to the kitchen, he was greeted by the enticing sight of his lover's backside sticking up in the air as he pulled a pan of something out of the oven. His kitchen had never felt so welcoming, and it scared him. He could get used to this far too easily. His mind warned about caution, but he stifled the voice. He'd promised Roan that he'd really give this a try.

Roan had soft music playing from the radio on the counter. The table was set with dishes he didn't recognize. A glass of wine was already poured and sitting on the table, waiting for him. His mind screamed, 'Run before you get in too deep', but he suspected it was already too late. Snagging the glass, he took a deep swallow to drown the nagging voice before walking up quietly behind his lover and snaking an arm around his waist. "Honey, I'm home."

Roan jumped and then relaxed back against Patrick's chest, twisting his head for a kiss. When their lips reluctantly parted, clinging for a final, lingering taste, Roan grinned. "'Bout time. Dinner's almost done."

"It smells great. What is it?" Patrick asked, scanning everything scattered over the counter. Chilies sat chopped on a cutting board. Food, bowls, and pots covered every other inch of available surface.

"Enchiladas Suisse," Roan announced, turning back to the chilies he had just pulled from under the broiler. With a practiced hand, he continued to peel and chop them, scattering them over the rolled enchiladas stacked in a clay casserole dish.

"Where'd all the dishes, glasses..." Patrick raised the hand-blown wine glass in his hand, "...and pots come from?"

"They're mine," Roan answered, snagging a pan from the stove and pouring a thick white sauce over the enchiladas. "They were sitting in boxes up in Dad's attic. I came over to start dinner, and you had one sauce pan, three mismatched bowls and a handful of water glasses." He stared accusingly at the older man leaning against the counter.

Patrick shrugged guiltily. "I don't eat here much."

"No shit. The refrigerator was even worse than the cabinets." Roan slipped one baking dish into the oven. "Why don't you take a shower while I run this over to Dad's?" he suggested, picking up the second casserole.

Patrick raised a questioning eyebrow. "Are you saying I need one?"

"Maybe...." Roan grinned. "Maybe I just want you smelling sweet for what I want to do to you later." He winked.

Patrick moaned, feeling himself harden in his jeans. He'd just been teasing. A bath was usually first on his list in the evening, but Roan's suggestive comment made it much more appealing. "Why is half of our dinner leaving?" he asked to cover his discomfort. He wasn't sure he was ready for Roan to know exactly how much power he wielded.

"Because if half doesn't go to Dad's, Dad comes over here, and I don't feel like sharing you tonight." Roan's voice deepened with husky promise. "This happens to be one of his favorite dishes, and when he found me picking chilies this afternoon, he guessed what I was making. You really don't want my father to watch while I do my best to seduce you, do you?"

Patrick shook his head mutely.

"Good," Roan chimed. "I'll be back. If you aren't done, I'll be joining you."

Patrick watched the young man almost skip out his door and wondered if that was supposed to be a disincentive. He headed upstairs to the bathroom with images of a naked... wet... soapy... slippery Roan in his arms.

Twenty minutes later, Patrick strolled into the kitchen barefoot, his hair still damp. Roan grinned at him. "I was just about to come get you."

Patrick pretended to turn around. "I can go back...?"

Roan laughed, wrapping his arms around his lover and pulling him towards the table, enjoying the playful flirting and not wanting to do anything to upset it. "No, no, no. Dinner is ready and best when hot."

"Like a lot of things," Patrick murmured, kissing Roan's neck.

Batting his hands away, Roan slipped on an oven mitt and carried the enchiladas to the table. "Eat food now, me later. You'll need the energy." His dark eyes focused on Patrick, leaving no doubt that he was very much looking forward to the experience.

Patrick did his best to concentrate on the food and surprisingly easy conversation while they ate. He'd forgotten how much they actually had in common. The voice in his head kept up a steady monologue as well, predicting catastrophe, but several glasses of wine managed to shut it up.

When every last enchilada had been consumed, Roan bounced up from the table. "Now the fun part," he announced, obviously pleased with himself. "I made sopapillas."

Patrick watched as the young man removed a basket from the warm oven, pulling back the cloth to reveal cinnamon and sugar-coated puff pastry. "Sopapillas? How long have you been cooking today?"

Roan's eyes shifted. "A while," he hedged. Instead of taking the seat across from Patrick that he had occupied during dinner, Roan sat down next to him, opening his legs wide to scoot the chair even closer, bracketing the cowboy between his thighs. Taking one of the warm treats out, he dipped it in a bowl of honey that had been sitting innocently on the table, twirling it to catch the tendrils of escaping stickiness, and held it up to Patrick's mouth.

Patrick hesitated, warning bells going off in his head again. "This is your date dinner, isn't it?" he teased, trying to break the sensual tension.

"Patrick, quit trying to distract me. I warned you that I was going to seduce you, so feel honored that you rated my *date* dinner. It's not poisoned, and it's going to drip all over if you don't eat it," Roan chastised, catching a drop of the honey on his finger and sucking it clean.

Patrick's mouth opened, his eyes fixed on Roan's finger between his lips. Eyes dancing sensually, Roan slipped the sticky-sweet confection past Patrick's lips. Tastes exploded across his tongue—the yeast of the dough, the sweetness of the sugar, the spice of the cinnamon and the tang of the honey. Just like Roan, Patrick thought. A unique combination that blended together to make the whole greater than any of its parts. His eyes drifted shut to enjoy the flavors, and then he jumped because of an unexpected swipe of Roan's wet tongue across his lips.

Patrick opened his eyes to stare into the coffee-colored ones mere inches away. He could feel the soft rush of Roan's breath on his face.

"Cleaning you up," Roan explained hoarsely. "They can be a little messy."

Patrick groaned, reaching for the basket with one hand and Roan with the other, slamming the door on the screaming voice in his head, twisting the lock and throwing away the key. He wanted Roan. Had wanted him for years. He wasn't a kid anymore, and Patrick was tired of being honorable.

A sharp tug on Roan's belt loop moved him from his own chair to straddling Patrick's lap. 'Oh yes, much better', the older man thought as the glorious weight of his lover's body settled against his swollen cock. Dipping one of the heavenly squares in the honey, not caring that he left golden trails across the table, he lifted it to Roan's mouth.

Roan opened his lips, extending his tongue for the treat. His hands caught Patrick's wrist, holding his hand in place while he licked and sucked each finger clean. Looking down, he smirked. "You made a mess."

Patrick's eyes dropped to the honey on Roan's shirt and jeans. "I think there's only one thing to do about that," he rasped, reaching for the buttons. "Your skin will clean up easier than your clothes."

Roan agreed happily, scooting back off Patrick's lap to shed his clothes quickly and efficiently. Standing, completely unselfconscious about his nudity, he pulled Patrick to his feet. "You, too," he requested, pulling the soft cotton T-shirt up from Patrick's waist.

Patrick raised his hands obediently, letting Roan strip off the shirt and toss it onto a chair. His breath hitched as the long, tanned fingers settled on the button of his jeans. He'd always kept this last barrier between them, touching Roan but not letting Roan touch in return. In his head, it was the final point of surrendering himself to the man in front of him.

Roan held his breath, waiting for Patrick to stop him. When his lungs burned, he sucked a breath in harshly and popped the button, the zipper gliding open easily with a tug. Unable to help it, his eyes darted lower to watch as Patrick's body was revealed. His mouth twitched as he saw the foreman's lack of undergarments. To diffuse the tension and keep from falling immediately to his knees, he teased, "Being hopeful, old man? I know you know how to work the washing machine."

Patrick chuckled. If he was honest, he *had* been hopeful, in a small, unacknowledged part of his brain. "Just more comfortable after stepping out of a hot, steamy shower."

Roan smirked, sensing the lie and emboldened by it. Pushing the loose jeans over Patrick's slender hips, he stroked his hands over the hard planes of the older man's body – coarse hair, smooth warm skin, work-hardened muscles, and sensitive patches that trembled under his touch. It was the body that had filled his dreams for his entire adult life. "I want you so much," he croaked, unable to hold back the words that bubbled up in his throat, barely biting back the declaration of love that wanted to follow.

The admission snapped Patrick's paralysis. He grabbed Roan's shoulders, crashing their bare bodies together, causing murmurs of appreciation to rumble from their throats. Hands reaching down to cup Roan's ass, Patrick lifted him up and onto the table, pushing him steadily backwards with a hand on his chest until he was laid out like a part of the meal.

Smiling, Patrick reached for the bowl of honey. Dipping his fingers into the gooey, golden liquid, he began to fingerpaint – lines down Roan's chest, circles around his nipples, an outline around the tattoo in the hollow of his hip.

Roan gasped as the rough fingers began to decorate him with honey, though he was slightly disappointed when his lover stopped with his tattoo. He knew what was coming next and feared that just the thought of Patrick's tongue lapping the sticky substance from his skin was going to be enough to make him come. The feel of Patrick's warm, rough tongue gathering the honey from his chest chased all rational thought from his mind.

Roan's fingers burrowed deep into Patrick's hair, guiding the cowboy's movements as Patrick's tongue methodically cleaned the honey from his bare chest and belly. Placing an open-mouthed kiss over each nipple, Patrick alternately sucked and tongued them clean as Roan ground with increasing fervor against his hip.

When the last drop was gone, Roan pulled Patrick down on top of him to reach his mouth, attacking it. His tongue thrust deep into his lover's mouth, chasing the sweet taste of the honey. "You have got to fuck me!"

Patrick's eyes pulsed with desire, black with only the tiniest rim of blue visible. "I'm going to, but... not... quite... yet," he drawled, punctuating his words with kisses down the midline of

Roan's chest, stopping just under his belly button. "You got any of that sugar left?"

Roan whimpered, nodding towards the counter. "Don't use the cinnamon," he warned.

Patrick laughed. "How do you know I want to use it on you? Maybe I want it for the sopapillas."

"You'd better not—" Roan's words broke off with a hoarse groan as Patrick licked a broad swipe up the underside of his cock. "Oh that's nice," he sighed, falling back on the table again.

Patrick chuckled, suckling the hard shaft. When he had it good and wet, he started sprinkling the sugar. Pulling back, he admired his work. A lopsided grin appeared when he caught the glare coming from his frustrated lover. "Kids. So impatient," he sighed.

As Patrick's mouth licked at his cock like a sugar-coated lollipop, Roan wondered exactly how much pleasure would drive him out of his mind. He thought that at the pinnacle of pleasure you just came, but somehow Patrick had pushed him past that point into a realm of sensation and anticipation he'd never experienced before. His legs felt like lead. In fact, every muscle in his body seemed heavy. He *had* to come.

Lifting his legs so that his feet rested on the tabletop, Roan flexed up, pushing deeper into Patrick's mouth. Taking advantage of the new position, Patrick slipped a hand between Roan's legs, running a dry finger along his cleft. "Hmmm...," he hummed, the vibrations from his musings drawing a sharp cry from the man on the table.

Rubbing his fingers through the softened stick of butter sitting on the table, Patrick returned them to his lover's entrance. With steady pressure, he pushed inside, circling and stretching the tight muscle. Roan mewled, rocking his hips. "More," he panted.

Patrick gladly complied, adding one and then two more fingers. Crooking them just so, he brushed the sensitive bundle of nerves that sent Roan skyrocketing.

Curling up, Roan grasped at Patrick's hand. "No, too close. Want you inside me."

Patrick slid his fingers free, moaning at the way the muscle clenched and twitched, trying to hold him inside.

"I brought lube," Roan said, waving a hand in the general direction of his jeans that were lying on the floor.

"Too much trouble," Patrick breathed, coating his fingers with butter again and slicking his cock. Pushing against Roan's knees, he bared the tight, butter-covered hole. Impulsively, he sprinkled a pinch of sugar on the pink skin and bent to lick it clean.

Roan bucked up from the table at the feel of Patrick's tongue rimming him. He wanted to come so badly, and he knew he could just let go. It would be so easy to just come, but it wasn't what he really wanted. As if he was reading his mind, Patrick took one last swipe and stood, positioning himself and pushing inside his lover with a single, slow plunge.

"OhfuckPatrick... justlikethat... Godyesharder," Roan garbled, his head thrashing from side to side, his fingers scratching at the table, unable to find purchase.

Patrick watched as Roan fell apart. One hand braced on the young man's pelvis, framing his cock and holding him still, he pounded harder and harder into the clenching passage. "I wanna see you come," he rasped, tilting his hips to aim for the spot that had jolted Roan off the table the first time. When Roan's hips snapped up so hard he couldn't hold them down, he knew he'd found it.

"God... need!" Roan cried.

"Come for me, baby." Patrick wrapped a callused fist around Roan's cock, forming a channel and letting Roan fuck his hand. Hot, white jets shot from the pulsing shaft, covering Patrick's hand and Roan's chest.

Patrick's head fell back, his mouth opening in a silent scream as he came, filling Roan's body. He rocked into the slippery hole again and again, his seed escaping with every stroke. His knees started to shake, and he fell forward over Roan to keep from collapsing. Catching himself on his elbows, he stared down at the love-drunk expression on Roan's face.

Unfocused, chestnut eyes opened and blinked at him lazily. "I admit, your dessert was better than mine," Roan quipped in a sated voice.

Patrick smiled and kissed him tenderly. "I'm afraid we made a mess," he said, looking around but not making any move to change their positions.

"Yeah, I'm more than a bit sticky."

"You're the one that brought out the honey," Patrick teased.

Roan batted his eyelashes playfully. "I didn't say I was sorry…" he clarified, yawning.

"You should get a shower before you fall asleep. I'll clean up the kitchen." Patrick pulled back reluctantly, helping Roan to his feet.

Roan stood, not sure what to do. Was Patrick inviting him to use his shower? He fidgeted, hoping for a clue, but the foreman was pulling on his jeans. "I hate to leave you with the dishes," he started.

Patrick pulled him into a tight hug. "Only fair. You cooked. I'll clean." Letting him go with a peck on the tip of his nose, he started to collect plates.

Roan pulled on his jeans, gathering his other clothes in his fist. "I guess I'll go then…."

Patrick turned and looked at Roan standing there with his clothes in hand, and felt a lurch in the pit of his stomach. He wanted to ask him to stay, but couldn't make his mouth form the words. Instead, he pulled him close for a searing kiss. Pulling back just far enough to look down into Roan's eyes, he stared, drowning in the dark depths, still unable to find the right words.

"Night, Patrick," Roan finally whispered, hugging him quickly and disappearing out the door. Happy. Sated.

And confused.

Chapter Five

THE warm, yellow sunlight streaming in his window alerted Roan to the fact that he'd overslept. Turning onto his back, he stretched under the crisp sheets. His dad really loved him. Roan had crawled into his bed last night, straight from the shower, to find fresh, clean sheets.

Swinging his legs over the side, he ran a hand through his unruly curls. Bah, he should never go to sleep with his hair wet. It was always a mess in the morning. His body ached pleasantly, reminding him of each and every touch from the night before. The world would be just about perfect if he'd woken up in Patrick's bed, in Patrick's arms, instead of his own. He still wasn't sure what had gone wrong.

Everything had gone exactly as planned. Dinner was great. They'd really enjoyed each other's company. The sex had been fantastic, and he hadn't felt Patrick pull away once, not until the very end and even then, he hadn't felt anything bad. Patrick had held him and kissed him goodnight. He just hadn't asked him to stay.

"Grow up, Bucklin", he chastised himself. "One night of mind-blowing sex doesn't mean he should be asking you to move in with him."

Walking to the window, he looked down on the yard below and the cabin shaded by three large oaks. "I would, though," he thought. "I'd live with you there forever if you'd let me in."

Shaking his head to clear the melancholy, he grabbed some clean clothes and a comb to try and tame his curls.

Unsurprisingly, Roan found the kitchen and barn empty. Everyone was already out. Wandering into Patrick's office, Roan scanned the desk. Patrick almost always had a 'to do' list lying around. He found several notes, but nothing that seemed recent or urgent. Maybe he'd ride out. He was bound to run into someone.

Walking around the door that was still jammed against the floor, he paused. That was one thing he could do. Gathering the tools he needed, Roan pulled the door off its hinges and set to work, whistling the entire time. If Patrick's office had a functioning door, they might be able to sneak a few private minutes in the middle of the day.

PATRICK dragged his weary body into the barn. He was getting too old for this shit. One of the horses had gotten tangled in some barbed wire down by the creek, wire he knew hadn't come from the Bucklin ranch. His men were always careful to remove any wire they replaced, but not all the ranchers in the area were as conscientious. It had probably come downstream and washed up onto the bank.

The mare was going to need stitches, at the very least, and might end up partially lame. Patrick was worried about one leg in particular. He had field dressed it the best that he could and sent Jeff with her over to the nearest road. Reece had ridden in to grab the truck and horse trailer to get her back to the barn with a minimum of movement.

Patrick had called the vet from his cell phone to have him meet them back at the ranch. Glancing at his watch, he decided he had just enough time to grab some lunch and maybe find Roan before everyone converged back at the barn. He'd been missing his lover since he sent him home last night. He wouldn't make that mistake again. He'd thought they'd both sleep better in their own beds, but he hadn't slept a wink.

Everything felt empty without Roan— his arms, his bed, even his work day. He'd been tempted to go rouse the slug-a-bed this morning so they could ride out together like they had two days ago, but he'd been afraid Roan's ass might not be up to a day in the saddle after last night, so he'd let him sleep. Staring out the barn doors towards the house, Patrick wondered if he was still in bed. He'd expected to find him in the barn or yard.

Roan attacked Patrick from behind, pulling the surprised foreman backwards into his office. With one foot, he toed the door shut and flipped the lock.

"Roh!" Patrick squawked, staring at the door. "How'd you do that?"

"Do what?" Roan asked, his lips attacking every inch of skin visible above Patrick's collar.

"Get the door to close," Patrick explained, squirming as his body responded to the attention.

Roan sat on the edge of the desk, pulling Patrick between his thighs and turning him around. "I fixed it." Kiss. "So we can…." Kiss. "Do this. I can't wait all day for a chance to touch you, so we need a place to be together where we won't be disturbed."

Patrick looked over at the door again. "I didn't even know it had a lock," he mused.

Roan laughed. "Why would you? Not much point in a lock if you can't close the door."

Patrick laughed, allowing himself to be pulled into another kiss. "I missed you this morning," he admitted, taking control of their kisses until Roan was breathless.

"I woke up late. Someone must have worn me out."

"Hmmm…." Patrick nuzzled Roan's salty neck. "I could have used you. We found a horse down."

Roan immediately drew back from the embrace. "Bad?"

Patrick dragged him back, his lips returning to the spot they'd been suckling before he'd pulled away. "She'll be okay. Jeff and Reece are bringing her in, and Doc's already on his way."

"So we have a few minutes…." Roan's question trailed off suggestively.

Patrick chuckled. "Yes, you hussy." But his body was already pressing Roan back onto the desk, his nimble fingers opening the buttons on his shirt and releasing his belt buckle. "What do you think we should do with our private moment?"

"I think you should fuck me over your desk."

Patrick moaned, one hand dropping to squeeze Roan's tempting ass. "Turn around," he ordered gruffly.

Obediently, Roan turned, pushing his jeans down his thighs and bending over Patrick's desk. He shot the foreman a come-and-get-me look over his shoulder.

"Fuck, you'd tempt Christ," Patrick murmured, his fingers pulling impatiently at his own jeans. "You still have that lube from last night?"

A shadow crossed Roan's face. "No," he admitted. "Guess I'll need to add your office to the 'stock with supplies' list."

Patrick growled, spreading his lover's white cheeks with his thumbs. Falling to his knees, he licked a wet trail up the musky cleft. "Think you can take me with just spit?" Patrick's tongue plundered Roan's hole, stabbing and sucking as he reached between the younger man's legs to fondle his balls and cock.

"Fuck, I'd take you dry if you promised you'd kiss it and make it better like that," Roan moaned, shoving his ass back towards Patrick's face.

The foreman teased the tight pink hole with his tongue and fingers until Roan was wet, loose, and impatiently whining to be fucked.

"Don't want to hurt you." Patrick curled his finger, stroking firmly over Roan's prostate and licking the dimple at the base of his spine.

"You won't hurt me, but if you don't fuck me now, I'm gonna come all over your desk."

"You're gonna do that anyhow," Patrick promised, standing and rubbing the blunt head of his cock up and down the wet cleft, adding his own fluids to ease the way.

Roan whimpered, bracing himself with his elbows. He could feel the pressure and then the burn as Patrick breached the outer muscles. Relaxing, he opened to his lover, letting him sink home with one steady push.

"Fuck, Roh." All the breath in Patrick's lungs hissed out through clenched teeth as he pulled back and sunk even deeper.

Roan's muscles clenched around him as the slow withdrawal stroked directly over his sweet spot. "Fucking hell! Like that! Again!"

Patrick's fingers dug deeply into the slender hips, watching as Roan's body stretched to accept him. Every stroke ratcheted the tension in his balls until he couldn't keep from pounding into Roan, hard and fast.

"God, harder." Roan's fingers scrabbled for purchase on the smooth surface of the desk, papers flying off in every direction. He finally collapsed completely onto his stomach, his cheek pressing against the cool wood as his body rocked back and forth with the force of Patrick's thrusts. Fingers clenching, he tried to force his muscles to move and failed. "Touch me."

Patrick pulled Roan's torso up to his chest, bending one of his legs and resting it on the desk. Roan cried out, locking his arms to keep from collapsing forward again as the new angle stimulated entirely new areas. The new position also gave the foreman easy access to his nipples, which he pinched and twisted ruthlessly before sliding his open hand down to circle the base of Roan's cock.

"Yeah… oh God, yeah…." Roan thrust his hips forward forcefully. Patrick closed his hand around the stiff shaft, letting Roan fuck his fist as he fucked Roan's ass.

"Shit," Patrick panted, his forehead resting of Roan's shoulder. "So fucking tight. Can't hold back."

"Don't. Come inside me."

"Wanna see you come first." Patrick's hand sped up, tightening and running the rough pad of his thumb over the sensitive ridge along the head of Roan's cock.

The younger man screamed, his back arching as ropes of creamy liquid splattered all over Patrick's desk.

Biting into the fleshy muscle covering Roan's shoulder, Patrick's throat rumbled with a deep groan as he slammed into the clenching channel. His body trembled as he pulsed inside his lover, the slippery seed allowing him to slide easily as aftershocks tightened his balls and caused his cock to twitch until Roan was whimpering with every jump of the semi-hard shaft.

"Still," Roan pleaded, reaching behind him to clutch at Patrick's hips.

Patrick froze, holding Roan tight, buried deep in his body. He could feel himself softening and hissed as he slipped free.

"God, I hate that part. Wanna keep you inside me forever," Roan mumbled, sated, turning to rest on Patrick's chest.

"Nice idea." Patrick brushed his fingers through Roan's damp curls, pushing them back from his face. "Not very practical, but a nice idea."

"Fuck practical."

Patrick chuckled. "Unfortunately, on the practical side of things, we're going to be overrun with people here soon, and I don't relish greeting them with my pants down." He slapped Roan's bare butt to get him moving.

"Spoil sport." Roan reached down for his jeans. "Just for that, you get to clean up the desk."

"I think I might just keep it that way." Patrick leered at his lover. "It'll make daydreaming over paperwork a lot more fun."

ROAN crawled up into the cab of Finn's truck, looking back at the barn through the window.

"Ease up, boy. They'll be fine. Doc's here, and there are only so many bodies that'll fit 'round a horse," Finn said, putting the truck into gear and pulling away. "I need a back stronger than mine, and you've been elected to baby-sit the old man."

"You aren't old," Roan replied automatically. "Where are we goin'?"

"Twisted Mesquite Ranch. Charlie Reynolds is selling out. They've got some equipment and a few horses I want to look at before he sends the rest to auction."

Roan nodded, staring out the side window.

"Nothin' out there you ain't seen before," Finn stated.

Roan smiled. "One of the things I like about this place. Not much changes."

"Some things do. You've grown up and Patrick seems to have finally noticed."

"I'm still not sure he's really seeing me," Roan sighed.

Finn glanced over at his son thoughtfully. "I thought with dinner and everythin' that things were goin' better."

"I did, too."

"So what's causin' the frown?"

Roan's mouth opened and closed twice while he considered and discarded words. "You know, it's not easy to discuss your love life with your dad."

Finn chuckled. "You shoulda seen Patrick. Blushed right up to the roots of his hair when he told me about the first time he touched you."

Roan felt himself flush as he thought back to that day at the pond, but he wasn't sure it was embarrassment. "I can't believe he told you about that."

"He didn't exactly volunteer the information. I had to drag it out of him, but he was beatin' himself up sumthin' awful 'bout it."

Roan thought back to that day at the pond. Senior Skip Day. They'd all passed their finals and were simply biding their time, waiting for the last day of school. Tommy Johnston had told him he'd go down on him, but wanted Roan to do it to him first. He'd been on his knees with his mouth on Tommy's cock when Patrick had driven up. Tommy had run, taking Roan's truck, leaving him stranded with the irate foreman.

Honestly, Roan had felt like flinging himself in Patrick's arms and thanking him for rescuing him, but he'd been too young and full of himself to actually do it. Every time Tommy had thrust into his mouth, he'd gagged, and his throat hurt like hell. He'd figured that only the person getting blown enjoyed it, so he'd persevered, but he wasn't unhappy that Patrick had cut it short. The only down side had been not getting to come himself, which is what he threw into Patrick's face.

He'd watched as the foreman he had always thought of as a steady rock cracked. Eyes blazing, Patrick had pulled him up and kissed a line of fire down his neck that had melted his knees. Sure hands had invaded his jeans, stroking and pulling on his cock in a way that had his head spinning. He'd jacked off more times than he could remember, but his own hand had never felt that good.

Face pressed into Patrick's neck, he had trembled, begged, cursed, and cried as the rough hand worked him. "Next time you want to feel like a man, don't go to a boy," Patrick had rasped in his ear.

In an embarrassingly short period of time, Roan had been screaming and coming all over Patrick's hand. He'd gotten a little dizzy, and Patrick had lowered him to the ground against the willow tree.

And then he was gone.

Roan had opened his eyes to find Patrick's truck, but no Patrick. He'd waited a long time before getting in the truck and driving home. Patrick hadn't come to graduation, and three days after, Roan had left for College Station.

Shaking his head to clear the confusing memory, Roan muttered, "I don't understand him any better now than I did then."

"If it's any comfort, I'm not sure he understands himself any better either," Finn offered.

"We made love last night, but I'm not sure if he really wanted it, or if I finally just pushed him into it. At the time, I thought he wanted it, but then…." Roan swallowed. "It was like he patted me on the head and sent me to bed. *My* bed."

"Ahhh… I wondered about that when your door was closed this morning. Sort of figured you'd come wandering in with Patrick for breakfast." Finn shrugged. "Or not. Wouldn't hurt the old coot to take a morning to sleep in."

"But then when I saw him today, the chemistry just sort of exploded again. It's fuckin' confusing."

"Don't over think this, Roan." Finn reached out and laid a hand on his son's leg. "Patrick wants you so bad he can't see straight. Has for years, but you've got to understand that Patrick's been a bachelor for more years than you've been alive. He's still worried about the age thing. He thinks you're gonna work him out of your system and be on to the next guy. He's trying to hold a part of himself back so when you leave, he'll have something left that's not broken."

"I'm not going to leave him!"

"So when we get home, go convince him of that," Finn said.

ROAN skipped up the steps to Patrick's cabin. The door was open and, normally, he'd have walked straight in, but Tyler's truck was parked in the side yard. A million insecurities surfaced at the thought of the blond man in Patrick's home.

Before he could raise his hand to knock, snatches of conversation floated through the screen door. "...showed up out of the blue." "I won't walk away from you over this." "...kid..." "...just trying to come between us, but it won't work." "I'll always be by your side."

Moving stealthily along the dark porch, Roan peered in the front window. Patrick sat in the corner of the couch with his arm around Tyler's shoulders. His eyes immediately blurred with tears and he turned, running from the pain. As he flew down the stairs, he hit the board that creaked. Not wanting to have to face Tyler, standing next to Patrick as he fell apart, he jumped to the dirt and sprinted into the main house.

"What was that?" Tyler asked, pulling his head off Patrick's shoulder.

"What?" Patrick looked around the room. "I didn't hear anything. Probably just one of the animals in the barn."

Tyler wiped disgustedly at the moisture on his face. "I hate that she can still fuck with my life this way."

"I know. You don't deserve it. You're a good dad. You'll fight this and win, and I'll be beside you every step of the way," Patrick promised. "You need to get some sleep, though. You look like you're starting a dark circle collection. You'll never snag another sucker... er... lover lookin' like that."

Tyler laughed like he was supposed to. "Can I bunk here tonight? I really don't want to be near my phone."

Patrick put a reassuring arm around him and started to steer him towards the stairs. "You are always welcome. You know that."

"I don't know what I'd do without you."

"Yeah, well, you are never goin' to have to find out, unless I let you feed me that horrible giblet casserole again," Patrick teased.

ROAN'S dark circles the next morning put Tyler's to shame. He hadn't slept one minute. From the moment he left Patrick's porch until dawn when he'd watched Tyler get in his truck, he'd had conversation after conversation in his head. They had run the gamut from Patrick having a perfectly good explanation for what Roan had seen, to the older man falling on his knees and begging Roan's forgiveness, to him telling Roan that it had all been a mistake and he really wanted Tyler.

Roan had planned the perfect cool and collected conversation starter. Unfortunately, the moment he saw Patrick, it flew right out of his mind. "You had a mighty busy day yesterday," he sniped. "I guess fucking me over your desk wasn't enough. You and Tyler have fun?"

Patrick looked at his young lover like he'd been slapped. "Fun? Not really. Roh, what…?" He reached out to him, but Roan pulled away.

"Oh, don't even try it," Roan sniped. "I was on your porch last night, coming to kiss you goodnight. To tell you…. Oh, fuck it!" He snorted at his own naivety. "I saw you with Tyler."

"Roan, Ty was just—"

"Just save it! How could you? You'll fuck me on every surface of the cabin or barn, but only Tyler is good enough to take up to your bedroom, huh?"

"But—"

Roan held up a hand, dismissing Patrick's attempts to explain. "All you had to do was say you wanted to date other people. Would've been fine with me. Adam called and left me a message yesterday."

"Roan, listen to me—"

"We'll both just date whomever we damn well please, all right?" the young man announced.

Patrick stood dumbstruck as Roan spun around and stormed out of the barn. Gathering his wits, he started to run after him, hesitating when Jeff called out to him.

"Boss, Marigold is down. She's foalin', and it doesn't look good."

"Shit," Patrick swore, whipping his hat off his head and running his fingers through his hair. With a last distressed look in the direction Roan had headed, he turned to Jeff. "Call Doc and radio Reece and Ben back in. We may need their help."

Chapter Six

ROAN cringed and pulled back slightly as Adam's breath blew across his face. The slightly intoxicated cowboy kept leaning closer than necessary to talk to him. It was loud in here, but not *that* loud. Of course, Roan recognized his ploy. A few weeks ago, he would've even encouraged it with a hand around his waist and similar behavior, but tonight it was getting on his last nerve.

Roan had psyched himself up for this date, determined to go home with Adam and let the handsome cowboy pound Patrick out of his system, but now all he could think about was finding a way to escape. Unfortunately, there weren't many options. Adam had picked him up, so he didn't have his own truck. He told himself to just relax and try and enjoy the night. He was doing his best to focus on picking up the thread of Adam's lengthy monologue about winning the rodeo buckle he was wearing when a golden head caught his eye.

Tyler.

Shit, did that mean Patrick was here, too? Of course, he'd known it was a possibility when he'd called and asked Adam out. He'd even picked The Red Dog to really rub Patrick's nose in the fact that he could have a different date every night of the week if he wanted. Moving closer and laying a hand on Adam's chest, he watched Tyler move across the room to the bar and exchange a laugh with Randy as he ordered a drink.

Adam responded to the unintentional encouragement by starting to kiss Roan's neck. "Maybe it's time to get out of here," he whispered, pushing the dark curls out of the way to reach more skin.

Roan used the hand on the cowboy's chest to push him firmly away. "I'll be right back," he said distractedly, heading towards the men's room and scanning the bar for Patrick.

Passing Tyler, Roan was surprised to hear the blond address him. "Your decision to explore a relationship with Patrick didn't last very long, I see," he stated flatly.

Roan turned, suddenly so angry he saw red. How dare this asshole sit there and make comments about Roan's commitment to Patrick when the night before he'd been doing his best to lure Patrick away from him? "What in the fuck gives you the right to judge me?"

"Patrick's my best friend, and I care about him. When I see him being played for a fool, I get more than a little pissed," Tyler answered, getting to his feet. The two men were about the same height, but Tyler had several pounds on Roan.

"Take it outside, guys," Randy warned from behind the bar. Many years of dealing with hot-headed cowboys had given him a sixth sense for trouble brewing.

Roan turned on his heel and stalked towards the door, leaving Tyler to follow in his wake. Stepping into the neon-tinted night, he moved away from the door so they wouldn't be overheard. "*I'm* not the one who decided that monogamy wasn't necessary… as you very well know. That was you two!"

Tyler's forehead wrinkled in confusion. "What are you talking about? Patrick would walk over cut glass – barefoot – to keep you from being hurt, and I'd never mess up something that Patrick wants as much as he wants you."

That sucked some of the wind out of Roan's sails, and his self-righteous anger faltered a little. "You were with him last night, and he sure as hell wasn't thinking of me then," Roan accused.

Tyler's expression changed slightly. "Last night? I was upset about my girls. My ex-wife, Abby, is trying to keep my youngest daughter from me because she found out about my affair with Patrick. Patrick and I've been best friends since I moved to town— of course I ran to him to talk it out! Are you saying that he's not allowed to have friends if he wants to have a relationship with you?"

Roan swallowed. Had the kid they'd been talking about been Tyler's daughter and not him? Why hadn't Patrick just told him this morning when he'd confronted him? 'Because you acted like an immature ass and didn't give him a chance to get a word in edgewise,' he groaned to himself.

"No... uhmm... that's not it. I just... well, I thought... he was holding you, and I heard him say that 'no kid was going to come between you'. You went upstairs with him." Roan stopped and waited for the older man to call him a fool.

Tyler leaned back against the side of the saloon and looked at his boots with a thoughtful expression. "You said all this to him, huh?"

If it hadn't been so dark, Tyler would have seen Roan flush. "Uhmm... well, no, not exactly. I sort of told him that I saw him with you, and that if he could see other people so could I, but he didn't tell me I was wrong."

Tyler snorted. "Did you give him a chance? Or just attack like you did with me?"

"He could've come after me."

"Patrick can be a little hard-headed. He's probably home right now, imagining you in someone else's arms and drinking his way through a bottle of scotch."

Straightening, Tyler invaded Roan's space, forcing him to retreat a step, his back connecting with the wall. "I'm only going to tell you this once. Patrick is one of the most loyal people I know. I will not see him hurt by your petty jealousy and juvenile temper tantrums." The blond poked at Roan's chest. "You don't deserve it, but I'm going to spell it out for you because you're obviously too blind to see it for yourself. Patrick is in love with you. Has been for a damned long time. We haven't been together since you've been back in town, and, yes, that means *before* you two were even being civil to each other.

"On the other hand, he thinks you're too good for him, and he's never going to beg or cajole you into being with him, when in his mind you'd be better off without him." Tyler took a deep breath and stepped back slightly. "And just for the record, I'd take him back faster than a bull could throw me. You've used up your chances in my book. Hurt him again, and I'll do everything I can to make him mine. Permanently."

Still fuming, the older man turned on the heel of his boot and stormed back towards the bar and his drink. He needed it right about now. Lack of sex and a confrontation with the person responsible was not doing much to lighten his mood. He was getting fucking tired of being noble. He should have staked his claim on Patrick the other night and driven Roan from his mind by fucking him through the mattress.

Several steps from the door, the blond hesitated. If he went back in there, he'd have to watch Roan come back in for the rest of his date with Adam. He didn't think his self-control was up for any more contact with Finn's son tonight. Changing direction, he headed for his truck. He had most of a decent bottle of scotch at home that would do.

Rolling to a stop at Old Highway Nine, he looked right towards home and left towards Wellington. He really didn't want to go home. Drinking alone and lonely in a house stripped of all personal effects by his divorce just wasn't healthy. Hadn't someone said there was a new bar that had opened just west of here? Stallion Station. That was it. Tonight was just the night to check it out.

Tyler spotted the rearing stallion sign with no problem, turning into the gravel parking lot. 'Respectable crowd,' he mused, looking around at the trucks in the parking lot. Pushing open a heavy carved wooden door, he stepped into the dim, smoky interior. It was smaller than The Red Dog, more of a pub than a dance hall, which suited Tyler just fine. Walking up to the highly polished bar, his eyes scanned the bottles. Nice selection.

"What'll it be, partner?"

Tyler eyes darted sideways, landing on a set of washboard abs covered by a tight, thin cotton shirt. Unable to help himself, his eyes traveled down over a subtle bulge that made his mouth water, and a pair of incredibly long legs. The denim clung to obviously muscular thighs. His gaze lingered every bit as obviously on the journey up, his mind fantasizing that the bulge was slightly larger due to his perusal. The chest was just as magnificent as the legs… broad shoulders… long, dark hair held back with a leather tie… full lips… and incredibly amused eyes. In this light, Tyler couldn't tell what color they were, but they were lighter than brown. He'd had enough of dark-eyed pretty boys for one night… and this was no boy.

Dark eyebrows rose, adding to the amused look on the bartender's face. "So… you want something or not?"

'You'd punch me in the nose for ordering what I really want,' Tyler thought. Clearing his throat, the blond ordered a scotch. He toyed with the idea of ordering top shelf, but decided not to waste the expensive stuff on getting blindly drunk. "Don't taste the difference after the third or fourth one anyway," he muttered.

"What?" the bartender asked, placing his drink on a napkin in front of him and scooting a bowl of pretzels closer.

"Oh, nothin'. Just talking to myself," Tyler replied, his fingers curling around the heavy glass and staring down into the warm amber liquid.

"As long as you don't start answering yourself, we'll be good," the younger man laughed, offering a warm smile.

Tyler shook off the feeling that he was being flirted with, deciding it was only wishful thinking on his part. Besides, he'd promised himself that after the ruckus his ex- was raising, he'd stick to women. It'd just be easier, since his relationship with Patrick had gone south anyway. Raising the glass to his lips, he took a large swallow, steeling himself for the burn. When the liquid slid smoothly down his throat, curling up like a contented kitten in his stomach, his eyes grew wide with surprise. "I've never known a bar that served Glendronach as a well drink."

"We don't, but you looked like a man whose tongue could discern the difference. I'm Karl." The dark-haired man extended his hand across the bar.

Tyler clasped the hand with his own, squeezing firmly, a dangerous glint in his eyes. "Ty, and you have no idea how talented my tongue is...." Tyler bit back the rest of the lewd comment.

Karl grinned. "Maybe if I keep feeding you Glendronach, I'll find out." He responded to a call from the far end of the bar, winking suggestively at Tyler as he turned his back.

Tyler's eyes traveled immediately to the tight ass that matched the rest of the man's incredibly fit body. "Fuck," he hissed, "the road to hell is paved with good intentions."

Tyler's gaze followed Karl, watching as he joked with customers, flirted with the waitresses, and easily managed the steady flow of drink orders. Everywhere he went, Karl would stop and make eye contact with him, smiling or winking in a way that sent the blond's stomach into spasms.

Karl took a quick swipe at the bar with a rag, looking around the room to determine what needed to be done next. Seeing nothing of immediate importance, he poured himself a Coke and wandered back to Tyler's end of the bar. Crossing his arms, he leaned against the counter. "Ready for another scotch?"

"Your boss is gonna object if I drink too much of his best at well prices." Tyler grinned and slid the empty glass towards Karl.

"Doubtful. Having a gorgeous blond sipping fine scotch at the bar is good for business. Besides, I am the boss. Bought this place when I couldn't take the pace in Dallas anymore. Decided that money wasn't worth three ulcers, no matter how much it was." Karl sat the refilled glass in front of Tyler and watched as the blond raised it to his lips, his eyelids dropping to half-mast.

"If you keep lookin' at me that way, I'm gonna start gettin' ideas," Tyler rasped, lowering the glass.

"Maybe I *want* you to get ideas," Karl replied, one eyebrow rising as he smirked. Turning his back on Tyler, he returned to the customers at the other end of the bar.

Tyler pulled at his shirt, fanning air against his chest. Damn, it was hot in here. The devil on his shoulder, who looked suspiciously like Patrick, started whispering in his ear. *Nothing wrong with a little friendly tumble. He's obviously interested... and drop dead gorgeous.* Gulping his scotch, Tyler turned away, watching the patrons in the bar while he listed all the reasons getting involved with Karl wasn't a good idea.

"So was the second not as good as the first?" Karl's voice rumbled from behind him, snapping him out of his reverie.

Tyler turned, looking down at his still half-full glass. "No, just got distracted, I guess." He took another swallow from his forgotten glass.

"What're you thinking about? Because I'm guessing that no matter how much she might want you to be, you aren't all that fascinated with Caroline." Karl nodded towards a slender cowgirl leaning against the jukebox, staring at Tyler like a coyote would eye a rabbit.

Tyler spun back to the bar, running his fingers through his hair. "Fuck."

Karl laughed, laying a hand on Tyler's arm. "It's okay, man. I won't let her have her wicked way with you. Your virtue's safe. Unless you don't want it to be...?" His fingers slid suggestively under the up-turned cuff of Tyler's shirt, playing with the hair on his forearm.

The last line had been added with an incredibly erotic look that melted Tyler from the inside out, taking the last of his reservations with it. "I'm not sure I've got much virtue left, but I'd be willing to lose what's there…" Tyler paused, eyes locking with Karl's, "…with you."

The smile started as a twitch at the corner of Karl's lips, traveling across the full mouth and up to his eyes. "Then I'd say we're both on the same page. Let me refill that glass and see what I can do about getting people out of here on time tonight."

Tyler didn't even try to keep his eyes off Karl for the rest of the time, and the bar owner played to him shamelessly, bending over to get bottles from under the bar, licking his fingers when some bourbon spilled over the side of a glass. Fuck. Tyler shook his head. It took all his restraint not to yell 'Fire!' at the top of his lungs and clear all the people out.

Last call was eventually announced and with many waves and lewd comments, the bar finally emptied. Karl disappeared from sight, and the lights across the room extinguished, leaving only the track lights on the bar illuminated. The country music blaring from hidden speakers changed to the soothing strains of classical. The brunette reappeared from a door on the other side of the dance floor.

"Rachmaninov?" Tyler asked, amazed.

"Ooooh… the man knows his music as well as his scotch," Karl retorted.

Unable to help showing off a little, Tyler added, "His *Second Piano Concerto*."

The bar owner grinned. "I do love a man with class."

"I've yet to see any proof of that." Tyler turned to face Karl, spreading his legs and leaning back against the bar on his elbows in challenge.

Karl's eyes narrowed dangerously. "Oh, you are playing with fire. You have no idea how much I want you."

"Obviously not enough or you wouldn't be clear over there."

A muffled 'ooofff' pressed out of Tyler's lungs as Karl impacted against him with full force, his lips attacking the blond's, his hand positioning Tyler's head so his tongue could plunder at will. Teeth grazed his lips as Karl sucked at them deeply, and Karl's hand slipped from Tyler's hip around to cup his ass, raising him to meet the relentless thrusts of his hips.

It took several seconds for Tyler's naturally dominant nature to assert itself— somehow it felt disturbingly right to submit to Karl's control. Pushing back against the bar, he spun them around, pinning Karl against the padded rail. Pulling sharply on the ponytail of dark hair, he exposed a long length of neck. Nibbling on the strained tendons, he rasped, "I'm going to fuck you so hard they'll hear you in Dallas."

"Do it," Karl said as he started to pull at Tyler's clothes. It took a matter of seconds for shirts to be unfastened and hands to slip inside, jeans to be opened and pushed out of the way, and then Karl was bracing himself against the bar, thrusting hard into Tyler's fingers and groaning shamelessly. "Fuck me."

Tyler slid his hard cock between the gorgeous tight cheeks, the head bumping behind Karl's balls and making the brunette moan and writhe. Biting into Karl's shoulder, he hissed, "You ready for my cock? Tell me you want it."

"Fuck me," Karl begged. "Stick that giant cock in my tight ass."

Tyler groaned, closing his fingers tightly around the base of his cock to keep from coming all over Karl's ass as he brushed against the pink opening. With fumbling fingers, he pulled a condom from his pocket and spit into his fist to add to the lubrication. One finger pushed at the tight hole, massaging it. "Relax, baby. Let me in," he crooned.

Karl did, and Tyler's finger slipped inside. "Fuck, you're so tight," the older man moaned, rocking his cock against Karl's hip as he fingered the tight opening, loosening the muscle.

"I'm good. Want you in me," Karl moaned as Tyler's fingers played over the sensitive walls of his ass.

Tyler pressed the head of his cock against the pucker. Grasping Karl's hips firmly, he pushed forward. "Aww… shit…!" His head fell forward onto his lover's back as the strong muscle gave, clenching tightly around the head of his cock as it slipped through. "Give me a second," he found himself saying. Fuck, wasn't that the bottom's line?

"Take your time," Karl hissed, pushing back, impaling himself on Tyler's shaft. "I'll just fuck myself on your cock while I wait."

"Fuck!" Tyler swore, fingers bruising Karl's hips as he pounded into his body. Hard and fast didn't describe the pummeling Karl's body got as Tyler raced towards his climax.

Karl pulled erratically on his own cock as Tyler fucked him over the bar. In no time at all, he was coming so hard his stomach muscles convulsed. His inner muscles clenched, and he pushed back against his lover, taking him as deep as his body would allow. "Oh… Ty… Oh, fuck…."

Tyler cried out as Karl's body gripped him, triggering his own climax. "Fuckin' hell!" he screamed, his fingers tangling in Karl's long hair, wrenching his head around for a kiss. His hips stuttered forward, each thrust punctuated by a moan swallowed between them.

Jerking muscles quieted to quivering. "Come home with me," Tyler whispered, rubbing his cheek against Karl's back, unable to find the energy to move away.

"We should go to my place," Karl chuckled, hissing as Tyler slid from his body.

"Why?" Tyler asked, curious about Karl's amusement.

"Because I live upstairs. We wouldn't have to get dressed, and we could be in bed in less than five minutes."

"Fuck," Tyler swore. "Why in the hell didn't we do that in the first place?"

Karl turned away from the bar, pulled Tyler up against his sweaty body, and rubbed their spent erections together. His hands slid down into the open jeans to cup the tight ass and pull Tyler closer. It wouldn't take long to rejuvenate interest. He grinned at the way Tyler's body responded to his. "You could have waited?" Karl drawled, nudging Tyler's lips open for a slow kiss. "I sure as hell couldn't've."

Tyler felt himself flush, and his eyes darted around for a safe place to focus. He couldn't look at the gorgeous bar owner for fear of giving away exactly how strong a reaction he was having. "No, don't reckon I could've, but now that it's the closer option...." His voice rose in suggestion.

Karl stepped away, pulling his jeans up but not bothering to fasten them. "This way."

Chapter Seven

PATRICK toed the old swing into motion again as he slowly sipped on his fifth scotch. The rhythmic creaking of the old hinges always soothed him, but not tonight. Tonight, it was seriously getting on his nerves.

Four hours ago, he'd watched Roan hop up into Adam's truck as he made his way from the barn to his cabin, tired, dirty, and sore. Marigold and her foal were both going to live, but it had been touch and go. This would be the mare's last foal. She had suffered too much damage to breed her again.

Roan still wasn't back. As he stared out the bay window while he ate dinner and caught up on some bookkeeping, Patrick'd told himself that he was enjoying the rising moon – not watching for Roan to return. At midnight, he'd given up all pretense and moved his sorry ass and scotch to the front porch swing. He'd had too much of the latter to be able to concentrate on feed expenditures anyway.

Stopping the swing, Patrick rose to his feet, stretching the muscles that had stiffened while he kept his vigil. "You are a pathetic old fool, Lassiter," he cursed. "You need to stop this nonsense and go to bed. Roan may not even be planning to come home tonight. He's not a kid anymore. He doesn't have a curfew you can count on. Are you going to sit out here all night just to catch a glimpse of him as he walks into the house after a date with someone else?" He shook his head. God, the voice of reason could be annoying.

Glancing over his shoulder as he pulled open the screen door, he spotted headlights turning into the lane. "Fuck." He returned to the swing, misjudging the distance and setting it swaying wildly as he sat back down.

Patrick planted his bare feet on the wooden floor to still the swing, watching as Adam's 4x4 pulled to a stop in front of the main house. He tensed, knowing that if it sat there too long, he was going to be hard pressed not to stride over and yank his Roan out of it. 'He's not your anything anymore,' he reminded himself. He exhaled gratefully when the passenger door opened almost immediately and Roan swung to the ground with a wave.

Patrick continued to watch silently, thankful to be hidden by the deep shadows of his porch.

Roan stood in the moonlight, staring at Patrick's cabin for a long time. It had taken him longer to get Adam to bring him home than he had hoped. Patrick was surely asleep. Tomorrow would be a better time to talk. He turned and climbed the first two steps of the main house before reversing direction and walking towards the rough-hewn cabin.

Patrick took in his appearance as he crossed the moonlit yard, looking for clues about what he'd been up to while out on the town. Roan looked exactly like he did on most days, scuffed boots, worn Wranglers, and a Western-cut shirt. Patrick couldn't quite make out the moon-washed color of the shirt, but the pearl snaps were unfastened halfway down, displaying a large section of smooth chest. Patrick felt a knot of jealousy form in his stomach, wondering if Roan had deliberately put himself on display to entice Adam or if the wrangler's hands had been responsible for opening the snaps.

Roan hesitated a second time at the bottom of Patrick's porch steps before grabbing the railing and bounding up them in two leaps. He pulled open the screen door and was raising his hand to knock when Patrick spoke from the shadows. "Bit late to come visitin', don'tcha think?" The scotch made his drawl more pronounced.

Roan started, turning towards the disembodied voice. Picking Patrick's shadow from among the others, he smiled tentatively and moved towards the swing. "Well, I obviously wasn't going to wake you," he replied as he sat down next to Patrick on the swing.

"Hmmm…." Patrick hummed, acutely aware of Roan's body so close to his side.

Roan gestured to the glass in Patrick's hand. "Whatcha drinkin'?"

"Scotch."

Tyler had been right about that, at least. It rankled slightly that the other man knew Patrick so well. Roan was feeling obnoxiously sober. It had been painfully obvious that Adam had been disappointed when Roan had declined his offer of a beer back at his place, but Roan had finally convinced the wrangler he wasn't just playing hard to get, that he really wanted to go home.

His heart had belonged for as long as he could remember to the quiet man sitting next to him, resolutely not looking at him. It was way past time to do something about it, just like his dad had suggested. "Can I have a taste?" Roan asked.

Patrick shrugged, not meeting Roan's eyes. If he had, he might have recognized the mischievous glint in them before his lap was full of the slender young man and his mouth was full of a demanding tongue. Patrick's head swam as all of the blood in his body rushed for his groin. With a thud, the glass tumbler fell to the porch floor as Patrick's fingers wound into thick, dark curls. Roan tasted like beer and something sweeter, a unique taste that belonged just to Roan and reminded Patrick of the sweet, clean smell of mown hay.

Roan straddled Patrick's lap easily, moaning softly as he ground his hips against the older man's, rocking the swing in a gentle arc. This they could do. This they were good at. When everything else is falling apart, go back to your comfort zone. He could always make Patrick want him. Bracing one hand on the back of the swing, he captured Patrick's head with the other to prevent his escape. Easily slipping his tongue past startled lips, he sucked the taste of scotch from Patrick's lips and tongue.

Wrenching his mouth away from Roan's to gasp for air, Patrick placed his hands flat on Roan's chest. "What in the fuck? Adam not enough for one night? You just can't—"

"Can't what?" Roan asked, rocking his hips harder against the other man. "Make a mistake? I did, you know. I should have trusted you. Let you talk this morning. Asked you why Tyler was spending the night. Not attacked you. I've never felt the way I feel about you about anybody, and it makes all my reactions a little… intense."

Roan slowly dragged his thumb up the ridge covering the zipper of Patrick's jeans. "Shit, you feel good. You are so fucking hard for me. It makes me want to strip us out of these jeans and ride you 'til I scream."

Patrick groaned, unable to resist arching up against the hardness hidden by Roan's jeans. "Sex isn't going to fix this," he moaned, his body ignoring his mind and seeking more contact.

"It might not fix everything," Roan said, leaning back with his hands on Patrick's shoulders. "But this seems to be the way we communicate best. We'll work on the rest, yeah? For now, let's use what works. Show me how you feel about me, Patrick, and let me show you how sorry I am."

Roan's lips descended to Patrick's neck, nibbling a trail towards his ear. He strained forward as strong hands caught his head, attempting to pull him away.

"Roan, stop!" Patrick caught at his roaming hands, trapping them at his sides. "Not talking is what got us here. We can't—"

Roan didn't need his hands. His tongue exploring the curve of Patrick's ear was sufficiently distracting. A deep groan rumbled up from Patrick's chest. Roan's lips curved into a smile against his ear and he blew softly, extracting his hands as Patrick's grip grew slack.

"Roan, Ty was…" Patrick said.

Roan moved his lips over the foreman's, stilling his mouth, determined to change 'Roan' back to 'Roh'.

Rough hands cupped his face, immobilizing him. "I need you to listen to me," Patrick stated.

Roan motioned towards the door, climbing off Patrick's lap. "Okay, let's go inside." He took Patrick's hand, afraid to break the physical connection and give his lover too much time to think. Inside the house, he led Patrick to the couch, sitting next to him, one leg curled over his lap.

Patrick's hand rested open on the denim-clad thigh. "I don't know what you saw last night, but Ty and I aren't together anymore. We haven't been since—"

"I came home. I know. He told me."

"Tyler?"

Roan focused his eyes on the hand stroking his thigh. "I ran into him at The Red Dog tonight. I kind of went off on him, and he set me straight."

"So you're here because Ty sent you…."

Feeling Patrick pulling away, Roan crawled back into his lap. "No, I would have come as soon as I managed to pull my head out of my ass. I acted like an immature brat. I'd spent all day thinking about you after we made love in your office. Hell, I spend all day every day thinking of you. I couldn't wait to get home to you, and seeing Tyler in your arms felt like someone kicked me in the stomach. I spent all night thinking about him in your bed, a bed I haven't even seen."

"Oh, baby…."

"I'm not quite as juvenile as all this looks. I came down this morning intending to have a perfectly calm discussion with you. I had even come up with a reasonable discussion starter, but all that other crap came streaming out instead. Every time you opened your mouth, I thought you were going to tell me you'd made a mistake being with me and you were back with Tyler, so I kept cutting you off." Roan paused, forcing himself to give Patrick a chance to respond.

Patrick stared into Roan's eyes like he was trying to read his soul. "What had you planned to say?" he finally asked.

The question surprised Roan. "Well... I was going to take you into your office and tell you that I had seen Tyler at your house last night. I was hoping at that point you were going to jump in and give me a perfectly rational explanation, but if you hadn't, I was going to ask you if you still had feelings for Tyler. I had even practiced my reaction if you said you did."

"Silly boy." Patrick pulled Roan towards him, initiating contact for the first time since Roan had messed everything up. Their lips met gently at first and then with increasing ardor. Patrick's hand pulled at the cotton shirt until he could slide his hands up Roan's sides and over the planes of his chest.

Roan whimpered, pressing Patrick's hand to his chest when it tugged on a sensitive nipple. "I want this. God, I want this, and I know I don't have any right to ask you for anything, but...."

"I can't deny you anything. Don't you know that by now?" Patrick asked, nuzzling the warm hollow at the base of Roan's throat.

"Take me to bed, Patrick. I want you to make love to me in your bed." He swallowed the knot of fear that had risen in his throat. "I want to wake up in your arms."

There. He'd said it. He'd asked outright for what he wanted. Patrick's silence finally forced him to meet his lover's eyes, not being able to wait one more second to gauge his reaction. His breath caught in his throat at the depth of love he saw reflected in their blue depths.

"I love you," Roan blurted before he could bite it back. He almost added the word 'too'. The emotion pouring from Patrick's eyes was as clear as a verbal declaration.

"Come with me," Patrick whispered, pushing Roan off his lap.

Silently, they climbed the stairs hand in hand. Roan's memory briefly flashed back to Patrick leading Tyler up these same stairs just the night before, but he firmly pushed his jealousy aside. Patrick paused outside his bedroom door, obviously unwilling to enter.

"Why are you so reluctant to show me your room?" Roan asked. "Are your dirty shorts slung all over the furniture or something?"

Patrick bit his bottom lip. "Well... not exactly." He paused with his hand on the doorknob. Taking a deep breath, he pushed it open.

Roan stepped into the room and gasped. The room was furnished simply with heavy pale pine furniture, a four-poster bed and six-drawer dresser. What caught his attention, though, were the photographs that covered the walls – Roan, Roan and the first horse he'd broken, Roan at graduation, and a breathtaking shot of the pond at sunset centered over the bed. "It's the pond," he said, ignoring the other images.

"Yeah," Patrick answered, waiting for Roan's reaction.

"Who took it?"

"I did."

Roan turned to stare at Patrick, flabbergasted. "I didn't know you took pictures. I've never seen you with a camera. How...?"

Patrick shrugged carelessly. "Well, I don't get much chance. When we first bought the ranch, I carried one with me everywhere I went, but it was hard on the cameras."

"I'll buy you a new one every year if you'll keep taking pictures like this one," Roan promised.

Patrick pulled his lover away from the wall, kissing him gently. "No chance. I took that picture the day you left for college. I wouldn't go back to that pain for anything. Instead of a camera, how about I keep you in my hands instead?" Patrick suggested, sitting on the bed and pulling Roan into his arms.

"Piss poor trade-off if you ask me."

Patrick's hands ran up Roan's thighs from knee to groin. "Now, are we going to sit here and discuss my photographs or are we going to make love?"

Happily distracted by the hands sliding over his body, Roan moaned. "Oh, make love, definitely."

Chapter Eight

"GOOD, because I think it's long overdue." Patrick's hands settled in the open V of Roan's shirt. With a sharp tug, the remaining snaps popped open like a string of firecrackers.

"Glad I didn't pick a shirt with buttons," Roan smirked, pushing Patrick flat on the bed and straddling his body. "Long overdue, huh? Exactly how long have you had thoughts about ravishing me?"

Patrick glanced away, unable to meet the young man's eyes. "Too long to be proper."

Grasping Patrick's chin, Roan tilted his face up to meet his gaze. "No more hiding between us. You were my first wet dream, and I doubt your feelings went back that far."

Roan's smile eased the tightness in Patrick's chest, the shame he had felt all those years ago slowly fading away. The man poised above him was all grown up and here of his own free will. If that just happened to coincide with every closely guarded fantasy Patrick cherished, well, bully for him. "No, probably not that far," Patrick conceded.

"So, have you laid in this bed and thought about me?" Roan asked, tilting his head and running his fingers up Patrick's chest, grazing his nipples through the soft cotton.

"God, yes," Patrick moaned, gasping as Roan's hands opened his shirt, slipping inside and connecting with bare skin.

"Tell me." Roan's fingers brushed through the dense curls on Patrick's chest, circling the small puckered nipples, pinching one and then both before leaning down to claim one with his mouth. Sucking the pebbled flesh hard into his mouth, he captured the nub with his teeth, biting firmly until Patrick cried out, his back arching off the bed. "Tell me," Roan repeated.

"If you want me to talk, you're gonna have to quit doin' that." Patrick's fingers wound tightly into Roan's curls, preventing him from doing just what he had asked for.

Flicking his tongue repeatedly, Roan wrung several erotic sounds from Patrick before sitting up and sliding his own shirt off his shoulders. Patrick's hands immediately moved to the flat stomach and higher onto the sculpted chest. He attempted to roll them over, but Roan resisted, pushing him flat on the bed again. "Uh-uh, when you take control, my mind shuts down and I'm incapable of doing anything but moaning and coming. I want to touch you all the ways I've been dreaming about."

"Well, if you insist," Patrick sighed, relaxing into the pillows. "Still want me to tell you my fantasies?"

Just the way Patrick said the words 'my fantasies' made Roan tremble. He rocked forward, pressing his throbbing erection against its mate through two layers of denim. Even though he wasn't sure he could actually handle the description without coming in his pants like a teenager, he managed a strangled, "Yes… please."

Patrick closed his eyes, focusing on the feeling of Roan's hands on his body. "There are dozens of them – of us together all over the ranch, here, the barn, the pond. You don't know how close I came to stealing your virginity that day at the pond."

"You wouldn't have been stealing. I'd have given it to you gladly," Roan said, his fingers deftly opening Patrick's jeans and working them down his hips far enough for him to be able to kick them to the floor. Standing quickly, he shed his own boots and jeans before returning to his position over Patrick.

"I think that's the thing that kept me away. I always knew you wouldn't stop me, so I had to have the control."

"You know that you can let that control go now, right?" Roan asked, his lips brushing the crest of Patrick's hipbone.

"This…" Patrick gasped.

"This what?" Roan's tongue circled a crescent moon tattoo low on Patrick's belly that he hadn't even known existed.

"My fantasy. One of them… hell, lots of them… I'd get out of the shower and stretch out on the bed, let the breeze from the window dry the last of the moisture from my skin. I'd close my eyes and imagine your tongue licking at the drops of water… blowing… oh fuck, Roh…." Patrick's voice dissolved into a groan as Roan licked the head of Patrick's cock, blowing warmly over the sensitive skin in an imitation of Patrick's words.

Opening his mouth, Roan slid the smooth head past his lips, letting it slide to the back of his throat and then pulling back slowly, his tongue lingering at the slit to savor the unique taste of his lover. "Do you fuck my mouth?"

Patrick's hips surged upward, his cock sliding easily into Roan's mouth. "God! No, not usually, but I may next time."

Roan chuckled around the shaft in his mouth, causing another involuntary thrust from his lover. "So what *do* I do?"

Patrick's legs fell open wider. "You keep licking."

The deep rasp of Patrick's voice and the vulnerability of his position drew Roan's eyes up to connect with his. Holding the smoldering gaze, he extended his tongue, licking a long stripe down the underside of Patrick's cock, suckling gently at the soft skin holding the twin globes. "More?"

"More." Patrick's eyes fluttered shut, unable to stay open as Roan's tongue dipped behind his balls and into the crevice between his cheeks.

Roan raised one of Patrick's legs, turning him onto his side to give him greater access. "So damp. So hot," Roan whispered against the lower curve of Patrick's ass, playing into the fantasy. "Tastes so sweet."

Patrick squirmed against the teasing sensation of Roan's tongue tickling the sensitive curve of his ass. He yelped as sharp teeth nipped at the skin, thumbs spreading him open wider. Every muscle clenched from Patrick's jaw to his calves. Opening himself this way just wasn't in his nature.

Roan ran a soothing hand up Patrick's muscular back. "Mine. Mine," he chanted after his tongue probed the small opening. "Let go. Trust me."

A shuddering sigh stuttered from Patrick's lungs as Roan's tongue sank deeper and deeper into his body. With each release of breath, he relaxed further, letting his lover claim more of his body... more of his soul. When Roan's hand slid between his legs to stroke his cock and balls, he collapsed forward, trapping it between his body and the bed to stop the motion. "Stop... can't... don't want to come yet."

Roan withdrew his hand, but continued to lap at Patrick's entrance before pausing to ask, "What if I want you to come undone at my touch?"

Patrick turned, grabbing his curls and pulling him up into a sloppy, wet kiss. "Then let me make love to you."

Roan whimpered as Patrick sucked their combined tastes off his tongue. "Fuck, yes." Rolling onto his back, he pulled Patrick between his legs. "Want you."

Patrick's hand searched randomly over the top of the nightstand for the lube, unwilling to look anywhere but at Roan. Finding the small bottle, he quickly used its contents to stretch and lubricate the furled opening. "Please tell me you're ready," he begged, removing his fingers and pulling Roan's thighs over his own.

"I've been ready for ten years." Roan planted his feet on the bed and lifted his lower body to help Patrick position himself. With one steady push, he felt his body resist, relax, and stretch to accommodate his lover's shaft. "Nothing... nothing feels like you inside of me... so full... so complete."

Patrick stared down at his body finally joined with Roan's. They had done this before, but this time was different. The words made it different. The place made it different. The feelings made it different.

Roan tightened his muscles, rocking up to encourage Patrick to move. "Patrick... please...."

Locking his arms, Patrick pulled back, plunging forward with enough force to shift Roan higher in the bed, the blunt scrape against his prostate causing him to cry out. Patrick repeated the motion, a slow retreat followed by a carefully angled thrust. Roan's legs curled around his waist, his hands searching for something to anchor himself to.

"Me. Hold on to me." Patrick pulled one of Roan's legs to his shoulder, plunging even deeper.

Roan clung to Patrick's shoulders, trying to pull him closer for a kiss. Their bodies moved in perfect synchronization – stroke, lift, drag, arch. Slowly they climbed towards the inevitable culmination.

Thighs trembling uncontrollably, Patrick grabbed his lover firmly by the hips and rolled them both over, keeping their bodies joined. "Ride me," he croaked.

Roan started to move, head thrown back, eyes pressed tightly shut, taking his pleasure from Patrick, his cock leaving sticky trails across Patrick's belly. He yelped when a work-roughened hand circled his hypersensitive flesh, but he quickly started rocking between the sensations, back onto the hard shaft and forward into the tight grip of his lover's hand. He wasn't going to last long this way.

Opening his eyes, Roan looked down. Patrick's face was contorted with the effort to hold off his orgasm, his teeth sunk so deeply into his lip that he'd drawn blood. "Come for me, lover," he whispered, cupping Patrick's cheek with his hand.

Sapphire eyes opened, locking with Roan's. "Roh! Oh... fuck... Roh!" Patrick thrust up into his lover's clenching body, his body jerking with the force of his climax.

Watching Patrick come undone was all it took to push Roan over the edge. Adding his hand to Patrick's, he squeezed tightly, coming all over their fingers and Patrick's chest. Uncaring of the mess, he slumped forward, rubbing his cheek against the coarse hair as Patrick's arms held him close. "God, I love you," he purred, his eyes drifting shut and sleep pulling him under.

Patrick shifted, allowing Roan to slide to his side. He held him tightly until his soft, shallow breaths confirmed that he was deeply asleep. Moving cautiously, Patrick slipped into the bathroom for a warm, wet towel, cleaning himself and then returning to clean up Roan. Tossing the cloth towards the open bathroom door, he crawled back into bed, pulling the quilt over both of them.

Patrick lay awake, his body sated, but his mind restless. He stared down at the man asleep against his chest. He looked so peaceful... so innocent... so fucking young. How could he hope to hold Roan's interest for longer than a brief fling? Roan might want him now, but in fifteen years, Patrick would be sixty. Should he continue to pursue a relationship and enjoy every minute that he got, counting himself lucky, or give up the chance to be with Roan at all and hope to salvage some part of his heart?

Tyler might not cause the deep clenching in his heart that Roan did, but their friendship was strong. Wouldn't pursuing a deeper relationship with him make more sense? They were the same age, wanted the same things out of life, and the sex was great.

'Nothing like Roan,' the emotional part of his brain supplied. He'd always known that making love to Roan would be special, but he'd underestimated exactly how incredible it would be by a long shot. Every touch pulled him closer to not being able to walk away. To potentially being destroyed when Roan did.

Patrick's eyes drifted shut, swamped by the memory of making love to Roan. Even just holding him as he slept touched a place in Patrick's heart he hadn't known existed before tonight. But intense didn't necessarily mean better. A roaring fire might give off lots of heat, but it will scorch your front while your backside freezes. A good bed of glowing coals will cook your dinner and keep you warm through the night.

Patrick grinned as he thought about Tyler's reaction to being compared to a cooking fire and then sighed, unconsciously pulling Roan closer. All the logical parts of his brain told him that he'd be better off with Tyler and that he should set Roan free. Better to push him away now than to fall deeper and deeper in love, only to watch him leave. His heart, however, screamed at the very idea of releasing Roan.

Every time Roan said, "I love you," he'd had to bite back an echo of the words. He knew Roan had to know how he felt, but he was scared to actually say the words. To him, the words meant forever. He'd never actually said them before, though he seemed to be thinking them a lot lately. He just needed a little more time – a little time to decide what was best for both of them.

As the clock turned 4:45, Patrick kissed the sleep tousled curls. Sliding silently out of bed, he reached for his jeans. He knew he'd never be able to resist a warm, half-asleep Roan when those chocolate eyes opened. He needed some space, maybe a chance to talk to Tyler or Finn and sort out his thoughts.

PATRICK heard his name as he was closing the gate to the back pasture. All of the animals were fed and the horses out. A quick glance at his watch told him it was only quarter to six, early even by his standards, and the reason for his efficiency was stalking towards him.

Stopping to check a board in the fence, the older man managed to keep his back to Roan until he was directly behind him. He already knew the board was rotted. It had been on his repair list for the last month, but it gave him a good excuse not to look at the expression that was sure to be on Roan's face.

"You got up and started awfully early this morning." Roan tried to keep the accusation and hurt out of his voice. He'd learned something from his blow-up over Tyler. Waking up alone had been like a knife to the chest after putting his heart on the line and asking to wake up in Patrick's arms. It made him question everything they had experienced, everything they had shared the night before, but maybe he'd been deluding himself. It terrified him that it might have been one-sided. He'd been so sure it was love he saw in Patrick's eyes. But he'd said, 'I love you,' and the words had gone unanswered.

"The horses get up at the same time no matter how late I stay up," Patrick mumbled, pushing to his feet and brushing his hands off on his jeans. For all his thinking, he was no closer to knowing how to deal with his feelings for the young man staring at him accusingly.

"They could have waited another thirty minutes." Roan silently cursed the quaver in his voice. "Or you could have got me up. I would've helped." Patrick still hadn't met his eyes, and the feeling of dread he had woken up with was beginning to overwhelm him.

"Roan, you know how a ranch works. I'm not...." Patrick reached for his anger out of habit. It was the closest thing he had to a defense against what he felt for the man in front of him, but all he found was fear. Fear of losing the thing that he was doing his best to push away.

"Oh, no," Roan interrupted him, "you aren't pulling that shit on me. I could take it when the only time you'd touch me was when I goaded you into it. I felt like I deserved it when you acted this way afterward, but last night, you didn't touch me in anger or out of lust. We talked last night. We *made love* last night, Patrick."

Roan stopped and used his hands to cup Patrick's face, raising his chin to make him meet his eyes. "You loved me all night long, and you can feed yourself whatever line you want, but I know that you felt everything I did. Don't do this," he pleaded.

"Don't do what? You've known all along who I am. Is one night in bed supposed to change that?" Patrick said stoically. The flash of hurt in Roan's eyes almost undid his resolve, but he had to slow things down. He had already lost his heart. Hell, truth be told, it had belonged to Roan since before he left for college. Patrick was used to living with loving, but not having, Roan. Last night, he had realized how addictive *having* Roan could be. If this continued much longer, letting Roan go wouldn't be an option. Roan needed someone his own age, not a broken down, way-too-settled rancher.

Roan curled his hand in Patrick's shirt like he was about to haul off and punch him. Of course, it reminded Patrick of the way he'd pulled him onto the bed last night, and he felt himself start to swell against the fly of his jeans. "You're a fucking coward," Roan accused, beginning a long, angry tirade.

Patrick just dropped his eyes to the dirt and let the profanities and accusations wash over him. He deserved every one of them. When Roan finally fell silent, he dared to look up. He expected to find anger burning in the dark depths of Roan's eyes; instead they were resigned and flat. It appeared he had finally extinguished the young man's passion, and the idea scared the hell out of him. He forced his hands into his pockets to keep himself from reaching out, pulling Roan to him, and saying all the words the younger man had been waiting to hear.

"You aren't going to say anything, are you?" Roan spat. "Fine, the weather service says we've got bad storms rolling in. I'm goin' out to Turner's Flats to bring the herd over to this side of the creek, so if it floods, they won't be cut off. We don't want to lose any of them trying to make it back to the barn if the creek swells."

Patrick simply nodded. Roan just shook his head sadly and headed into the barn to saddle Shadow. The high-strung stallion suited his mood today.

Patrick got his tools and pretended to look busy fixing the broken board, watching furtively as Roan mounted up and rode out of sight.

Standing from fixing the last in a long series of boards that seemed to need repair once he'd paid attention, Patrick glanced up at the sky, trying to figure how much time had passed. A frown crossed his face at the dark clouds rolling in from the west. He'd skipped breakfast altogether, so he hadn't heard any of the weather reports this morning. It looked like it might be bad enough to bring the horses back into the barn, and he could do that quicker mounted. Grabbing the toolbox, he whistled to Lakota.

An hour and a half later, all the mares and foals were safely stowed back in their stalls, the mamas happily munching on an extra can of oats. Affectionately stroking Artemis's nose, he chuckled, "Spoiled rotten, the lot of ya."

The loud clanging of the dinner bell made him jump. He glanced at the clock on the barn wall, confirming that it was only 9:15. He sometimes lost track of time, but the bell ringing in-between meals was their warning system. Heading out of the barn at a full run, he met Finn halfway across the yard.

"Tornado's comin'," the older man yelled against the wind that was already gusting heavily, pelting both of them with sporadic bouts of stinging rain. "Two 'ave been spotted. One touched down at the old Saunder's place, headin' this way."

"Shit!" Patrick cursed, scanning the yard. His first thought was Roan.

Like he had read his mind, Finn asked, "Where's Roan?"

"Turner's Flats." Patrick didn't have to expound on what that meant. "He left hours ago, Finn, and he knew bad weather was headin' in. He should be back across the creek by now."

"Did he take a radio?"

"Should've." But he was upset, so probably not, Patrick added silently. "Where are the other men?"

"I sent Zeke to the storm cellar. He's slower than I am. Jeff is securing the house and Reece grabbed the jeep to fold down the windmills closest to the house. Told him not to be a hero. Do what he could and then head to ground. Ben's off."

Patrick nodded, looking longingly in the direction Roan had taken. But the young man had grown up around twisters and knew how to take care of himself. Pushing his hat down firmer on his head to keep from losing it, Patrick turned back to the barn. "Grab the dogs and head down to the storm shelter. I'll try and reach him on the radio and be right behind you. He'll be okay, Finn," he added, not sure which one of them he was reassuring.

Patrick closed the barn doors as he went through, sliding the bolt in place. Reaching the office, he tried to raise Roan on the radio but got only static. The hollow feeling in the pit of his stomach grew. There was one handset missing from the charger, but it could have been left out by one of the other hands. It had been a couple of days since Patrick had looked after them. He grabbed one and clipped it to his belt, just in case.

Leaving the barn as secure as he could get it, he headed for the shed to kill the main breaker. They collected both solar and wind energy and if the county's power went out, the flow would reverse, draining their stores. Depending on how bad the storm was, they'd need them to run the freezers and water pumps. After the last bad storm, they had run on solar power for almost two weeks before the lines were back up.

From there, he headed to the chicken pen. After five minutes of chasing chickens already nervous from the storm, he had a total of two out of the hundred or so back in the chicken coop. "Stupid fuckin' birds," he cursed. "Fine, blow away." Stomping out of the pen, he sent up a silent prayer. 'God protects fools and drunks. Let's hope that extends to chickens.'

A low rumbling and the cessation of rain told him it was time to quit fooling around and get down into the storm shelter. He was jogging towards the house when he spotted Muffin with a tiny kitten in her mouth, headed towards the porch.

"Fuckin' hell! She must've had her kittens last night." Breaking into an all-out run, he scooped her up with one hand, leaping to the porch over all three steps. "Where'd you put 'em, sweetheart?" A soft mewling, barely audible over the thundering wind, led him to the screen door. Muffin had wedged her kittens between the screen and kitchen door. "Not a bad choice," he muttered in admiration, "but how 'bout we take them with us?"

Pulling his hat off his head, Patrick loaded it with six, day-old kittens. He had to put mama down, but he knew she'd follow her babies. Looking to the west pasture, he spotted the twister, dark and ominous, pulling down out of the clouds like it was being sucked into a giant drain in the earth. No more than eight steps to the shelter. Thank God. He swung over the porch railing, closed the distance, and hauled on the iron handle. Finn pushed from the inside, and Patrick slid through the opening with Muffin between his legs.

"Take the scenic route?" Finn asked.

Patrick grunted, unloading the kittens into a box in the corner and staring at the sturdy wooden door. Silently he sent out the thought, 'Roh, find shelter. Come home to me. I love you.' The only response he got was the howl of the wind. Why were they always one step out of sync? Given a chance, he was going to fix that.

PATRICK had never been claustrophobic, but if he didn't get out of this cellar soon, he was going to lose it. It felt like the walls were closing in and his skin was crawling with nervous energy. Changing the station on the radio for the fourth time in the last five minutes, he ran across an updated weather report.

The weather service had downgraded the Tornado Warning to a Tornado and Severe Storm watch. Patrick told Finn and Zeke to stay put and pushed the heavy door open with Jeff, unsure of what they would find. The first thing he noticed was that both houses and the barn still had their roofs, a very good sign. Chickens were free and scratching all over the yard. A tree had fallen on their fence, setting them loose. He called out an all clear to Finn.

All four men headed straight for the barn, leaving the storm cellar door open for the animals to find their own way out. Sliding back the door, Patrick sighed at the sight of the slightly agitated but physically safe horses. "Jeff, check 'em out. Grab some carrots and apples out of the pantry. It'll get their mind off the storm."

He pulled out his saddle and tack as he listed what needed to be done, telling Zeke to ride over to check on the neighbors. It took less than five minutes to saddle Lakota. Reece had shown up by the time he was done, but he hadn't seen or heard from Roan.

"Someone stay by the radio," Patrick called, heading out of the barn. He didn't have to say where he was going. He was just happy that Finn hadn't insisted on going with him. He had some things to say to Roan that would be easier to say without Finn around to hear them.

The foreman pushed the paint as fast as he could safely go over the rain-soaked ground. There was a line cabin near Turner's Flats, built right into the side of a small butte. It would be the safest place for Roan to have taken cover.

Approaching from the east, Patrick felt the dread begin to settle in a heavy knot in his stomach, the twisted and broken trees showing that the tornado had followed this same path. His eyes searched constantly for any sign or movement that might lead him to Roan. The high pitched whinny of a horse in distress made him wheel Lakota around, heading towards a clump of trees to the north at a gallop. Skirting the edge to the far side, Patrick spotted Shadow, snorting and rearing, his reins caught in a tangle of mesquite branches.

Carefully riding up next to the agitated horse, Patrick clucked and soothed the animal with a patter of nonsense. When he had the horse free, he ran his hands over every inch, looking for injury. "You seem okay, old boy. Now where is Roan and why isn't he with you?"

Long habit kept his voice calm so as not to spook the already scared horse, but inside he felt himself start to give in to his own fear. He gave the horse a little slack and said, "Roan."

It was a long shot, but Lakota would've taken Patrick straight to him if he'd known where to go. Shadow was a different horse. Given his head, he sidled sideways and tossed his head to get free. Patrick took a deep breath. Pulling off Shadow's bridle, he swatted the horse on the rump. "Home!"

The horse took off for the barn, and Patrick turned east towards the cabin. Clearing the last of the trees, he spotted what was left of the place he had hoped would shelter Roan. Broken planks of wood and the skeletal structure of the plumbing sticking out of the ground made him pray Roan hadn't been here.

Eyes scanning every inch of the landscape, but seeing nothing, Patrick felt the tightness in his chest increase until it was impossible to take a full breath. Swallowing the lump in his throat, he blinked rapidly, clearing his eyes of the unwanted tears. Panic would not help Roan. He needed a clear head... and help.

Pulling his rifle from the back of his saddle, he fired three shots in the air. He waited for a response to the signal. If anyone from the ranch had been within hearing distance, they would have fired two shots in return.

Silence. Nothing but the ratchety chirp of insects after a storm. He now knew it was one of two things. Either Roan couldn't hear him, or Roan hadn't carried his gun. Snapping the radio off his belt, he called back to the ranch for a search party.

Looking out over the fields, green and refreshed from the rain, he whispered, "Hang on, Roh. We'll find you."

Chapter Nine

MOUNTING Lakota, Patrick turned towards Turner's Flats. He'd start at the beginning. Keeping a running count of the horses that he passed as he approached the creek, he determined that Roan had finished getting all of them across before the water level rose. He was irrationally irritated that the horses Roan had come out here to save were obliviously grazing, content and safe.

Slipping from his mount's back at the edge of the creek, he stooped to get a closer look at the soft ground. The rain had washed away most of the prints in the mud, but the number and direction of them clearly showed that Roan had driven the horses across the creek. Walking slowly away from the bank, he spotted several partial prints from Shadow, the only horse wearing shoes, leading away from the creek. Roan had finished his task and made it back across safely, at least.

Patrick was so engrossed in looking for tiny details that he never heard the sound of approaching hoofbeats. "Well, Tracker, anything interesting down there?" came an amused drawl.

Startled, Patrick looked up into familiar green eyes. "Ty!"

The blond dismounted and walked over to look at what Patrick was examining. "Shadow came into the barn. Doc checked him over, and he's fine. You radioed in that you found Shadow without Roan, but I think seeing the horse ride in, saddled with no rider, still shook Finn. The sheriff's set up quadrants and search teams."

"Do we have an assignment?"

"Finn figured you'd want to freestyle. My assignment is to baby-sit you."

Patrick snorted, standing and pointing at the ground. "Roan got the horses across and made it back to this side of the creek. The impressions are deep. It must've already been raining pretty hard."

"So… caught in a bad storm he can't outrun, where would he head?" Tyler asked.

"The line cabin."

Tyler could barely hear his friend's voice. "So let's go."

"It's gone," Patrick said stoically. "The tornado turned it into a pile of matchsticks." Patrick placed his foot in the stirrup and swung into the saddle.

"He wouldn't have known that," Tyler said, mounting his horse.

"Nope. The most direct route to the cabin is that way. I found Shadow about thirty degrees south." Patrick pointed.

"Is there anything in that direction?" Tyler nodded to where Patrick had found the riderless stallion.

Patrick shook his head. "Not that I can think of. Of course, I'm not exactly batting a thousand when it comes to reading Roan's mind of late."

"It'd take more than a crystal ball and a handful of Tarot cards to do that," Tyler snorted. "Best just go with what makes sense. Roan was headed to the line cabin and something separated him from his horse."

Patrick clucked his tongue at Lakota to get him moving, keeping him at a steady walk so he could watch the ground. "If we plot a line north from where I found Shadow, we may find where he and Roan parted company."

"Lead on, McDuff." After several tense minutes, Tyler fidgeted in his saddle. "So, you and Roan get a chance to talk this morning?"

Patrick shot a look at his friend over his shoulder. "He came and found me last night. Said you set him straight. How'd that happen?"

Tyler shrugged. "Ran into him at The Red Dog. So everything okay?"

"Well, it was… until I fucked it up this morning." 'Please give me a chance to make things right,' Patrick sent up a silent prayer.

Tyler sighed. "What'd ya do?"

"Just got to thinkin' too much. Same old shit, really. I'm too old for him. He's gonna leave."

"Fuck, Patrick! He *will* leave you if you keep acting like an insecure teenage girl. And I won't blame him. And I *won't* be taking you back, either." Tyler's voice lowered to a mumble. "Danged fool cowboy. Doesn't know a good thing when it lands in his lap."

Patrick grinned slightly at Tyler's disgruntled tirade. "I know. Trust me, when Finn hollered that we had a tornado coming and I knew Roan was out here somewhere, my whole perception of what was important changed."

"Well, then, let's find the kid so you can beg his forgiveness and I can get back to the gorgeous brunette I left in bed to come out in this godforsaken mess."

"Brunette?" Patrick asked, one eyebrow raising and pulling the corner of his mouth with it.

Tyler blushed slightly. He wasn't in the habit of picking up men at bars, and he wasn't sure if this counted since the man had been behind the bar instead of a patron. "Oh hell, I'll tell you all about it later. Could be nothing but a one-night stand. Didn't have time to see how the morning-after was gonna go."

"Okay, but I want—" Patrick's words cut off as he spotted something on the ground. Swinging off Lakota, he retrieved the shiny object. "Looks like a watch crystal," Patrick said, scanning the area. "Lot of disturbance on the ground. Rain's washed away anything really useful. I found Shadow almost due south of here."

Patrick scanned the area. The nearest thing to the south was the cluster of trees where he'd found Shadow. East was flat. Over the rise was what was left of the cabin. To the north, there was a crag of rocks. "Let's go check over there," Patrick suggested, motioning north. "If Roan got thrown and Shadow bolted, he could have headed that way to get out of the rain." He didn't mention that if Roan were okay, he would have headed towards the ranch on foot after the storm passed. There were no boot marks in the dirt.

"I'll go around to the east. You take the west," Tyler suggested. Patrick nodded, already turning his horse.

Tyler rode as close to the rocks as he could, dismounting several times to check crevices. Occasionally he'd call Roan's name, but his voice just echoed back to him. Spotting another niche, he swung down, getting excited when he saw marks in the dirt. Pulling his rifle from his saddle, he went to explore. Someone or something had been this way recently, and in case it was an animal not in the mood to be disturbed, the gun made him feel better. He spotted the boots first, a rush of adrenaline sending his pulse skyrocketing. "Roan!"

A soft groan answered his shout, and Roan's eyes fluttered open as Tyler knelt at his side. "I never thought I'd be happy to see you," the young man said.

"Fuck you, kid," Tyler said back, amused. If Roan could be snarky, he wasn't hurt that badly. "I've got someone with me I bet you'll be glad to see. I know he'll be glad to see you."

Roan's eyes opened completely for the first time. "Patrick?"

"Who else is crazy enough to be glad to see you?" Tyler stepped away from Roan until he could see blue sky, firing three shots into the air.

"You sure he'll be happy to see me?" Roan asked, just as two answering shots rang out.

"I reckon, since he's been out here searching for you for hours. Don't go holding this morning against him, whelp. Just mark yourselves even. You had your moment of madness and so did he. Now I'll just duck out to hold the horses and let him come see to you," Tyler said, turning back to where he'd left his mount.

"Tyler?" Roan called out.

The blond turned back. "Yeah?"

"Thanks."

Tyler smiled. "I guess I can put up with you if you make him happy."

"I'll do my best," Roan promised.

"I think you will at that," Tyler whispered under his breath, careful to make sure the kid didn't see his smile.

Patrick's boots hit the ground before his horse had come to a stop. "Where is he?"

Tyler jerked his head, reaching for Lakota's reins. "In there. He's okay. Take a deep breath before you scare the kid to…." Tyler's words trailed off as Patrick disappeared from sight.

Roan's eyes were closed again as Patrick approached, eyeing the pale color of the younger man's skin with worry. Sinking to his knees, his hands searched Roan for injury.

"It's my left ankle," his tired voice stated.

Patrick's eyes shot up to lock with dark chocolate ones. "Broken?" he asked. Now that he'd found Roan, all the things that he wanted to say seemed to be sticking in the back of his throat. It was easier to deal with the crisis at hand, assessing Roan's injuries and getting him back to the ranch.

"My ankle or my heart?" Roan asked, grasping Patrick's hands and stilling them against his chest. "Patrick, I—"

"Roan, I—"

Both men stopped, and Roan laughed. "You first."

"I'm sorry I was such an asshole this morning," Patrick stated simply.

"Okay..." Roan answered. "But why? What happened? I thought—"

Patrick interrupted. "I love you."

Roan was momentarily speechless, his eyes filling with tears and his throat closing up. "You love me?"

Patrick nodded, pulling Roan's hands up to his lips and kissing his knuckles. "And it scares the bejesus out of me."

A smile broke over Roan's face. "I think we can handle that. Just don't push me away. Talk to me when you start getting scared. Think you can handle that?"

"Sounds too simple."

"Hardly," Roan squeaked, wincing as he tried to sit up, overwhelmed with the urge to kiss his lover.

"Easy," the older man soothed. "Now tell me where you're hurt and what happened."

"Left ankle. It might just be a sprain, but I heard something snap. The boot's keeping it pretty stable, but it's swelled up like a balloon inside. They're gonna have to cut it off, and I love these boots," Roan whined.

Patrick chuckled. "If that's all you're worried about, I'll buy you a new pair. How bad's the pain? Think you could ride with me?"

Roan grimaced. "I don't think so. It hurts like the devil."

"Okay, we'll wait for the truck to make it out from the ranch. Let me go make sure Tyler was able to reach them by radio." Patrick started to get up, but Roan clung to his hand.

"I know it's stupid, but don't leave me," Roan requested, looking embarrassed. "I dragged myself in here to get out of the rain, and then all I could think of was no one would be able to find me, but it hurt too much to get turned around and back outside."

"What happened?"

"I was on my way to the line cabin to get out of the storm. Shadow spooked at some thunder and threw me. Stupid, huh? Thrown like a green kid."

"If you spend enough time on horses, you get thrown," Patrick stated matter-of-factly, "and it was a good thing you didn't make it to the cabin. Tornado flattened it."

Roan's eyes grew wide. "Really?"

"Really."

Both of them stared silently at each other for a few minutes, grateful for the series of events that had prevented Roan from being in the cabin, realizing just how close they had come to a real disaster.

"Guess instead of selling him for dog meat, I owe the ornery rascal some sugar cubes. Everybody okay?" Roan asked.

"Everybody but you," Patrick said, brushing the dark curls back from Roan's face. The storm had cooled the temperature, and the young man's clothes were wet from the rain. He was shivering and sweating heavily. "We need to get you to the hospital. Hang on a sec."

Patrick turned and hollered, "Ty!"

The blond appeared around the corner, anticipating the question. "I can see them comin' now."

Patrick squeezed Roan's hand. It was going to be okay.

EIGHT weeks later, Roan was about to climb the walls. He'd been restricted, by Patrick's orders, to the house, cabin, or yard. He'd wandered in and out of the barn a couple of times, but he wasn't allowed to work, which was worse than just staying away all together. No riding or hard, physical labor – at all – until his ankle was pronounced healed. Patrick had laughingly informed him that he was welcome to take over the books. Roan had stuck his tongue out in what was supposed to be an act of petulant defiance, but ended up being the prelude to a careful but intense session of lovemaking. Roan shivered at the memory of Patrick licking, kissing, and suckling at every part of his body until he'd come, nearly blacking out in the process.

But the end of the forced vacation was in sight. Finn had taken Roan to the orthopedic clinic that morning, where he had finally traded his walking cast for a brace that he had to wear for another two weeks. He still wasn't allowed on horseback, but he could take it off to sleep and shower. Indulging in a long, hot shower with a loofa to remove all the dead skin from his lower leg and finally end the perpetual case of itching was the first thing he'd done when he got home.

Sitting at the kitchen table, he stared longingly out at the horses in the pasture. This was the longest time he'd gone without being on a horse since he had moved to the ranch when he was ten. It didn't help his overall restlessness that Patrick hadn't fucked him since his accident. He'd made love to him with his hands or with his mouth, but he hadn't actually felt Patrick's cock inside him for eight weeks. It was about to drive him crazy.

Coffee. Fresh coffee sounded good, and it'd be ready for when Patrick got home. His sweet foreman was going to need the extra energy tonight because Roan was coming to bed minus his plaster anchor, and he was going to get fucked if he had to tie Patrick to the bed and ride him. The swelling in his jeans suggested that maybe tying Patrick up wasn't such a bad idea. The doc had said 'no' to riding horses, but he hadn't said a thing about foremen.

Reaching for a mug, Roan swung the cabinet door back and forth several times, listening to it squeak. Getting the WD-40 while the coffee brewed, he sprayed the hinges. Patrick's cabin had never been in such good shape. Roan had worked his way through his dad's 'to do' list for the house and then started on the cabin. It kept his hands busy, which was good since the young man wasn't used to being idle. As long as he stuck to small tasks or made sure the evidence of the bigger projects was cleaned up by the time Patrick got home, he had gotten away with it. Who knew that Patrick could be such a mother hen?

Patrick climbed the steps, pulling off his hat. Brushing his fingers through his sweat-damp hair, he toed off his mud-caked boots. The heat had been blistering today, and he was desperately looking forward to the cool of the cabin, a shower, and his lover's arms. Eager, he threw the front door open, putting his shoulder into it. The door swung freely, banging with a resounding thud against the foyer wall and knocking several chunks of plaster to the floor.

"What the fuck?" Patrick cursed, moving the door back and forth to examine the ease with which it swung.

"Patrick?" Roan called. "I'm in the kitchen!"

Wandering into the room that was quickly becoming his second favorite − next to the bedroom − Patrick whistled at the sight of his lover dressed in nothing but a worn pair of blue jeans, a white brace replacing the familiar heavy boot on his injured ankle. "What happened to the front door?" he asked, wrapping his arms around the tanned torso and running a line of kisses down the exposed neck.

"I fixed it. I'm running out of things to fix since I've been on labor restrictions. Damn thing hasn't opened right since before I left for college."

Patrick grunted. "The wall needs to be fixed now."

"What? What's that mean?" Roan asked confused.

Patrick thought about it, shrugging. "Literally or existentially?" Patrick replied, pulling the love of his life into his arms and pressing their lips together.

Roan forgot all about the door, the wall, and the world as Patrick's tongue claimed his mouth. Relaxing against his lover's chest, he sighed his approval, leaning back against the counter and raising his braced foot to hook behind Patrick's knee and pull him closer.

The feel of Roan's foot made Patrick pull back. "Your cast's gone," he said, sitting in a chair and raising Roan's foot to his lap to examine it.

Roan hopped around to sit on the table's edge before he lost his balance. "Yep, all healed."

Patrick raised a suspicious eyebrow. "Hardly, or you wouldn't still be wearing this contraption." His fingers explored the Velcro straps that held the brace in place.

"I only have to wear it a couple more weeks, and I can take it off when I bathe, sleep, and anytime I'm not on my feet. I bet I could even ride a little."

"Liar," Patrick accused, looking up at his lover with an indulgent smile. "Finn told me the doc said no riding. You must have sworn him to secrecy about the cast. Am I gonna have to ask for written proof after your next visit?"

Roan pouted, and Patrick laughed, pulling him down onto his lap. "I know you miss the horses, baby, but the last thing we need is for you to mess up your ankle so badly that you can never ride again."

Laying his head on Patrick's shoulder, Roan sighed. "I know. I just feel so bloody useless."

Patrick pressed his cheek to the top of Roan's curls. "I wish there was something I could do to make you feel better."

Roan's fingers slipped between the buttons on Patrick's shirt, playing with the soft hair on his chest. "Oh... but there is…." Flipping open several of the buttons, Roan captured a pink nipple with his teeth, flicking his tongue over the tight peak.

Patrick groaned, his fingers sinking deep into Roan's hair. "I need a shower."

"I prefer salty to sweet," Roan murmured against Patrick's skin, sucking at one of the nipples.

Patrick's breath hissed out between his teeth. He'd been holding back with Roan and was just as frustrated as his young lover. He finally had the man of his dreams in his arms, in his bed on a permanent basis, and he hadn't been able to make love to him once. Part of him felt like it was divine retribution for his stupidity, but Roan was really testing his control. "I *really* need a shower, Roh."

"Fine, I'll come scrub your back." Roan stood, grabbing Patrick's hand. "No restrictions on getting wet now."

Patrick followed as Roan pulled him up the stairs to the master suite. "Roh, I don't think—"

"Good. Don't think."

"You shouldn't—"

"Oh, yes, I very much should." Roan sat on the counter and removed the brace, standing and pushing his jeans to the floor.

Patrick's mouth went dry as Roan's cock popped free of his jeans, already stiff, the head a deep red. He couldn't help reaching for it, his fingers skimming the surface and causing Roan's breath to hitch and his fingers to clutch the edge of the counter for balance.

"See! You aren't steady on your feet. Putting you in a slippery shower is not a good idea."

Roan pulled Patrick close, beginning to work on removing his clothes. "It's not my ankle that makes me unsteady when you do that."

"Yeah, but if we get in that shower together, there is no way I'm gonna to be able resist doin' all those things that make you sway," Patrick argued.

Roan whimpered, pushing Patrick's jeans off his hips. "God, I hope so." His hands circled the heavy shaft that rose proudly from its nest of curls. At least one part of Patrick's body agreed with him.

"I've got an idea," Patrick suggested, stepping away from Roan's exploring hands. They'd be making love on the cold tile of the bathroom floor if his lover kept that up. "How about the tub?"

Roan's eyes slid over to the extra-large Jacuzzi tub and an almost pained moan slipped through his parted lips.

"You get to scrub my back, and I don't have to worry about you standing on that ankle," Patrick continued, like he still had to convince Roan.

"Fill the fuckin' tub," Roan finally growled, sliding on his brace and disappearing while Patrick did as ordered. When he returned, Patrick was in the tub, most of his body hidden by frothy bubbles, the hair on his chest curled in wet swirls. Roan opened the cooler in his hand and offered him a cold bottle of beer.

Patrick looked at the label of his favorite beer and laughed. "Aren't we supposed to be drinking champagne by candlelight?"

"I can go get champagne if you want," Roan offered, pretending to turn towards the door. "I just figured you'd rather have beer."

Patrick snatched at Roan's hand, pulling his lover towards the tub. "There's only one thing I want, and he's too far away. Now, take off that brace."

Roan lowered himself into the hot water, arranging himself in front of Patrick so that his back pressed against Patrick's chest. "God, no wonder Amanda hated you," he sighed. "You got this and she got Dad, not much of a bargain."

Patrick chuckled, his lips running up the side of Roan's neck. Roan tilted his head to the side, offering the tanned column to Patrick to explore, and in doing so, caught sight of them in the mirror. Patrick's sun-bleached hair was in direct contrast to his dark head. Both muscular, but Roan slender and smooth. Patrick's mouth dipped lower, his teeth grazing Roan's collarbone. Roan saw it in the mirror a second before he felt the touch, doubling his anticipation and his pleasure. His head falling back on Patrick's shoulder, he moaned, pressing his hips back into the erection swelling against his ass.

Patrick couldn't get over the feeling of having Roan in his arms. He hadn't shared it the night Roan asked about his fantasies, but they were about to fulfill a long-standing one. His arms slipped below the water, circling Roan's body and tracing light and random patterns over his chest, capturing his nipples between his fingers and tugging on them until they hardened into pebbles. Every gasp from Roan encouraged him to pinch harder until the young man was squirming against him, pushing hard against his arousal.

Tracing the cut of the muscles down Roan's well-developed torso, Patrick slid his fingers into the crease between thigh and body, brushing his thumbs up and down the sides of Roan's cock. "Fuck, Patrick," Roan complained. "Touch me!" His legs fell open, allowing him further access.

Patrick gladly obliged, his hands touching, teasing, preparing, and finally turning Roan around to face him. "Wanna see you react to my touch," he rasped. "Hand me that blue bottle." Unwilling to remove his hands from Roan's body, he indicated a little shelf with his eyes.

Roan grabbed the bottle. "Silicone lube? I'm thinking I don't want to ask why you have this by your tub."

Patrick curled a hand around the back of Roan's neck, forcing him down for a hard kiss. "I bought it last week in hopes that I would find myself in just this position." He nudged at Roan's cheek with his nose, stealing another quick kiss. "I've never slept with anyone here at the cabin but you."

Roan looked up, startled by that admission. "But Tyler—"

"Has been here, but I always spent the night at his house. He's crashed here a couple of times, but always in the spare bedroom. This place, like my heart, has always been too full of you to share with anyone else."

Roan swallowed the lump that had risen in his throat. He was not going to cry. God, a little romantic sentiment and he was acting like a girl. "So, you gonna use this stuff and fuck me, or are we gonna sit here and talk about Tyler?"

Patrick laughed, pouring gel into his hand and nudging Roan up on his knees. When his first finger probed the furled opening, Roan groaned and sank down onto it. "I take it that feels good," Patrick teased.

Eyes closed, head back, balanced on his knees and supported by Patrick, Roan moved up and down in the warm water, relishing every stroke of the fingers inside his body. "God, I've missed this."

"You're…" Patrick cleared the hoarseness from his throat. "…not the only one."

One finger soon became three, and Roan's movements sped up until he was fucking himself on Patrick's fingers and the foreman was wondering if he could come just from watching the pleasure on his lover's face.

Patrick slid forward, giving Roan's legs room to slip around and behind him. Roan reached for his solid length, his hand trembling as he mapped the familiar contours. Patrick hooked his hands under Roan's arms and lifted, positioning the younger man directly over his cock. Roan grasped Patrick's shoulders and slowly lowered himself onto the hardened staff, crying out as it unintentionally brushed his prostate.

"Holy hell, you're tight," Patrick commented, teeth clenched as he fought to retain control.

"That's what eight weeks of no sex will do to a boy. Make sure it doesn't happen again," Roan teased, dropping his forehead to Patrick's shoulder as he rocked forward.

There was no way Patrick was going to refuse that offer. Grabbing Roan's hips, he moved in steady increments, forward and back until he was fully sheathed inside of the tight channel. "Am I hurting you?"

"Fuck, no. Move!" Roan yelled.

"Are you sure? We could move to the bed."

Roan clenched his teeth. "If you stop what you're doing, I won't be held responsible."

Patrick laughed and kissed him. He lifted Roan's hips slightly, thrusting in even deeper, making his movements as slow as he could possibly bear. The kiss continued, his tongue plundering Roan's mouth at the same pace as his cock plundered his body. Adjusting their position, he placed them directly over one of the jets, spreading his legs and letting the water pulse directly on Roan's opening, hundreds of tingling bubbles rising to tickle his balls and cock.

Roan let out a cry and started moving quickly and erratically against him. Patrick couldn't hold back any longer. He squeezed Roan to him tight, moving inside of him in short, well-placed jabs until the younger man froze, his body convulsing around Patrick. Groaning, he followed Roan over the edge into a sea of sensation.

When Patrick began to become aware of his surroundings again, the only sounds were the splash of the jets of water and their harsh pants. He loved the feeling of his lover draped over him and was in no hurry to move, but the bed would feel even better. "Wanna go take a nap before dinner?" Patrick asked, his lips moving against Roan's curls.

"Hmmm… guess so," Roan murmured, sated and sleepy.

Standing, Patrick helped Roan from the tub, rubbing him down with a large, fluffy towel.

"Keep rubbing me like that and we'll be going to bed to do more than nap," Roan warned.

Patrick ran the towel over himself haphazardly and swung Roan up into his arms to carry him to the bed.

Laughing, Roan curled his arms around Patrick's neck. "What is this, my wedding night?"

"Could be," Patrick remarked, the mood turning suddenly serious. "Would you marry me?" he asked, laying his lover on the bed and crawling in beside him.

"Can we do it by the pond?"

Patrick's eyes sparkled. "Seems fittin'."

"Hell, yes!" Roan screamed, throwing his arms around Patrick's neck and pulling him over on top of him. "I love you, you know."

"Not half as much as I love you."

"I love you more," Roan shot back.

Patrick ended the argument by giving Roan a better use for his lips.

Epilogue

PATRICK stood with Tyler beneath the willow tree next to the pond. The evening was surprisingly cool for mid-September. Judging by the tendrils of pink already climbing into the sky, it was going to be a glorious sunset.

"You couldn't have ordered a prettier night," Tyler commented, pulling at the cuffs of his Western-cut tux.

"I'm sorry about the monkey suit. Roan wanted them for some danged fool reason." Patrick adjusted the turquoise slide on his tie.

"Don't apologize to me." Tyler grinned, looking over at the dark man in the last row of chairs, staring at him with smoldering eyes. "This get-up's gonna get me laid tonight. Probably the same reason Roan wanted you in one. We look damn good."

Patrick laughed. "That's what I like about you, Tyler, your humility."

"Humble doesn't get you ridden hard by a man like Karl."

Patrick glanced over at Tyler's new boyfriend. Apparently, the one-night stand had developed into more after all. "Obviously a lot of fire there. Think there could be more?"

Tyler shrugged, always uncomfortable with talk of 'more'. "He's smart, fun, and great in bed. I'm good for now."

Patrick laughed like he was supposed to, but wondered exactly how much damage Tyler's failed marriages had caused. He knew Tyler was fighting for shared custody of his youngest, and having every intimate detail of his life open for public scrutiny was hard on the private man. His musings were cut short by the arrival of a shiny new Chevy 4x4.

Finn swung down from the driver's side, dressed in a slight variation of the tux Patrick and Tyler wore. It looked good on the tall man, emphasizing his broad shoulders and copper hair. Patrick suspected that more than half of Finn's hair was grey, but mixed with the copper strands, it looked sun-bleached.

Hurrying around to the passenger's side, the Irishman helped a stunning brunette down from the high truck. Finn had met Frances, a nurse at the local hospital, while he had been transporting Roan in for physical therapy. Patrick suspected that the crafty old fox might actually have met his match in the part-Navaho woman.

Patrick scanned the small group of friends. It looked like everybody who'd been invited was here... everyone except Roan. His lover had been surprisingly closed mouthed about how and when he would be getting to the ceremony. He'd just kissed Patrick as he got out of bed this morning and promised to see him at sunset.

The sky was now a wash of pale pink and orange. He was about to ask Tyler if he'd spoken to Roan when he caught the silhouette of a rider out of the corner of his eye. As it drew nearer, Patrick was able to clearly identify Roan's slender frame and wild curls. He was riding Taranis and leading Lakota. Walking the horses right up through the crowd, he stopped close enough to Patrick that Taranis put his head down and nudged him with his nose.

Patrick grabbed Taranis's bridle to steady himself. "You're riding." His eyes shifted to Finn and found his longtime friend smiling a knowing grin.

"Doc cleared me yesterday," Roan said, sliding to the ground and wrapping his arms around his lover's waist. "Surprise."

Patrick beamed; he had his Roh back in his arms, safe and whole. Bending his head, he captured the soft lips. What was supposed to be a quick kiss of greeting deepened as Roan stepped close to his body, tipping his head and opening his lips. Patrick grabbed the slender hips, hauling Roan up against his body firmly.

A burst of cat-calls and applause broke the two men apart. Patrick rested his forehead on Roan's shoulder, trying to calm his breathing, his hands still firmly holding the young man against him. "Guess it's time to get hitched, huh?"

"No backing out now, cowboy," Roan teased.

"You're not gettin' out that easy. Took too much work to get you hog-tied." Patrick passed the horses' reins to Jeff, who walked them over to the side.

The four men, Patrick and Roan in the center, Tyler and Finn flanking them, gathered under the willow tree. Mort Grantham, the preacher at the local Christian church, had offered to officiate, but neither man felt the need for someone else to tell them they were married or to kiss their spouse, for that matter. They'd written their own vows. And standing face-to-face, staring into each other's eyes, they stated them, promising to love, cherish, and protect each other until the day they died. After the words had been said, the power of the moment lingered. Eyes still locked, they stood silent until a shrill whinny from Lakota broke the moment and a joyful shout went up from the gathered friends.

Patrick's lips crashed into Roan's, both men kissing through broad smiles. His arms circled his husband's body, lifting and spinning him in a circle. "I think Lakota approves," Patrick laughed.

"Yeah, he told me that if you hadn't gotten your head out of your ass, he was going to kick some sense into you the next time you tried to clean his hooves," Roan replied.

"Let me hug my son," Finn said, slapping at Patrick's shoulder and pulling Roan out of his arms and into his own.

Tyler met Patrick's eyes over the embracing couple. Nodding his approval, he smirked. Darting his eyes towards Karl, he indicated that they'd be leaving soon.

The guests started moving towards their trucks, heading up to the house for barbeque and beer. "You comin' up to the house?" Finn asked, releasing Roan, who gravitated back to Patrick's arms.

Roan looked up at his new husband. "No, I don't think so, Dad. You can save us a plate in the fridge, but I haven't been on a horse in more than three months, and I'm in the mood for a ride."

Finn couldn't quite hold back his snort of amusement at his son's double entendre, but Frances was at his side, poking him hard in the ribs. "Let 'em be," she scolded. "It's their wedding night, after all. Why would they want to spend it up at the house when they could be enjoying a glorious evening like this?"

The sky had darkened to a deep orange, surrounding a crimson sun and cotton candy clouds. Finn and Frances climbed up into his pickup, leaving Roan and Patrick standing alone.

"So, cowboy, fancy a ride?" Roan asked.

"Depends on what I'm ridin'," Patrick answered with a cocky grin.

"I was thinking we could head out towards the flats and then follow the creek back to the pond."

Patrick tucked Roan close to his side, moving towards the horses. "Seems like we always end up back at the pond, doesn't it?"

"Maybe when you make love to me under the willow tonight we'll finally finish what was started here," Roan suggested.

"Baby, we are *never* gonna finish what we started here."

Justice

AUTHOR'S NOTE

As a child, I watched old westerns with my granddad every Sunday afternoon. I fell in love with the hard headed cowboys, who faced down every outlaw and physical hardship with bravery and tenacity. What I could never understand was why they would fall in love with the women, who were usually shown shrieking or swooning at the slightest provocation.

The answer is…

They didn't.

WELCOME TO JUSTICE

Chapter One

ADAM ABRAMS was tired and dusty. Glancing quickly to his right and left, he confirmed that his brothers looked as disheveled as he felt. Passing a sign cheerfully welcoming them to Justice, population 324, he sent up a silent prayer that the name of the town was a good omen. Maybe here, he and his brothers would find what they were seeking.

The dust-colored buildings drew closer and so did Nathaniel and Noah, tightening ranks like they did every time they were faced with the unknown. For a town boasting a fairly small population, Justice seemed to be incredibly prosperous. Businesses lined the main street. Colorful signs swung in the breeze. Hitching posts were full, and well-dressed people bustled about industriously.

Pausing in the center of the street, the three men surveyed their surroundings. As no threat seemed imminent, Noah spoke up, "We need food, sleep, and a place for the horses."

"I need a drink," Nathaniel added. Nathaniel was the youngest of the three brothers, but not at all shy about voicing his opinion.

"Fine, you go get a drink... *one* drink," Adam warned pointing towards the saloon. "Noah and I will take care of the horses and meet you at the hotel." Adam knew he spoiled his baby brother, but he felt guilty that the younger man had been denied the love of a mother and father – stuck with the fumbling attempts of an older brother.

Noah rolled his eyes as Nathaniel dismounted, tossed his reins to Adam and strode towards the bar. He loved both his brothers, but knew that Adam was too serious and Nathaniel too frivolous. He hoped once this damn quest was over they could settle somewhere for more than a few weeks and things would change. Adam was almost forty. He needed a lover to share his life with, not just younger brothers.

"You comin'?" Adam yelled over his shoulder, snapping Noah out of his musing.

Dismounting outside of the stable, Adam looked around, admiring the obvious care that went into the upkeep of the place. The owner obviously knew his business. Wrapping the reins around the hitching post, he headed into the cool interior of the barn. His eyes adjusted quickly to the dimmer light. Just like the exterior, the interior was clean and organized.

At the far end of the barn, mucking out the last stall, Adam could see a slender, denim-clad form. "Hey! Who do I talk to about boarding three horses for a few days?" he called out.

The figure straightened and turned. 'Damn, it's a woman,' Adam thought as she moved towards him. Quite a woman at that, she had long blonde hair tied conveniently off her face, curves in all the right places, and long slender legs. If he'd been into women, this one would have been a keeper.

"That would be me. Name's Miranda, but you can call me Randy," she offered, tugging off a glove, wiping her hand on the thigh of her jeans and extending it in greeting.

"Ah... I...." Adam took the offered hand. "I... I'd rather talk to the owner. The stallion is a little high-spirited and needs a firm hand."

Randy smiled like she had heard those exact words hundreds of times. "I *am* the owner, Mr... ?"

"Oh, Adam... Adam will do." He shook his head. This little bit of a thing owned this stable. If he hadn't been so impressed with the way it looked, he would have immediately thanked her for her time and left to find other arrangements. Sometimes hotels kept a barn for their patrons.

"So Adam, why don't we go meet this 'special' horse of yours?" Randy knew without asking that the stallion belonged to this man and not his brother standing quietly in the shadows. This man deserved a 'special' stallion.

Sampson meant more to Adam than he would ever care to admit. They had found the proud black stallion at one of the first towns they came to after leaving California. He had been abandoned just outside of town by the man they were following, Elias Riddley, the man who murdered their parents. The stallion had been starved and mistreated.

It had taken Adam the better part of two years to earn the horse's trust. Unwilling to be ridden, Sampson had followed behind Adam's horse at first. Healing the stallion had been therapeutic. If Adam could heal the damage done to the horse by Riddley, then maybe there was hope that the damage to him and his brothers could be healed as well.

Sampson whickered softly as Randy approached. He was a large horse, 19 hands, and dwarfed the stable owner... not that she seemed to notice. She approached the horse at a slow but steady pace, murmuring lilting nonsense the entire time. She came to a halt on the mounting side of the stallion, asking his permission before touching him.

Adam stood in awe as Sampson granted approval by nudging Miranda strongly with his head, almost knocking her off her feet. Adam's body tensed, ready to leap to her aid and step between her and the unpredictable horse. Randy just laughed as she regained her balance, scolding the horse in a voice that said she was anything but angry. Starting with his silky mane, she ran her hands over every inch of the beautiful horse's body.

Adam stood spellbound as the horse's muscles twitched under her soothing touch. He loved his horse dearly, but right this minute he was insanely jealous of him. As he watched Sampson respond to the touch of this slip of a woman, Adam's body tensed for a completely different reason. A desire to be touched flowed through his veins. He wanted someone to stroke his body like Randy was touching his horse. He wanted to accept a touch with trust like Sampson was doing. If Sampson could find someone to trust in this town, maybe he could, too.

Adam sensed Noah's approach before he saw the shadow fall on the ground next to him. "She's got quite a touch there," Noah drawled lazily, smiling at his older brother's discomfiture.

"Come on. We've got to meet Nate at the hotel," Adam growled. The two brothers started to unfasten the bags from their saddles. Adam talked with Randy about care for the three horses and hurriedly made his escape. Striding towards the hotel, Adam easily shouldered the weight of both his own bags and Nathaniel's. Noah let him since Adam was the one who'd let Nathaniel out of his responsibilities before they even checked into the hotel.

NATHANIEL opened the door to the saloon, setting off a bell. By the time he reached the bar, a sandy-haired man was there to greet him. "Welcome. What can I get ya?"

"Whiskey, thanks," Nathaniel replied, throwing his leg over a stool and pushing his long duster out behind him as he settled.

The barkeep returned with a glass and a bottle Nathaniel recognized as damn fine whiskey. 'I like this town already,' he thought, pouring himself a shot.

"I'm Luke Coleson. What brings you to Justice?"

"Nathaniel, but Nate'll do. My brothers and I are just passing through and needed a break. Your town seems fairer than most. Good a place as any to settle for a spell." Normally Nathaniel would have ignored the question. Adam had taught him to be wary of a stranger's inquiries, but this man with his wind-blown hair and smiling blue eyes seemed to put him instantly at ease.

Luke nodded and turned back to the box on the floor, removing bottles and placing them carefully on a shelf. Nathaniel couldn't help but stare at the incredible view every time Luke bent over to retrieve another bottle. 'God, the man has an incredible ass.' His mind filled with daydreams of reaching over the bar and running his hands over the stretched denim, squeezing the firm flesh. Somehow Nathaniel knew that sex with this man would be raw and powerful.

Trying to distract himself from the throbbing in his jeans, Nathaniel nodded towards the painting of a dark-haired boy behind the bar. Apart from the fact it was of a boy instead of a woman, it was a typical bordello scene. The boy was stretched out on a velvet couch, shirt open to expose his bare chest and body positioned in a very sexually suggestive way. "Unique painting you've got there."

Luke smiled at the painting and turned back to the brooding stranger. "My bar, my painting, my choice." His answer was stated in a calm, quiet voice, but there was an underlying tone that brooked no argument.

"You painted that?" Nathaniel asked, surprised.

Luke looked at the man seated at his bar for several long seconds before answering. He could sense no mockery in the question, so he took no offence. "Yep. I dabble in painting and photography. Most of the paintings you'll see around town are mine."

"You sell them?"

"Nope," Luke laughed. "Give them as gifts mostly."

"He's a beautiful boy," Nathaniel commented, gesturing towards the picture again.

"Thank you," came a soft, rich voice from over his shoulder.

Nathaniel jumped to his feet and turned to face the unknown voice. Years of looking out for himself and his brothers in bad situations had left him with a serious distrust of having people sneak up behind him. Especially people he didn't know. His mouth fell open as he came face to face with the image in the portrait made flesh... and oh, what flesh.

Nathaniel could feel his knees shake and his mouth fill with saliva. Unconsciously, he licked his lips. If Luke was raw sex... leather and lust, this nymph was pure sin... satin and elegance.

The slender man with dark curls stood in front of him, tilting his head to one side before smiling and extending his hand. "Jamison Moore."

It took Nathaniel a minute to register that the vision was speaking. Shaking himself, he met the hand with his own. "Nate."

"Nice to meet you, Nate," Jamison purred as he glided around the bar to Luke's side. "Are you passing through or looking for a place to settle?"

"Ahh... not sure yet." Passing through was the correct answer. Nathaniel normally would have said it without a second thought, but something about the two people he'd met so far in this town made him almost desperate to say 'I'm staying.'

Looking down at the half-empty bottle, Nathaniel shook his head... another promise broken. "How much do I owe you?"

Luke smiled and waved off Nathaniel's coin. "Consider it a 'Welcome to Justice' present. Bring your brothers back with you next time, and I'll do the same for them."

Nathaniel thanked him and headed out the door toward the hotel. Before the door was even shut, Jamison had Luke pressed up against the bar and was kissing him ravenously. When they broke for air, Luke chuckled, "Wake up from your nap a little horny?"

Jamison just growled, winding his fingers into Luke's hair and pulling his head to the side so he could place a trail of bites from his ear to his shoulder. "Want you," Jamison growled.

Luke moaned and started walking Jamison backward toward the office without allowing any space to come between them. His lips plundered, and his hands made short work of Jamison's clothes. "What do you want?"

"Your great big cock buried in my tight ass," Jamison answered without hesitating a lick.

"You slut!" Luke pushed Jamison against the desk and lifted his long legs to wrap around his waist, grinding the hard bulge of his jeans into Jamison's groin.

"That's my job, and you wouldn't want me any other way." Jamison smiled cockily as he pinched Luke's sensitive nipples through the fabric of his shirt. "You need to be naked. Now!" Jamison ordered, clawing at the buttons on the barkeep's shirt. He managed to slip two free before losing patience and tearing open the shirt and sending buttons skittering to the corners of the room.

Bending to capture one furred nipple with his mouth, Jamison dropped his hands to work at Luke's belt. The leather wouldn't be as easy to defeat as the shirt had been. As soon as he had the buckle free and the buttons on the pants undone, he slid his hand inside and circled the thick length of his lover's cock. Stroking it from base to tip, he groaned, "Need this inside me... *now!*"

Jamison had come downstairs barefoot, a habit he had caught from Luke. Unless he was headed outside, Luke could be found behind the bar or pretty much anywhere in the saloon barefoot. Luke easily stripped the loose jeans from the younger man's hips, throwing them carelessly towards the chair. Running his hands back up the smooth thighs, he framed Jamison's sex with his fingers, pressing underneath the tender sac with his thumbs. An incoherent gurgle broke from deep in Jamison's throat.

Luke grabbed the bottle of oil that was still on the desk from their afternoon lovemaking the day before. Pouring some on the smooth tan belly, he trailed his fingers through it, coating his fingertips and drawing random shapes in the oil.

"Bloody hell, Luke, are you going to fuck me or paint me?" Jamison gasped exasperated.

"Hmmm… painting you sounds like fun…."

"Fuck you! If you don't ram that hard cock into my body right now, I'm gonna go find someone who *will* fuck me. Think it'd take me long if I walked out of here like this?" Jamison taunted.

Nothing provoked Luke faster than the idea of Jamison leaving him for any reason. "You wouldn't find a soul, because I'd shoot them before they could drop their pants," he growled dangerously.

Jamison pouted, sticking out his bottom lip and looking up at Luke through sooty lashes. Hell, Luke knew it was an act, but responded to it anyway. Leaning down for a kiss, he sucked that pouting bottom lip into his mouth and nipped at it lovingly. He coated his cock with the oil and began to rock it into Jamison's tight sheath. He hadn't prepared him with his fingers, so he took his time pushing in and then rocking out, only to return and push in a little farther.

With each push, Jamison's moans got more frantic. He lay back onto the desk and thrust his hips up towards Luke, trying to get deeper penetration. "Fuck, Luke! Give me all of it!" Desperately needing relief, Jamison grabbed his leaking erection and started to stroke himself.

Luke grabbed his hand and moved it away, placing it on the cool wood of the desk. "Mine," he ordered. "Don't touch." Firmly grasping Jamison's hips, he angled his thrust and pounded in and out, repeatedly striking his lover's prostate and making him scream out in pleasure. Normally he would touch and stroke Jamison's arousal, but he was enjoying watching it bob against the flat stomach, leaving a puddle of moisture just begging to be tasted. Unable to withstand the lure, Luke pulled back until he could lap up the small puddle of pre-come. Not bothering to try and avoid touching Jamison's sensitive head, he lapped at the soft, smooth skin like a kitten, his tongue every bit as rough.

Jamison groaned and grabbed Luke's hair. Pulling up, Jamison looked deep into Luke's eyes as he re-sheathed himself. "Fuck... coming!" he shouted almost immediately. Shortly after his warning, he came in long bursts all over his stomach and Luke's chest. He clenched his thighs tighter, pulling Luke deeper inside his body and urging him with his heels to move faster.

Luke's head tilted back with a wail, and he let loose, pounding Jamison so hard that the desk shook. Several things fell with a crash, but neither man paid any attention. Single-mindedly seeking that burst of pleasure, Luke focused all of his attention on the naked man stretched out below him. Jamison rippled his internal muscles, and Luke cried out his release, collapsing forward onto Jamison's chest while his body twitched and shuddered through its aftershocks.

Easing his arms underneath Jamison, Luke held him tight to his body and fell backwards into the big chair, pulling his lover with him to land straddled over his lap. As their breathing returned to normal, Luke ran his fingers through Jamison's damp curls. "So what do you want?"

Jamison pulled away from Luke's chest and smirked. "I don't suppose playing dumb would work."

"Nope."

"Nate."

"It's been a long time since we've taken anybody else into our bed. Are you sure? We don't know anything about him." Luke's questions weren't meant to discourage, just explore.

"Tell me you didn't feel it too, and I'll drop it." Jamison looked seriously at his lover.

The corners of Luke's mouth pulled up into a grin. "I can't do that, and you know it. That boy is special. I can't wait to meet his brothers. I want something in return, though."

"What?" Jamison asked curiously.

"You get to sew the buttons back on my shirt this time."

Chapter Two

SIMON looked up as two dark men walked into the lobby of his hotel. Both men had long dark hair and brooding eyes. Not many men made Simon feel small, but both these men were well above six feet tall with broad shoulders. He moved behind the desk and greeted them. "Welcome to Justice. Need a room for the night?"

Noah and his brothers had shared enough cramped quarters over the years that they appreciated a little space when they could get it. "We'd like to have three rooms if you can accommodate us," Noah answered, smiling at the blond man behind the desk. The sun streaming in through the front window made his hair shine like spun gold, and Noah was a sucker for gold.

"I'm sure that can be arranged. I've got three rooms empty at the end of the hall. Each room has fresh linens and its own tub. Shall I call for some hot water to be brought up?" Simon pointed to a blank line in the register, so the men could sign in.

"God, yes! I haven't had a decent bath with warm water in a month of Sundays," Noah moaned with anticipation. Adam laughed at his brother's theatrics.

Simon adjusted himself behind the counter. The tone of anticipated pleasure in Noah's voice had gone straight to his cock. "Is there anything else I can get you? Company perhaps?"

Noah looked at Simon, trying to decide if the older man was coming on to him. Simon's next words shattered that idea.

"I could have a nice, *friendly* woman sent to your room to help with your bath." The emphasis of Simon's statement said much more than the actual words.

Adam saw the spark of interest in Noah's eyes when he looked at the hotelier. He watched that spark flicker and die. "No, just the water will be fine," Noah answered, turning to climb the stairs to the rooms Simon had indicated.

Adam frowned. They had met with plenty of scorn and outright hatred over their sexual preferences in towns in the past. He had been hoping to find more tolerance - if not acceptance - in a town with a name like Justice. Shaking his head, he realized he had a lot of expectations for this town he had only just ridden into.

Simon watched Noah climb the stairs, shoulders slumped and looking dejected. Stifling the urge to run after him and hold him until the look went away, he turned to the quieter man. "Did I say something wrong? I didn't mean any offence. You aren't religious folk, are you?"

Adam chuckled at the idea of them being 'religious folk'. "No. You didn't do anything wrong. My brother just prefers his bath partners to be a little less feminine, if you know what I mean."

"Oh... I'm sorry, Mr. – Abrams." Simon glanced at the register the newcomer had just signed. "I'm sure Jamison could fill that desire, too, if your brother is interested."

The spark of hope flared again inside Adam. He extended his hand to Simon over the counter. "Call me Adam. The one that just left is my brother, Noah, and the one yet to arrive is Nathaniel. Who's Jamison?"

Simon laughed silently. "I'm Simon. Jamison runs the brothel over the bar. Best high-class 'ladies' this side of the

Mississippi. He doesn't have any gents living in the house, but I'm sure he has resources."

"What about Jamison? Does he...?"

"Oh, not for ages. He's been in a committed relationship with Luke for years now," Simon explained.

"Luke?" Adam asked, raising an eyebrow. It was unusual to hear folks talking about same sex relationships so openly.

Simon laughed at himself. "Hell, small town curse. You tend to talk about people like everyone knows them. Luke Coleson owns the saloon and usually serves as barkeep when he ain't painting or playing with the new fangled camera he ordered from back east. He's a little strange, but good as gold and loyal as a June day is long. He was raised by the local tribe, but moved into Justice when he was about twenty... wanted to explore his 'white' side."

"Jamison... well, I'm not sure you can sum up Jamison as easily. You'll have to meet him for full effect. He was traveling East with his folks when their wagon got swept down river. His dad was trying to cross while the water was too high. Luke found him on the bank, almost dead. He carried him to the village where he was raised. They raised Jamison up, too."

"I think Jamison might have stayed with them, but he was kidnapped and raped by a gang of rogue soldiers fleeing from the war. Luke tracked them and killed every one of them... brought Jamison back here and nursed him back to health. Stella, the madam before Jamison, took him under her wing, and the rest is pretty much history."

Adam was stunned, and it showed on his face. People he knew didn't go pouring out life stories to total strangers. "Seems like an odd profession for a boy who's been through that kind of a trauma."

Simon just smiled and shook his head. "Jamison doesn't like playing by anybody's rules. He claims it helped him take back ownership of his body. You'd have to talk to him about that. He'll tell you. One of his favorite stories is how he set out to catch Luke when Luke was being all noble and wanting nothing to do with the kid. Be sure and ask about that one. He'll have you rolling on the floor. Luke will be scowling, but he doesn't mean it. That boy is the best thing that ever happened to him, and he knows it. We're not a real secretive bunch."

Adam chuckled this time. "I've noticed. Folks don't mind that Luke and Jamison are so open about their relationship?"

"Nope. Like I said, we aren't secretive. Folks who have a problem with it tend to move on quick, and folks lookin' for an acceptin' town have been known to cross the country to get to us. Now, I'm keeping you from your bath, and I have some making up to do with your brother." Simon came from around the desk and extended his hand to Adam. "Welcome to Justice. I hope you stay awhile."

"Thanks." Adam turned towards the stairs, wondering… hoping Simon was intending to make things up to Noah in a way Noah would really enjoy. Simon was special, and Adam sensed things were about to really change for the better. Tromping up the steps, he actually started whistling.

SEVERAL minutes later a firm knock sounded on Noah's door. He was puzzled, two boys had been traipsing in and out with hot water buckets for the last fifteen minutes without knocking. Swinging open the door, he found Simon standing in the hall with two steaming buckets and a canvas bag slung over his shoulder.

"May I come in?" Simon asked simply.

"Um… sure… Mr.…?"

"Just Simon. No need for Mr.'s." Simon stepped past Noah into the room. Moving quickly to the tub, he tipped the last two buckets into the bath, topping it off. Dropping the bag to the floor near the tub, he started rummaging through it for the supplies he'd brought.

"Okay, Simon. If you return the favor. I'm Noah." He watched suspiciously as Simon placed a cake of spicy-scented soap on the edge of the tub and a large sponge next to it.

Next, Simon pulled out several big, soft towels. Finally, he pulled out several bottles with unidentified contents. When he was done, he stood and turned towards Noah. "I owe you an apology."

Noah's forehead creased. "What... why?"

Simon moved towards Noah until he was standing within a foot of the taller man. "I think I left you with the opinion that only a man interested in women would be welcome here." Noah opened his mouth to say something, but Simon boldly raised his hand and laid his fingers over Noah's lips to stop him. Noah's eyes got wide, but he remained silent.

"That's not true," Simon continued, taking a deep breath. If he was wrong about this, he was about to make things worse and likely be sporting a black eye come dinner. "If I was hasty with my words, it was because I was attracted to you. It's been a long time since I've had an instant attraction to someone, and I was trying my best to treat you like I would any other guest."

Simon let his fingers drop from Noah's mouth back to his side as he waited for the younger man to say something. Noah just stared into his eyes like he was trying to read his mind. Simon tried to put all he was feeling into his eyes for Noah to find. Neither spoke, but Noah's expression softened.

Simon didn't move his feet, but found himself leaning towards Noah, wanting to be closer. Noah met him halfway, and their lips met in a tentative brush. Again and again, their lips moved across each other, closed and dry. Simon didn't think he'd ever felt anything more enticing. His knees felt weak, and his stomach was doing somersaults.

Finally, Noah stepped towards Simon and brought their bodies into complete contact. It had taken him several minutes to give in to the feelings swarming through his body. He had not been raised to trust easily, but Simon had come to him, had been open and honest, and had stood, hands at his sides, waiting for Noah to accept or reject his offer, even after the kiss had begun.

Noah's step opened the floodgates. His fingers sunk into Simon's golden hair, grasping the silky strands as he tilted Simon's head so he could completely meld their mouths. His tongue ran along Simon's lips, turning the kiss from soft and dry to hot and wet. Simon groaned and opened his mouth to Noah's onslaught. Noah's tongue penetrated Simon's mouth, seeking his tongue. He found it, taunting it with quick jabs and long, stroking sweeps, begging it to come and play.

Simon accepted with a vengeance, chasing Noah's tongue back into his mouth and thrusting powerfully, reveling in the addictive taste. They moved back and forth from Noah's mouth to Simon's until their tongues had memorized every inch of the other. Then they moved on to exploring lips, cheeks, chins, jaws and ears. When Noah's mouth found the sensitive skin just behind and below Simon's ear, he moaned, grabbed Noah's hips and ground their erections together.

Noah was surprised and slightly disoriented as Simon stepped back from their embrace. "I promised you a hot bath and I never break my promises." He started to move towards the tub.

Noah pulled him back, sealing their lips again. "I need you far more than the bath," he whispered against Simon's lips.

"And you'll have both," Simon promised, a devilish green flame dancing in his eyes. "Strip down," he ordered, picking up one of the bottles and pouring some of the scented oil into the water. The soft scent of lavender and vanilla filled the room.

"I'm going to smell like a cookie," Noah complained as he toed off his boots and started unbuttoning his shirt.

Simon's only answer was a steamy look and a pass of his tongue over his lips. Noah started tearing at his clothes in an effort to get naked. "What about you?" Noah asked. "Aren't you going to join me?" He stood next to Simon and ran a hand over the front of his soft cotton shirt, wanting to see and feel what was under it.

"I hope so, but first I want to do this for you. Let me… please?"

Noah put a hand on Simon's shoulder to steady himself as he stepped into the tub. Sinking into the hot water was almost orgasmic in itself. Leaning back against the side of the tub, he was incapable of keeping his eyes from drifting shut.

Noah felt the rough sponge coat his chest and shoulders with slippery soap bubbles. He kept his eyes shut, concentrating on the feelings. Simon washed his arms and hands, pulled his legs up out of the water one at a time, washing his legs and feet. Returning to his chest, the sponge moved in circles. Noah felt Simon's fingers brushing his nipples through the soap foam, and his mouth opened on a soft moan. Unexpectedly, the touch disappeared, and Noah forced his eyes open to determine why.

Simon was pulling his unbuttoned shirt from his jeans, and Noah held his breath at the first sight of the broad, muscled chest. Simon obviously worked hard if one was to judge based on his body. "You're beautiful," Noah whispered, feeling instantly embarrassed. Men didn't say things like that to other men, even if they were about to fuck.

The smile that lit Simon's face made Noah want to say it again, along with hundreds of other words that would make Simon glow like that. "The sleeves were getting wet," Simon explained.

Noah grinned. "Probably ought to take the pants off, too - just in case."

Simon looked at Noah like he was full of shit, but his hands dropped to his belt anyway. Completely naked, he returned to the side of the tub and picked up the sponge. He started to kneel again, but Noah reached out and stopped him. "You could reach me better if you were in here with me," he suggested.

Simon stepped into the tub and straddled Noah's legs, re-soaping the sponge and moving it over his chest and then lower, under the water. Noah moaned and arched his back at the first brush of the coarse sponge over his heated erection. He'd been hard ever since Simon walked in the room, and the direct touch felt like heaven.

Simon wrapped the sponge around the shaft and started moving it up and down, setting his pace with the thrusts of Noah's hips. He was mesmerized by the look of bliss on Noah's face. He watched as pleasure overtook his dark lover and swore to bring that look to Noah's face as many times as he was allowed.

Simon dropped the sponge in the water and continued to stroke Noah with his hand until he lay soft and completely sated. Noah opened his eyes and looked at Simon with a satisfied but sheepish grin. "Boy, that was selfish of me."

"That's what I wanted. You're young. I'm sure you'll recover quickly, and if not, I'll just have to be the one doing the fucking," Simon replied.

Noah moaned at Simon's words. "I want you to fuck me. I like the idea of you inside of me." He turned over in the water and pulled his knees under him.

Simon's body moved forward unconsciously, pressing his hard length against the crack of Noah's ass. Both men moaned and pressed into each other. "Fuck, Noah, you undo me."

Reaching for one of the bottles on the side of the tub, Simon poured some of the clear oil over his fingers. Slipping a finger in between the hard cheeks, he found the puckered opening and circled it teasingly. Noah pushed back into the touch, and Simon let the tip slip inside before pulling it back. He repeated the motion again and again with one, two and finally three fingers, never letting them penetrate more than a couple of inches. Noah whimpered and tried to push them deeper. He was completely hard again and feeling desperate. "Simon... please...."

"What do you want, lover?" Simon answered.

"You! Fucking hell... want... need... you!" Noah panted, screaming when Simon pushed his fingers completely in and curled them to stroke Noah's pleasure center. Noah's muscles gave out completely, and Simon caught him around the waist.

Repeatedly, he stroked the same spot inside Noah until they both were trembling with unfulfilled desire.

Simon slowly slid his fingers from Noah with one last lingering brush against his smooth gland. Noah moaned, beyond being able to utter words of protest. Coating his cock with more of the oil, Simon circled the stretched opening with the tip of his cock before allowing it to slip inside.

Noah was well stretched, but Simon's cock was so much larger than his fingers. He sank in about halfway and paused, waiting for Noah to relax around him. "You okay?"

Noah nodded, biting his lip. "More," he croaked.

Simon pushed the rest of the way in, moaning at the feeling of being completely buried in Noah's hot, tight ass. "Fuckin' hell... need to move, baby."

Noah answered by pulling away and slamming back against Simon's groin. The unexpected move almost made Simon lose control right then. "Oh fuck...!" he cursed, starting a furious downhill race towards his climax. He wanted to make Noah come again, but he was being chased by an out-of-control freight train. Angling his thrusts, he searched for the spot that would push Noah over the edge quickly.

"Hell yes!" Noah screamed as he hit it. He gripped the side of the tub to brace himself.

Simon reached around and grabbed Noah's length under the water, pumping it hard, making him cry out, curse, and thrash about. Water sloshed in all directions. Simon felt Noah's cock harden and twitch, spilling his seed into the water. The corresponding clenching of the muscles around Simon's oversensitive flesh pushed him over the edge. He growled, biting down on Noah's shoulder as he filled his lover with his come.

Both men fell forward into the slightly cooler water, panting. Simon pulled Noah up against his chest and laid his chin on the top of his head as he held him close, trying to catch his breath.

Noah peered over the edge of the tub at the water covering the floor. "We made a mess."

Simon chuckled and pulled him back against his chest. "Don't worry. I know the owner."

NATHANIEL opened the door to the room he'd been directed to by the young girl behind the counter. She'd also told him that Noah and Adam had the next two down the hall. Running his fingers through the hot water filling the tub, he sighed. Sure that his brothers were indulging in the same activity, he stripped off his clothes and lowered himself into the water.

Clean, relaxed and ready for another drink, Nathaniel dressed quickly after his bath and knocked on the door next to his, using his signature knock to let Adam know it was him.

"Come in!" Adam yelled from the opposite side of the door. Nathaniel opened the door and smiled at his brother. Adam was lounging in his tub with his arms on the sides, smoking a fat cigar.

"Aren't you a sight?" Nathaniel teased sitting down on the bed.

Adam just clamped the cigar with his teeth and grinned around it. Taking in a mouthful of smoke, he blew it out in Nathaniel's direction. "I could get used to being a man of leisure. You look cleaner than when I last saw you, so I'm going to assume you didn't *just* leave the saloon."

Nathaniel smiled. "Unlike you, I didn't linger in my bath. Isn't the water getting cold?"

"They've been up twice with buckets to heat it up. This may be the best hotel we've ever stayed in. How was the whiskey?" Adam asked.

A dreamy, lust-filled expression moved over Nathaniel's face. "The barkeep served up the good stuff without me even asking and didn't even charge me. Said to consider it a 'Welcome to Justice' present. He also offered the same to you and Noah if I brought you in tonight."

"So this 'barkeep' responsible for the sappy look on your face?" Adam did a double take as Nathaniel blushed. His bad-assed baby brother did not blush. "Well?" he prompted.

"Sort of... I guess...."

Now Nathaniel was stuttering... blushing and stuttering in the same day. "Was this barkeep named Luke?" Adam asked curiously.

"Well, yeah, and then there was this other man named Jamison. How'd you know...?"

Adam sat up in the water. "So you met both Luke and Jamison, huh? It isn't one of them you're attracted to, is it? From what I've heard, they're a couple."

Nathaniel swallowed, not meeting his brother's eyes. "I got that feeling. They just seem to have an energy around them, you know? But at the same time, I definitely felt something directed at me. Luke is hot as hell, but Jamison...." Nathaniel's voice drifted off and the dazed expression returned to his face.

Getting to his feet and stepping out of the tub, Adam said, "I guess you're old enough to make your own mistakes. Just don't go getting yourself shot by a jealous lover, okay? I'd hate to have to kill someone for shooting you if you deserved it." Adam looked out the window. The streets weren't as busy as they'd been earlier. People at home eating dinner, he assumed. His stomach rumbled in response to that thought.

"You gonna get dressed?" Nathaniel asked.

"What? You getting shy? It's nothing you don't have. I am hungry, though. Shall we hit the diner or this saloon of yours?" Adam asked, shrugging into his shirt.

"I promised I'd bring you and Noah back to the saloon. I'll go get him." Nathaniel got up and started towards the door.

"No, don't bother him. He'll catch up with us later."

Nathaniel turned a curious look towards his brother but didn't ask. He knew all of Adam's 'voices' and some were not meant to be questioned. "Okay, I'll meet you downstairs."

Five minutes later, Nathaniel found himself holding his breath as they walked through the door of the Lazy Dog Saloon. The same bell rang, but the room was much busier. Pretty girls bustled between the tables, laughing and flirting with the customers while they delivered drinks and plates of food. A man with spiky blond hair played the piano. Luke was behind the bar, but he had two other young men with him serving drinks. Jamison was nowhere to be seen.

"Well, we just going to stand here in the doorway, or do we get to sit down?" Adam asked sarcastically.

"Oh, sorry," Nathaniel apologized, moving into the room. There were only three tables left unoccupied, so he picked the one closest to the bar. Pulling out a chair, he dropped his hat on the table. Before he could even sit down, his hat was joined by a full bottle of the whiskey he had drunk earlier and three glasses.

"Welcome back, Nate. Didn't you say you had two brothers?" Luke asked in soft, friendly voice. Nathaniel hadn't noticed how soft spoken Luke was earlier when the place had been empty.

"Oh yeah, this is Adam," Nathaniel introduced, pausing and allowing the two men to shake hands. "Uhm… Noah is…."

"Busy," Adam finished. "I reckon he'll be along later and hungry enough to eat a bear." Nathaniel shot Adam a puzzled look, still not understanding Noah's absence and Adam's jovial mood about it.

"Well, I don't serve bear as a rule, only when someone has to shoot one because they come into town after garbage. But I can offer you some tender venison steaks."

"That'll do." Adam nodded to Luke with a smile. Both men watched the barefoot barkeep walk away. "He does have a certain energy about him, doesn't he?" he commented to Nathaniel after Luke was out of earshot.

"Yeah, and wait until you meet Jamison."

The steaks had been consumed with half of the bottle of whiskey when Noah arrived. He pushed through the door and stood in the exact same position Nathaniel had as he surveyed the room. His hair was still damp, and he looked more relaxed than Nathaniel had seen him in months.

Noah spotted his brothers and nodded at them with a smile, but didn't come to join them. Nathaniel got to his feet, but Adam tugged him back down. "Sit. He'll be here in a minute."

The bell on the door rang again and a good-looking blond man came in. "Simon!" was shouted from multiple locations around the room. Simon raised his hand in greeting, but joined Noah as they walked across to the brothers' table.

Nathaniel looked at Adam, hoping for some sort of an explanation, but Adam's eyes didn't leave the two men walking towards them. When they reached the table, Noah reached out a hand and ruffled Nathaniel's hair. "So little bro, you still here from earlier?"

"Fuck you!" Nathaniel spat, swatting at Noah's hand. Noah just laughed, pulled out a chair, and folded his long legs under the table. Nathaniel looked pointedly at the blond and huffed. Extending his hand, he introduced himself, "I'm Nate, by misfortune of birth related to these two monkeys."

Simon laughed and clasped Nathaniel's hand. "I'm Simon. I own the hotel you are currently residing in, and I'd say fate dealt you a winning hand when she chose your kin."

Nathaniel couldn't help but smile as Simon's laughing green eyes filled with light. Shit, what was it with the people in this town? His eyes caught the movement of Noah's hand as it rested on Simon's thigh under the table. His eyes never moved from the piano player, but Nathaniel could see it moving slowly back and forth in a sensuous stroke. 'So that's what Noah's been up to this afternoon.' He turned an appraising eye back to Simon. Was he good enough for Noah? Adam obviously thought so, and Adam was rarely wrong. Relaxing, he used the spare glass to pour a drink for Simon and then refilled and passed his own glass to Noah.

Whistles and catcalls filled the room, drawing all four men's attention. Jamison was descending the stairs with two of the prettiest girls Nathaniel had ever seen. He couldn't take his eyes off of Jamison. He was dressed all in black and the smooth surface of his shirt reflected the light. Nathaniel wondered what it would feel like to run his hands over it. Luke stepped out from behind the bar and did exactly what Nathaniel had been imagining. He slid his hands up Jamison's arms, over his shoulders and down his back, pulling the slender man into his arms for a deep kiss. Nathaniel had felt the sexual energy around them earlier, but seeing it played out before his eyes had him close to coming in his pants.

"Fuck me," he whispered softly.

A soft chuckle from Simon snapped him out of his trance. "They are something, aren't they? Doc reckons the birthrate doubled once they got together. You watch them for a little while and just get this overwhelming need to go make love." Simon's eyes slanted to Noah, and his hand dropped to squeeze the hand still resting on his thigh.

Adam whistled softly, watching Luke and Jamison walk hand in hand towards their table. "Well, I think I see what you mean, baby brother."

Luke extended his hand to Noah as Jamison dropped into Simon's lap. "Welcome to Justice. I see you are already keeping good company."

Noah shot a glance at Simon and then smiled at Luke. "I never found a town quite so friendly."

"We like to think we're unique," Luke replied, pulling a chair over from a neighboring table. Jamison planted a wet kiss on Simon's cheek before shifting to Luke's lap. Luke's arms settled around the slender man in a gesture of familiar intimacy.

Simon chuckled as Noah watched Jamison lap crawl. "Be careful. He'll be on your lap next."

Nathaniel felt a bolt of jealously shoot through him at the idea. Jamison was obviously with Luke, but if any of the brothers had a chance to touch him, even casually, it was going to be Nathaniel. "You haven't eaten yet, Noah," Nathaniel reminded, distracting Noah from Jamison.

"Yeah, and I'm hungry enough to eat a bear."

Luke laughed and pushed Jamison to his feet so he could stand. "Seems to be a favorite dinner for you boys. Will a venison steak work for you too?"

Noah and Simon both agreed to settle for venison. Luke and Jamison walked off towards the kitchen. The dinners were consumed, and the noise level in the saloon rose as it got later and more crowded. The room darkened as the last of the daylight left the sky, leaving just the gas lamps for illumination. Noah and Simon had shifted closer and closer to each other until Simon was sitting sideways in his chair, leaning back against Noah who had his arms possessively wrapped around the blond's chest.

"Hey, it's 9:30, who's got 'Rose Duty' tonight?" Phillip called out from behind the bar.

"It's Simon's turn," Charlie answered from the piano.

Simon groaned and sunk further back into the comfort of Noah's arms. "Can't be. I did it almost all last week." A lively discussion ensued about whose turn it was.

"What is 'Rose Duty'?" Adam asked, taking a sip of his whiskey.

"Rosey's our town librarian, a bit forgetful. Forgets things like eating, going home, that sort of thing. If Rose doesn't show up here for some food by now, one of us goes on a rescue mission, and tonight it's *not* going to be me," Simon insisted, taking another sip of his whiskey.

Forever the big brother, Adam got to his feet. "Where's the library? I'll do it." He hadn't seen Noah this happy in a long time and didn't want anything to disturb it.

Simon examined Adam speculatively for a minute before smiling. "Six buildings down on the right. You can't miss it."

Chapter Three

ADAM placed his hat on his head firmly and headed for the door. The streets were almost empty, and his boots rang out on the wooden planks. He spotted a sign with an open book on it and noticed lights glowing in the windows. Pushing open the door, he called out, "Hello." The last thing he needed was a scared woman swooning and shrieking. There wasn't an answer.

Moving farther into the library, Adam spotted the source of the light coming from a back office. He tried calling out again. Nothing. Pushing open the door, he stepped into the cluttered room. Every surface was covered with books and papers. A figure was bent over the desk. "Miss?" Adam asked. "Miss Rose?" he tried a little louder.

Papers flew into the air, and the figure spun to face him. Unkempt copper hair the color of a desert sunset stuck out in every direction. Blue eyes blinked owlishly at him from behind thick wire-rimmed glasses. "Aw, hell! You scared me. Library's closed."

The man pulled the glasses from his face, returning his startling blue eyes to a normal size, but leaving them no less striking. He stared at Adam, making a slow perusal from head to foot. Adam found his groin warming at the lingering look. "You're not here for a book, are you?"

Adam shook his head. "I'm looking for Rose. I'm supposed to help her home or at least to the saloon for something to eat."

The man's face broke into a sardonic grin. "Well, you've found *her*."

Adam sputtered, "You're Rose?" His voice rose on the last syllable until it almost squeaked.

A full chuckle broke from the copper-haired man. Moving towards Adam, he extended his hand. "Yep. A dreaded nickname from childhood. Most people call me Dale, unless they're teasing me."

Adam was glad the room was dark as his face flushed at his mistake. Silently he promised to kill Simon. "Oh… I'm sorry. I'm…." He clasped Dale's hand and felt a flush of heat for an entirely different reason. Small charges of awareness skittered up and down his arm, finally settling low in his groin and making his cock pulse and hum. He completely forgot what he'd been about to say.

"You're?" Dale asked with a quizzical expression on his face.

"Oh… I'm Adam."

Adam and Dale stood silently, hands clasped for far longer than was appropriate. Dale finally stepped back. "Well, if they're sending someone for me, it must be late. Come to think of it, I am hungry."

Dale looked directly into Adam's eyes as he said the words, making Adam wonder exactly what Dale was hungry for.

Adam cleared his throat. "Uhm… well… I guess…." He shifted from foot to foot. "Are you done here? Should I…?"

Dale smiled, dropping his glasses on top of the open book he'd been bent over when Adam entered. "Let's go. If you've come all this way to rescue me, the least I can do is not hold up your return to the saloon."

When they exited the library, Dale turned to the right instead of the left towards the saloon. Adam, not knowing what else to do, followed him. Anxious to fill the silence, Adam gave in to his curiosity and asked, "How'd you end up with a nickname like Rose?"

Dale might be beautiful, but he was every inch a man. Adam admired his well-built frame and wondered if you could get shoulders and arms like that from lifting books. The feminine nickname bothered him. He wondered... hoped... dreaded that it might have something to do with Dale's sexual orientation. He'd love for the younger man to be available, but hated the idea of him enduring any teasing for it.

Dale laughed. "When I was a kid, I had a sister who loved to make flower crowns. You know, the kind you weave out of flowers. Well, she'd invite me to tea parties and make me wear them. She and Mom would bake cookies and the only way to get any was to attend a tea party. It was blackmail, but they were really good cookies. Anyway, one day, I realized about halfway through the party that I was late for a baseball game. I forgot to take the crown off. With red hair and this skin, when the guys spotted the flowers, I blushed deeper than the reddest rose." Dale turned and smiled ruefully up at Adam before shrugging and laughing.

Adam admired Dale's ability to laugh at himself. He could just imagine the other boys' reaction to him arriving with flowers in his hair.

"I got off lucky. I know it. So now you have to share something embarrassing," Dale prodded.

Adam looked down at his boots. 'Great. Share an embarrassing moment. Not a wonderful way to attract the attention of someone you are interested in. Whoa. Did I just say I was interested in him? Am I interested? Well maybe this sharing thing could work to my advantage.'

"Well, when I first started dating, this friend and I decided to ask these two sisters out. We figured it would be less scary if we did it together. They said 'yes', and we took them for a walk and a picnic to this pretty little pond. While we were there, they dared us to go skinny dipping. At fifteen, a dare is serious business, so we stripped down and hopped in. Jacob was showing off and dunked me, so I had to get him back. It turned into quite a tussle, and somewhere during, I discovered that I liked Jacob a lot more than the girls we left on the bank. So there I was with my britches sitting several feet up on the bank, a raging hard-on, a friend who looked as confused as I felt, and two girls waiting for us to come out." Adam shook his head sheepishly.

Dale did a poor job of stifling his laughter and finally gave up, laughing so hard that he had to stop walking to hold his sides. "I'm sorry," Dale hiccupped. "I shouldn't laugh, but almost the exact same thing happened to me, only it was with my sister's boyfriend. You don't ever want to have a sister who thinks you are trying to steal her boyfriend. I slept with one eye open for months."

Adam smiled, feeling warm inside at the shared confessions. He'd kept himself apart for so long, he'd forgotten how good it felt to connect with someone other than his brothers. "Well, you obviously survived."

"Barely," Dale chuckled, starting to walk again. "You don't know my sister."

Adam noticed that Dale was walking a little closer now, allowing their arms and shoulders to brush as they moved. Every brief contact sent shivers through Adam's body. Adam was startled when Dale turned left towards a small two-story house just past the stables. "Oh, I guess you're home."

"Yeah," Dale said, standing on the bottom step of the porch to even their heights. Decisively grabbing the front of Adam's vest, he pulled the startled man close, wound his free hand into Adam's hair, knocking off his hat, and kissed him until they both were panting for air.

"Night, Adam. Thanks for walking me home," Dale whispered, tracing his fingers lightly over Adam's stubbled cheek.

Turning, Dale disappeared through the front door before Adam could find his voice. He was left standing on Dale's front walk, staring at the front door, shuffling his feet like a courting schoolboy. The feeling didn't dampen the 'cat that got the canary' grin on his face in the least. 'Damn, Rose is one hell of a kisser.'

Adam had decided to return directly to the hotel. He told himself that it was the prudent thing to do, get a good night's sleep so he could start early tomorrow on his search for any sign of Elias Riddley. It had nothing whatsoever to do with the pounding need in his pants begging for release.

The farther he got from Dale's house, however, the angrier he got. Dale didn't know him. He could be a cattle rustler or mass murderer. What was the idiot thinking, trusting a total stranger to walk him home and then kissing him goodnight? Turning back towards the saloon, Adam stormed inside. Nathaniel was standing at the bar talking to Jamison. Simon was draped over Noah's lap, still at the table listening to the music.

Adam strode over to the table and kicked one of the chairs around so he could drop into it backwards.

"Where's Rose?" Simon asked with a grin.

"Ha! Very funny! If I weren't so angry at him, I'd have a word or two to say to you about your small omission." Adam scowled at Simon.

Noah sat up a little straighter behind Simon. He was clueless about what was going on, but his brother was in a temper, and it seemed to be directed at his new lover. Noah felt it behooved him to pay attention. For the first time in his life, he found himself waiting for more information instead of just jumping into the fray on his brother's side.

"Do you know what that flighty... careless...." Adam searched fruitlessly for a word to sum up his frustration at Dale's reckless behavior. "Well... he let me walk him home... no clue who I am... and even kissed me... who in the hell...?"

Noah cut in at this point. "Hold on. He? I thought you were going to rescue a woman named Rose?"

Adam barked out a laugh. "Yeah. So did I! Didn't your boyfriend here fill you in after I left, so you both could have a good laugh? Rose is a *man*... named Dale... with copper hair... and blue eyes...."

Adam was ranting again and not really paying much attention to Noah or Simon. Noah looked at Simon who was smiling as he listened to Adam go on and on. Suddenly part of Adam's rant sunk in.

"Adam, did you say he kissed you?" Noah shouted, jumping up and almost dumping Simon onto the floor.

Adam stopped, startled. Looking over his shoulder, he saw Nathaniel looking their way. "Sit down," he ordered quickly. The last thing he wanted was for his nosy little brother to get interested in this. "Yeah, he kissed me. Grabbed me and kissed me right on his front steps. With no clue about who I am."

Simon held up a hand to stop Adam, who he could see was about to wind up again. "I'm sure he knew all about you before you even checked into the hotel."

"But how?"

Simon chuckled. "More of that small town curse. Dale is Randy's brother."

"Randy from the stables?"

Simon nodded.

"If she's got a brother, why is she running them all alone?"

"Randy inherited her daddy's touch with horses. Dale inherited his mother's love of books. He's set up the largest lending library this side of the Mississippi. We're pretty proud of that," Simon saluted Adam with his glass before finishing the contents.

"That many people read in this town?"

Simon nodded. "I can't think of anyone off the top of my head that can't read unless they're just too young. Kids around here start going to the library when they are about five. Dale has them reading within a year or two."

"Isn't there a school?"

"We have one of those, too. Eliza Taylor runs it out of the back of the dry goods store. She's really good with math and history. I imagine she'd do just fine with the reading, too, but Dale has that touch. He not only teaches the kids to read, but teaches them to *love* it. So, Dale teaches reading, and Eliza teaches everything else. Well, except languages."

"Languages?" Adam couldn't wait to hear this.

"Luke and Jamison teach the languages. Between the two of them they speak eight." Simon looked at the expression on Adam's face and laughed. "But it's not a structured thing. Anyone who wants to learn a language works here. That's what Phillip and Charlie are doing." Simon pointed to the slender dark-haired man behind the bar and the blond playing the piano as he named them.

Adam shook his head. Justice really was a unique town. Simon had managed to completely distract Adam from his anger, and he found himself suddenly bone weary. Tipping back the last of the whiskey in the glass in front of him, he stood. "I'm headed to bed. You get to round up Nate. I kept him out of your hair earlier."

Noah grimaced. With a swoosh of his dark duster, Adam was out the door.

ADAM woke the next morning to warm, yellow light streaming through the curtains. He could tell the day was well gone. Puzzled at the lack of urgency he felt, he rolled onto his side and let his mind run through the events of yesterday.

Justice was not what he'd expected. For the first time since his parents' death, he felt comfortable with where he woke up.

The burning need for revenge that had been driving his every waking thought was no longer alone in his brain. Nathaniel's infatuation was nothing new, but for the first time, Adam actually approved of the object of his desire. Adam had no desire to play second fiddle to the kind of bond Luke and Jamison obviously shared, but he had to admit second fiddle with those two was probably better than first with most people.

Adam just happened to want someone who belonged *only* to him... someone like Simon. He couldn't help but envy the way Noah and Simon had been looking at each other last night. It was a very real possibility that Noah had found the kind of man worth sticking around for... which would mean he'd be staying in Justice.

It all came back to the town. If Noah stayed in Justice, would Adam stay, too? The little voice in his mind supplied an additional incentive: 'Dale's here.'

Dale. Adam had never felt so instantly at ease with anyone in his life. He didn't even talk to his brothers the way he'd talked to Dale. With them, he had to be the strong one – the authority figure. It would be nice to have the luxury of sticking around long enough to get to know Dale.

Between the good night's sleep and the thoughts of Dale, Adam's body was feeling refreshed and more than a little randy. 'Aw hell... best part of the day's already shot anyway,' Adam thought, letting his hand drift down his belly and circle his half-hard cock.

Adam's mind supplied the image of Dale, moonlight reflecting off his hair, face turned up just before he kissed him. His hand glided up and down his thick shaft, enjoying the tingles building at its core. He remembered the feel Dale's lips pressed against his and thought about how they would feel on other parts of his body.

Dale might be a shy librarian, but when it came to claiming Adam's lips, there had been no hesitation or lack of skill. He felt a slight twinge when he thought about Dale gaining his experience. 'Dale's lips belong on mine. I don't want anyone else's hands on him.' Adam groaned and his hand sped up. 'I want him coming around *my* cock, screaming *my* name until he forgets anyone else exists. Until I forget anyone else exists....'

Adam convulsed upward with his climax, cupping his hand and catching his own seed. Indulging himself, he cleaned his hand with his tongue and imagined Dale drinking come from his fingers... leaning in and tasting himself on Dale's tongue. 'Oh yes... there are many things I want to share with darling Rose... and I will,' Adam promised himself.

Rolling out of bed, Adam hastily pulled on his clothes and rapped on his brothers' doors. "Meet me for breakfast at the diner in 10," he yelled at each door. Galloping down the stairs, he nodded at the girl behind the desk and wondered if Simon's absence meant he had spent the night in Noah's room.

Remarkably, both Noah and Nathaniel made the deadline, arriving at the diner in cheerful moods. A slender blonde greeted them with a smile, walking over to their table to pour them coffee and take their orders. She started with Nathaniel, asked Noah, and then looked at Adam. "What are you in the mood for, Adam?"

Adam frowned. "How'd you know my name?"

Meg laughed. "Small town. I had dinner with Randy last night. She wouldn't shut up about your horse, and then Dale walked in and wouldn't shut up about your ass...." Meg let her statement drift off with a laugh at her own joke as she walked back towards the kitchen.

Adam felt himself flush again. 'What the fuck is up with me? Maybe I'm coming down with something. I'm sure this town has a doctor.' Looking back from the door Meg had just walked through, Adam caught his brothers' amused stares. "What?!"

Noah coughed into his hand to cover a snicker. "Not a thing. So what's our plan?"

The three brothers discussed ideas for finding Elias Riddley for the next hour. Noah would go to the bank and general store to see what he could find out. The small town grapevine could work to their advantage or detriment, only time would tell. Nathaniel would talk to Luke and Jamison, and Adam would search through the town records, which were either at the courthouse or the library. They had made the same searches at multiple small towns and were good at spotting the various names and scams that Elias seemed to repeat wherever he settled.

NATHANIEL entered the saloon to the tinkling of the now familiar bell. The main room was empty, gleaming wood tables neatly surrounded by chairs awaiting the afternoon rush of customers. Nathaniel paused and listened. He couldn't hear anything. It wasn't near a mealtime so there weren't any preparation noises coming from the kitchen. Figuring that Luke probably used down time like this to do books, he headed for the door labeled 'Private'.

The door was open about six inches. As Nathaniel approached, he could hear a cacophony of noises, grunts, moans, and sighs. Stopping just outside the door, Jamison's voice was easily recognizable as he moaned Luke's name. Knowing he shouldn't, but unable to stop himself, Nathaniel slowly pushed the door wide enough to be able to see into the room.

Knowing that Luke and Jamison would be having sex on the other side of the door hadn't remotely prepared Nathaniel for the image that greeted his eyes. Luke lay on his back across his desk completely naked, his legs bent at the knee and hanging over the end. Jamison was straddling him, a knee on either side. His body was bowed backwards so that his hands rested on the desk by Luke's feet. His body moved up and down on Luke's cock like a slow motion erotic parody of a rodeo rider.

Stunned by sheer sexual force of the image in front of him, Nathaniel stood at the door, slack jawed and completely oblivious to his clear intrusion. Unconsciously, he adjusted himself, straightening his swelling length down one pant leg to eliminate an uncomfortable kink. His hand lingered, the base of his palm pushing hard against the bulge to the rhythm of Jamison's motion.

"Nate."

Nathaniel jumped guiltily at Luke's raspy voice. Tearing his eyes from Jamison's pleasure contorted face, he looked at Luke. He found no anger or condemnation in the steady blue gaze, only lust and a faint hint of amusement. Nathaniel's mouth worked silently, but he could think of nothing to say to explain his behavior.

"Nate. Come here," Luke ordered softly.

Stunned, Nathaniel obeyed silently, walking towards the desk. He sunk his hands deep in his pockets to keep from reaching out to touch. Stopping beside the couple, his nose was inundated with the strong musk of arousal and sex. His hands clenched the inner fabric of his pockets.

Luke chuckled at the look of abject desire on Nathaniel's face, a low deep rumble that caused Jamison to moan and speed up his pace. His eyes were still pressed closed, and Nathaniel assumed he was unaware of his presence.

"Touch him," Luke suggested.

Nathaniel did a double take from Luke to Jamison and back. "What?"

"Touch him." Luke motioned with his eyes towards Jamison's weeping erection that bobbed and swayed with his motion. "He needs to come. Help him?"

Nathaniel wasn't about to wait for Luke to change his mind. His eyes focused on Jamison's rigid length. Drops of pearly come were falling in threads to collect in a small puddle on Luke's stomach. Without thinking, Nathaniel bent over and licked the gift off Luke's stomach.

Luke moaned and clutched Nathaniel's head, winding his fingers into his hair. When Nathaniel pulled back, Luke's eyes were pressed closed, but Jamison's were open and burning with need and desire. Nathaniel gasped, the air rushing from his lungs.

Nathaniel's eyes locked with Jamison's. He slowly ran his hand up Jamison's smooth, muscular thigh, savoring Jamison's gasp as his rough fingers circled the base of the shaft, guiding the length towards his mouth. He never lost eye contact as his lips stretched around the tip and sank down the long, slender shaft.

Jamison moaned and rocked between the hot suction of Nathaniel's mouth and glorious stretch of Luke's cock. Moving faster, he moaned wantonly and reached up to pull at one of his flat nipples. When his moan was echoed, he looked down and realized that both Luke and Nathaniel were watching him. A seductive smile spread across his face. Sucking two fingers into his mouth, he wet them. He circled one nipple and then the other, making them glisten, and then pinched them until they were hard and puckered.

Reaching up to pull at the hardened nubs, Luke used his other hand to gently guide Nathaniel's rhythm. "Suck him, Nate," Luke ordered, thrusting up hard in counterpoint.

Jamison cried out and lost his rhythm, thrusting blindly up into Nathaniel's mouth as Luke pounded against his prostate. "Fucking hell... I'm coming!" Jamison shouted, filling Nathaniel's mouth while the muscles around Luke became almost unbearably tight, triggering his lover's climax.

Nathaniel sucked, swallowed and licked until Jamison's sated cock slipped from his lips. Luke growled ferally, grabbing Jamison's hips and pounding up into him as the younger man collapsed forward onto his chest.

Stumbling backwards into a chair, Nathaniel sat, chest heaving, still not quite sure of what he should do. Luke had invited him in... well, Nathaniel had sort of invited himself in, but Luke had offered more. Jamison certainly hadn't objected, but what now? Should he leave?

Luke nudged Jamison, who was quite content to curl up and fall asleep purring on Luke's chest. "Jamie."

"Hmmm... mrphrmmm...."

"We have company who is in need of some relief, I imagine," Luke whispered against Jamison's ear.

Jamison stirred at Luke's words. Luke felt Jamison's insatiable cock begin to harden against his thigh. Damn, but the boy was voracious. Jamison turned to look at Nathaniel panting in the chair, legs spread wide to ease the pressure on the large bulge in his pants. Jamison licked his lips, and Luke laughed.

Slipping quickly off the desk, Jamison knelt between Nathaniel's legs, immediately attacking the buttons of his trousers. At the first touch, Nathaniel's eyes flew open and then immediately fluttered closed as Jamison outlined his pounding hard-on with his fingers. "Oh, I do love a man who packs a large gun," Jamison hummed.

Nathaniel yelped as Jamison bit down through his trousers just hard enough not be gentle. Distracted by what Jamison was doing between his legs, he didn't notice Luke moving behind him until he felt the older man's mouth on his neck. Arching his throat back, he surrendered to the touch.

Jamison stopped to pull off Nathaniel's boots, socks, pants and undershorts. While he was working, Luke reached around Nathaniel's chest and opened all the buttons on his shirt, pushing the sides apart to explore his chest.

With easy access to all of Nathaniel's body, the two lovers started a joint attack on his senses. No words were exchanged, which left Nathaniel wondering for the brief period he was capable of rational thought if they could read each other's minds.

Jamison blew puffs of warm breath over Nathaniel's superheated groin, running teasing licks along his inner thighs and then tasting the slit of his cock. Luke stroked his chest with rough fingers, tangling in his chest hair and tugging slightly. When Jamison's lips descended over the head of his cock, sucking him deep into the velvety warmth of his mouth, Luke's fingers unerringly found both his nipples, pinching them hard and twisting. Nathaniel's hips came completely out of chair. "Oh fuck... oh God...!"

Jamison's mouth moved languidly up and down his cock, stopping to swirl his tongue over the soft head, through the slit, and then back down the underside as he sucked Nathaniel completely into his throat.

"Arghhh…" was the best Nathaniel could do as his fingers wound into Jamison's curls.

Luke's lips covered Nathaniel's ear, making shivers race up and down his spine. "He's good at that, isn't he?"

Nathaniel hoped that was a rhetorical question because he was completely incapable of making his mouth form words.

"Look at him," Luke whispered. "Look at those pink lips stretched around you, his nose buried in your hair. He can smell how close you are… the musk of your skin… your sex."

Nathaniel moaned again, trying hard not to thrust his cock farther than Jamison could take him.

"You can, you know," Luke rasped, switching to the other ear and sending a whole new set of shivers through him. "Go ahead. Fuck his pretty mouth. I promise he wants you to. He wants to feel you slam into the back of his throat."

Nathaniel thrust up tentatively. Jamison groaned around his cock causing the most delicious tightening in his balls, so Nathaniel repeated the motion. Jamison moaned and doubled his suction, breaking the last of Nathaniel's self-control. Grasping Jamison's head, he thrust up against every down stroke. Jamison moaned and hummed around his shaft, and Luke continued to purr into his ear.

"Oh, hell… fucking god… Jamison, please…." Nathaniel thrashed in the chair, Luke's arms around his chest literally anchoring him to the earth. With a keening wail, Nathaniel shuddered as he filled Jamison's mouth.

Jamison reduced his suction, gently tonguing Nathaniel's sated shaft while his hands stroked twitching thigh muscles. Allowing Nathaniel to slip from his mouth, he licked his lips, placing a kiss on the soft skin just to the side of the bed of curls. "Mmmm… thank you," he murmured against Nathaniel's hip bone.

Nathaniel's fingers tightened in Jamison's curls, the only action he could get his body to perform. His head was resting on Luke, who was stroking his upper body. Nathaniel turned his face, and Luke captured his mouth in a slow, burning kiss. Luke's tongue demanded entrance and laid claim to his mouth.

Nathaniel's eyes shot open when he felt Jamison's tongue begging to be allowed to play. Jamison crawled into Nathaniel's lap to be able to reach the kissing couple better. Several minutes passed in the messy exploration of tongues.

Luke pulled away when he heard the bell over the door. Jamison sighed and laid his head on Nathaniel's shoulder. Luke peered into the main room. Spotting the foursome of customers, he muttered, "Damn. Play time's over, boys."

Jamison crawled off Nathaniel's lap and stretched. Nathaniel's mouth began to water. Jamison naked, stretching like a sated mountain lion, might very well be the eighth wonder of the world.

Luke chuckled and patted Nathaniel on the shoulder. "Control, boy. You have to learn to postpone the pleasure a little or you'd be fucking him every minute of the day."

"This would be a bad thing?" Jamison asked coyly.

Luke laughed, loaded Jamison's arms with his clothes and pushed him toward a door off the side of the room. Nathaniel assumed it led straight to the private quarters. Standing as quickly as he felt his legs would support him, he dressed.

Hesitating, Nathaniel turned to Luke. "Urhmm … about this…" He wanted to ask if this would happen again, but he couldn't get his mouth to form the words.

Luke moved to stand right in front of his new lover. "You askin' if this was a one-time thing?"

Nathaniel nodded, dropping his eyes quickly to the floor.

"Jamison and I have been together for a long time. That boy is a part of my soul. Our life songs are intertwined, but there are a lot of different kinds of love … and relationships. We both desire you and like you. If you want this to happen again, it will."

Nathaniel nodded again, his confidence returning. He smiled at Luke and pressed a quick kiss to his lips before turning to leave.

Returning to the hotel, Nathaniel collapsed exhausted on the bed in his room. Adam had left a note that he was researching deeds at the library and not to wait on him for dinner. Thinking back to the diner owner's comment, Nathaniel thought, 'Library, huh? I hope he had the same luck I had.'

Just before he drifted off to sleep, he remembered that he'd never even asked Luke about Elias Riddley. 'Shit!'

Chapter Four

ADAM stood outside the library, trying to decide why he was really there. Was he there to see the maps of recent claims – or was he there to see Dale? Did it really matter? Was this anticipation over seeing the red-headed librarian again really such a bad thing? Maybe he should just accept and enjoy it.

Pushing open the door, he entered the cool interior. He heard muffled cursing coming from the back room and smiled before heading back in search of darling Rose.

Entering the dusty office, Adam was treated to the enticing sight of Dale's backside up in the air, his upper body hidden by the table he was crawling under. "You fuckin' cantankerous…."

"Tsk… tsk… tsk…what did that box ever do to you?" Adam asked with amusement dripping off every syllable.

Dale jumped, his head coming in contact with the bottom of the table with a hard 'thump'. Then the curses really started.

Adam pulled the shorter man from under the table and stood him up, running his fingers through his hair feeling for lumps. "I think you're going to survive. I don't feel anything," he pronounced.

"I do. Don't stop on my account," Dale said, closing his eyes and pushing his head against Adam's fingers. "Mmmmm... feels good," he purred.

Opening his eyes slowly, Dale examined the expression on Adam's face. He had his bottom lip caught between his teeth and his eyes were dark with lust. Taking the hand that wasn't tangled in his hair between his own, he moved it down to just below his belt. "If you are looking for lumps, mine seem to be a bit farther south than that."

Adam moaned, and his eyes dropped closed as Dale pressed his hand into very clear evidence of his desire. His fingers convulsed, squeezing the hard column of flesh and drawing a hiss from Dale.

"Dale, I..." Adam started.

A loud clatter made both men jump guiltily, reminding them they were in a public place.

"Come walk me home tonight?" Dale asked wistfully as Adam moved a respectful distance away.

Adam nodded.

"What brought you to the library today?" Dale asked in a louder, professional tone.

"I need to look at some land claim maps from the last couple of years," Adam answered, still trying to control his breathing.

"Right this way." Dale turned and walked through the door and to the right.

Soon after, Adam unrolled the first map, letting his eyes follow Dale's retreating back before leaning over the table and getting to work.

ADAM stretched, the muscles in his back cramped from extended time leaning over a low table examining maps. His first thought was of food, realizing he had skipped lunch. His second thought was of Dale. With a smile, he quickly rolled up the maps he'd been examining and set off to find his copper-haired vixen.

The library was completely deserted as he made his way toward the office where he expected to find Dale. He guessed that it was past closing time; although as he passed the front door, he saw the 'open' sign still in the window. With a flick of his wrist, he turned it to read 'closed'.

Entering the cluttered office, Adam paused for a moment to take in the image of the man he was rapidly becoming attached to. Dale was looking down at a book lying open on his worktable, a stack of papers clutched in his hands. His hair was sticking up at all angles, telling the tale of fingers running through it many times that day either in frustration or concentration.

"Are you hungry?" Adam asked suddenly.

A surprised squeak coincided with the stack of papers flying into the air. Dale spun, his face flushed and his chest heaving with rapid breaths.

"You scared the shit out of me!" he complained.

Adam chuckled a little at the completely startled look that covered Dale's face, enhanced by the glasses that made his eyes look three times their normal size.

Adam gave in to the impulse he'd had the night before, stepping towards Dale, removing the glasses and brushing his thumbs over the light stubble covering his cheeks and jaw. "You are adorable when you're startled," Adam murmured before leaning in to capture the pink lips with his own.

Dale groaned, melting against Adam and surrendering to the kiss. "Mmmm…are you sure you want to eat?" he asked, suggestively grinding his groin into Adam's thigh.

Adam caught Dale's hips with two large hands, pinning them still. "Yes. I'm starving, but I promise to have you for dessert."

Dale's eyes widened. "Oh, that sounds like a promise too good to pass up. Let's go."

Dale quickly grabbed a large ring of keys and headed for the front door. Adam pushed his hat firmly on his head and followed. Pausing on the wooden walk while Dale locked the door, Adam asked, "Shall we head to the saloon for dinner?"

Dale extended a hand to Adam and shook his head. "Nope. They might take exception to me wanting to strip you naked and nibble my food from your bare skin. Let's go to my house."

Adam's whole body reacted to Dale's words. His internal temperature jumped, leaving him flushed and sweating. His cock swelled to almost a full erection instantly, and his mouth suddenly felt very dry. Unconsciously, he licked his lips. Cautiously, he placed his hand in Dale's and let himself be led up the street.

As they approached, Adam noticed that the inside of Dale's house was flooded with light, unlike the night before. Entering through the front door, they immediately smelled the delicious aroma of baking cookies and heard the light laughter of female voices. Following the sound, they headed towards the kitchen. Walking through the door side by side, the two men came to an abrupt halt.

Meg was sitting on top of the counter, her blouse drawn down to her waist revealing a pair a creamy white breasts crowned with dusky pink nipples. Randy was standing between her knees, licking Meg's nipples, sprinkling them with sugar and then licking them clean again.

Erotic laughter and needy gasps filled the room. Meg was the first to realize they weren't alone, looking up at the men with laughter and passion in her eyes. Nudging Randy, she said, "We seem to have company."

Randy looked over her shoulder. "Oh good, then they can finish the last batch of cookies. Don't let them burn," she tossed over her shoulder as she pulled a laughing Meg from the room toward the stairs.

Dale shook his head and walked to the oven, peering inside to see how done the cookies were.

"Does that happen often?" Adam asked, still sounding a little dazed.

"Hmmm... I guess. Neither one of them is exactly shy. Randy just always seemed to have bad luck with men, usually falling hard for the men who didn't love her back. Meg is perfect for her... loves her deeply and keeps her from taking life too seriously."

"They look happy," Adam thought out loud.

"Yeah. They also have really good ideas. Come here," Dale ordered gently.

The seductive glint in Dale's eyes moved Adam forward immediately. "What are you up to?"

"You like cookies?" Dale asked flirtatiously, breaking off a piece of a cooling cookie and placing it between his lips.

Adam made a sound that was half affirmation and half moan, taking the cookie from Dale's mouth with his teeth. He quickly swallowed the bite, thrusting his tongue inside Dale's mouth to chase the rest of the taste.

"You're sweeter..." Kiss. "...than any..." Kiss. "...cookie."

Dale wrapped his arms around Adam's neck, pressing up against the taller man and aligning their groins. Dual groans echoed through the kitchen at the contact. "I know you're hungry," Dale panted against Adam's neck, nipping at the salty skin. "But I really need some relief."

Adam growled, lifting Dale onto the counter top and ripping open the buttons on his pants. Pushing the soft material to the side, his hand circled Dale's swollen shaft.

Dale gasped, his head falling backwards against the cabinet. Bracing his hands on the counter, he pushed up into the tight grip. "Fuck, that feels good."

Spurred on by Dale's obvious enjoyment and surrender to the pleasure, Adam moved his hand up and down the shaft, one hand reaching down and gently massaging the tightening sac. He watched, mesmerized, as the head grew darker and started leaking drops of pearly liquid. Extending his tongue, he swiped it over the head.

"Ohmyfuckinggod," Dale babbled, thrusting his hips up sharply and winding his fingers into Adam's hair.

Excited by Dale's unrestrained reaction, Adam lowered his mouth to the smooth flesh again, sucking the entire head into his mouth and lightly scraping it with his teeth as he withdrew.

"Fuck... Adam... I can't..." Dale panted.

Adam looked up into lust-fogged blue eyes. Maintaining eye contact, he whispered, "Oh yes you can. Come for me, Rose." Sealing his lips around the leaking cock, he lowered his mouth until he could feel the head bumping the back of his throat. Massaging the length with his tongue, he withdrew and returned, increasing his pace in time with Dale's cursing.

Dale's whole body seemed to curl up to meet Adam as he screamed his climax, every muscle in his body quivering, contracting and then releasing. "Holy fuck, Adam." He carded his fingers through Adam's dark hair. "My turn now, yes?" he asked, his voice still shaky from the strength of his climax.

Dale watched as shutters came down in his lover's eyes. His forehead creased in confusion. What had he said? "Adam?"

Adam ran a careless hand through his hair and moved back from Dale. He could still feel the attraction pulling him forward and had to consciously tell himself not to immediately step forward and take the ravished younger man into his arms. The look of loss and worry on Dale's face pulled at his heart.

He wasn't free to love like this. This wasn't a casual fuck. This was the beginning of a relationship where both partners would give and take in equal measure. Until he settled his past, he had nothing to offer except the imminent danger of his death.

Adam cleared his throat. His mouth didn't want to voice the words forming in his brain. "I'm fine." He looked around in a slightly panicked gesture. "In fact, I need to... need to go... ummm... it would be best." Before Adam managed to finish his incoherent excuse, he was turning to retreat through the house to the door, leaving a sated and very confused Dale to deal with an oven full of burned cookies.

Even as he was running away from Dale, there was no doubt in Adam's mind. Dale at the height of pleasure was more beautiful than anyone he had ever laid eyes on. He wanted to see that look again and again, which scared the shit out of him. Maybe it was time to head out of town for a while.

THE next morning, Adam left a note for his brothers explaining that he would be checking some of the locations he'd found on the maps and not to expect him back until later in the week. Throwing his pack over his shoulder, he headed for the stables.

Neither Randy nor any of the horses were in the barn, so Adam headed out the backdoor into the pasture. He had taken no more than three steps when a shotgun blast sounded. Jumping into the air, he had his pistol drawn and had turned towards the assailant before his feet hit the ground.

Randy calmly lowered a shotgun and stared at Adam with cold eyes. "Rattlesnake," she stated simply.

'Did Dale tell her about me running out last night?' Adam's forehead wrinkled as he tried to think of something to say to a pissed off sibling with a shotgun in her hands. The blast had struck not 18 inches from the front of his boots, and shotguns weren't known for their accuracy.

Randy simply walked past Adam headed towards the barn. "Been meanin' to kill that snake for weeks. Keeps spookin' the horses."

Adam looked down at a dead rattlesnake blown into several pieces. Randy may have just saved his life, but he had an unsettling feeling that hadn't been her only intention. He was pulled from his reverie by a terse question.

"What can I do for you?" Randy asked, her voice carefully modulated to be polite, but not the least bit friendly.

"I... uh... need my horse," Adam answered, still feeling unsettled and uncomfortable.

Randy turned towards him, letting her detached gaze run from his boots to his hat. "Leaving?"

Adam nodded, but added a clarification, "Just for a few days."

"Hmmm... his tack is in the tack room. Go ahead and pull it, and I'll whistle him in," she instructed.

Adam gaped as Randy stepped on the middle rung of the fence and whistled sharply. Sampson raised his head on the far side of the pasture and trotted to her quickly, nuzzling her stomach while she ran her fingers through his mane. At least her feelings towards him weren't affecting her treatment of his horse. Belatedly realizing he hadn't gotten the tack, Adam quickly ducked in and out of the stables, slipping a neck bridle over his horse's head.

Randy hopped to the ground and looked up at Adam. Her eyes softened briefly, and Adam wondered what had just run through her mind. "Travel quickly and come back safe," she whispered before leaving him standing alone beside his horse.

NOAH and Nathaniel fell into an easy rhythm during Adam's absence. They spent good parts of each day searching for information on Elias, had dinner at the saloon and explored their new lovers at night. Justice was beginning to feel like home.

Friday morning, Simon was walking from the storage shed to the back door of the hotel when a loop of rope fell neatly over his head and around his torso, tightening and pinning his arms to his sides. Looking over his shoulder, he spotted Noah holding the end of the rope with an enormous grin on his face.

"Look what I caught," Noah crowed cockily.

Simon just grinned and shook his head. "Well, now that you've caught me, what are you going to do with me?"

Noah walked closer, reeling in his catch. Just a few feet away, he gave a sharp tug on the rope, pulling Simon off balance and catching him to his chest with strong arms. Lowering his mouth right next to Simon's ear, he whispered, "I'm gonna fuck ya 'til you can't walk straight."

Simon groaned, pushing his ass back against Noah's crotch. "Don't need a rope for that."

"Yeah, but sometimes it's more fun with a little rope." Noah's hazel eyes danced mischievously.

Simon shuddered. "Let's go upstairs."

Since the first night the two men had spent together, they hadn't managed to keep their hands off each other for more than a few hours at a stretch. They spent every night and morning fucking, and the middle of the day frequently found Noah on his knees behind the reception desk or Simon's hand around Noah's cock in the barn.

Simon kept expecting the rampant need of new desire to wear off – or at least lessen – but it hadn't. If anything, it was getting stronger. The more he touched Noah, the more he wanted to touch him again.

Halfway up the stairs, both men were moving fast enough to call it running. Noah grabbed Simon's arm just as the blond man entered the room in front of him, swinging him up against the wall and kicking the door closed with his boot.

Lips sealed to lips; hands struggled with inconvenient and unnecessary clothes; and hard bodies strained to be closer.

"I. Want. You," Noah stated, watching Simon's eyes darken from emerald to forest.

Simon's hips surged forward, grinding his cock into Noah's. "So quit talkin' and fuck me."

Noah shook his head. "Nope." The dark head dipped and warm lips started nibbling behind Simon's ear.

"No?! Fuck, Noah, if you dragged me up here just to tease me, I'm gonna have to use that rope of yours to tie you to the bed and ride myself to heaven, because I need to come," Simon complained, thrashing against Noah's restraint as the nibbling mouth worked its way down his neck and onto his chest.

"Oh, I'm not goin' to tease you. I'm just not goin' to fuck you." Noah's mouth discovered a rosy nipple ringed with soft golden hair. Gently, his teeth pulled on the hair, causing the flesh to pucker. Licking the raised nub, he blew over the wet flesh.

Simon's body trembled under the touch. "Don't damn well care what you aren't goin' to do, just don't fuckin' stop doin' that."

Noah chuckled and switched his attention to the neglected nipple. Once he had it hard and damp, he rolled it gently between his teeth, tugging, suckling and then soothing it with kisses. Abruptly Noah stepped away, and Simon almost sank to the floor. "I'm not stopping anytime soon. Get on the bed for me, lover."

Simon gladly complied, stripping out of his remaining clothes and stretching out on the well-worn quilt, waiting for his lover to join him. Noah lost his clothes as well, but instead of joining Simon on the bed immediately, he circled the bed examining his lover from all angles.

Simon squirmed under the scrutiny. "Come over here where I can touch you," he pleaded, reaching out for Noah.

Noah just stopped and stared at Simon for a long time. "You are so fucking beautiful it takes my breath away."

Simon dropped his eyes and to his dismay noticed that the flush of pleasure and embarrassment he felt at Noah's words had spread from his face to his chest.

Noah sat on the bed beside Simon and gently stoked his fingers through the fine, gold hair on his chest. "I want to do this a little differently. Will you trust me?"

Simon nodded. Noah lay down beside him, pressing their bodies close. Returning to Simon's nipples, he picked up his thorough ravishing right where he'd left off. Simon moaned as the already sensitized disk was sucked strongly.

Noah left no inch of Simon's skin untouched. He brushed his cheek against the smooth skin of his shoulders, sucked at the tender skin inside his elbows, nuzzled the soft trail of hair leading down his stomach and placed open-mouthed kisses over his hip bones. Every brush of Noah's lips made Simon's body melt further into the bed.

Simon had agreed to trust Noah, which in his mind, meant letting the younger man take the lead, but he was running out of control fast. "Noah, lover, if you don't touch me soon, I'm going to explode," he rasped, pulling Noah up by his hair so he could seal his request with a kiss.

"I *am* touching you, love." Noah grinned smugly, but he stroked his palm over Simon's length anyway.

Simon's needy groan wiped the smile from Noah's face. "You really want me, don't you?" Noah asked sincerely.

Simon looked up and stared into his lover's hazel eyes intently. "With every piece of my being and for as long as you'll put up with me," he answered honestly.

Noah stretched his long body on top of Simon's, kissing him thoroughly. Slipping his fingers into his mouth, he began to prepare Simon's body with the same meticulous care he used to explore it moments before. When he couldn't hold back his own need any longer, Noah joined their bodies, entering Simon slowly and never breaking eye contact.

Buried to the hilt in Simon's clenching warmth, Noah desperately wanted to move, fucking Simon hard and fast until they both screamed. That was how they always ended up, but tonight Noah wanted to show Simon that he meant more than that to him.

Supporting his weight on his elbows, but leaving their bodies pressed together, Noah started to move, each stroke slow and deep. He pulled back until Simon's outer ring of muscle clenched around the head of his cock in a desperate attempt not to lose contact and then smoothly glided forward until their bodies were completely coupled.

Simon's eyes changed with each stroke. Noah could see the spike of pleasure when he brushed his lover's prostate, the almost panicked look when he came close to withdrawing and the blissful look of completion when he was buried to the hilt. He wanted to learn each and every one of Simon's expressions.

Even with the slower pace, the constant caressing of Noah's cock deep inside him was driving Simon closer and closer to his peak. Canting his hips to meet each thrust, Simon grabbed Noah's head to pull him near enough to kiss. The pressure of their bodies sandwiching his erection made him moan.

Noah snapped his hips forward, increasing the intensity of his penetration. Rolling his hips, he changed the friction on Simon's cock and balls, causing him to cry out and grip Noah's ass to bring him even closer.

Both men were breathing heavily, poised on the edge of pleasure. Noah's movements became shallower until he was barely moving, rocking repeatedly over Simon's prostate.

Simon's eyes fluttered as his climax overtook him. The slow build up led to a long, drawn out climax that slowly unwound from his groin instead of exploding in short bursts.

The trembling of Simon's body and convulsions of the muscles around his cock triggered Noah's release. A deep moan was torn from his chest, muffled by Simon's neck as his body arched like an unbroken horse trying to shed his rider, and then he collapsed against his lover.

After several minutes of harsh breathing, Noah slipped out of Simon, rolled to his side and scooted back, spooning their bodies together.

"Damn," Simon cursed reverently.

Noah drifted to sleep with a smile.

Chapter Five

LUKE felt strong hands touch his shoulders, gently kneading. "You've been working too hard," Jamison whispered next to his ear.

"Lots to be done." Luke turned his head from the books he'd been working on to capture his lover's lips in a soft kiss. "Always time for you, though." Luke pulled Jamison down into his lap.

Jamison curled up, laying his head on Luke's shoulder. "Doesn't feel like it lately. I never seem to get you all to myself anymore."

"Are you changing your mind about Nate?" Luke asked, tracing lazy circles on Jamison's side.

Jamison shrugged. "Not really."

"Well, what *do* you want?"

"I want you to myself for a while. Can we go home for a few days?" Jamison turned pleading brown eyes up at him, and Luke knew he was lost. He was never able to deny Jamison anything.

Swatting him on the ass, Luke pushed Jamison off his lap. "Go get ready. I'll arrange things with the guys to cover the saloon and see about the horses."

"Just Tanner. I want to ride with you," Jamison tossed over his shoulder as he left the office.

Thirty minutes later, Jamison walked into the barn dressed in a soft buckskin shirt, leggings, and moccasins. Luke was tossing a blanket on Tanner. He stopped and took a deep breath to get his body under control. Jamison dressed in soft, worn leather that molded to his body was an intoxicating sight. "You ready to go?"

Jamison nodded, jumping onto Tanner's back, moving forward to let Luke mount behind him. They both preferred to ride without a saddle unless they were doing something that required a place to tie off a rope. Luke squeezed his legs, and Tanner broke into a fast walk.

As soon as they were out of town, Luke took them up to a smooth canter. It was a beautiful day, the warm sun on his back and the cool breeze blowing the hair off his neck. The natural rhythm of the horse moved Jamison's ass against his cock in a very provocative manner.

Luke moved his hands from Jamison's thighs up under his tunic. When his fingers encountered bare skin, he clucked Tanner down to a walk. "Jamie?" he asked sweetly, stroking the bare skin around Jamison's hardening cock.

"Yes, love?"

"Why don't you have any pants on?"

Jamison moved back against Luke, searching for more friction from the hard bulge in Luke's pants. "I do. Only, the important parts are accessible."

Luke couldn't argue with that as his hand easily slid around his lover's erection. Jamison's tunic which came down over his hips had hidden the top of his pants which were really only chaps, covering his legs and hips but leaving his cock, crotch and ass completely bare.

Luke's hands gripped Jamison's hips, pushing him away slightly so he could look down at the smooth skin of his ass. His rough thumbs made circles on the skin, making Jamison moan softly.

Leaning forward onto Tanner's neck, Jamison looked over his shoulder. "Please fuck me."

"Oh hell, Jamie. How do you expect me to say 'no' to that?" Luke shuddered and the bulge in his pants grew painful.

"I don't expect you to say 'no'. I expect you to fuck me," Jamison stated.

Luke groaned and ground his cock against the tight little ass in his hands. With a quick scan of the horizon, Luke capitulated. Pulling Jamison back to his chest, he moved one of his lover's legs over Tanner. Jamison caught on and spun so he faced Luke, reclining against the horse's neck and putting his legs over Luke's.

Luke undid the buttons on his trousers, allowing his cock to spring free. He never did have much of a use for underclothes. It wasn't something he'd been raised to wear, and he never wore them when dressed in his tribal clothes. Grabbing Jamison's ass in his hands, he lifted the slender man up onto his lap as far as he could.

"When you were planning this little horseback seduction, did you think to bring oil?" Luke asked, gently stroking Jamison's cleft with the tips of his fingers.

Jamison smiled beatifically and slipped a small corked bottle out of a pocket in his shirt. Luke just shook his head and coated his fingers. Jamison's eyes fluttered closed as Luke's fingers breached his body. Luke worked him with both hands, one preparing his ass and one stroking his cock.

Jamison arched into the touches, purring contentedly. "This what you needed, Jamie?" Luke asked softly.

Jamison nodded and ground down on Luke's fingers. "As soon as you work that cock inside me," he panted as Luke's fingers played with his prostate.

Moving his hand to coat himself with oil, Luke positioned himself to breach his lover's body.

Jamison made low, encouraging noises in the back of his throat, tilting his hips to an accommodating angle. "Take me."

Luke surged forward, sheathing himself in one long plunge. Jamison's back arched up off the horse, allowing Luke to slip an arm under his body and pull him upright against his chest. They rode that way for a while, holding each other close, kissing and letting the rocking of the horse subtly shift their bodies together.

Jamison eventually got impatient, lifting himself off Luke's lap and slamming back down with satisfied moans. Luke supported him and let the younger man find his rhythm. He could feel his lover's body beginning to tense and tremble as he got closer to coming. Reaching between them, he added his hand to the sensations driving Jamison to the brink. With a hoarse shout, Jamison came all over Luke's hand, his shirt shielding Luke from the majority of the mess.

Luke laid the momentarily sated man back against Tanner's neck. Bracing the slender hips with his hands, he started a slow and easy pace in and out of the still clenching sheath, giving Jamison a chance to recover his breath.

He watched as Jamison began to squirm against his thrusts, his breath hitching as Luke repeatedly hit the perfect spot inside of him. Finally, his dark eyes fluttered open. "You ride like a white man," he taunted with a mischievous smile.

Luke matched his smile. With a cluck and a squeeze, he encouraged Tanner into a canter. Again and again, his cock drove deep inside Jamison. Luke pulled his lover to him with more and more urgency.

Needing Luke's hands to stabilize them at the faster pace, Jamison grabbed his own cock and fisted it roughly. He wanted to come with Luke and knew he didn't have long to catch up.

One of Luke's hands shifted to Jamison's shoulder, searching for even more leverage. His rhythm faltered and his head fell forward. "Come with me, Jamie," he groaned.

Jamison moved his hand faster and faster until it blurred, canting his hips onto Luke's cock, his moans and curses increasing in both volume and frequency.

Luke growled deep in his throat, throwing his head back in a silent howl. Burying himself deeply, he flooded Jamison's socket with pulse after pulse of his come until it leaked out to be absorbed by the rough blanket.

Jamison tightened around the pulsing shaft, wanting to feel every twitch. Within moments, his come covered his hand and mixed with Luke's. "Oh gods, yes!" he screamed, his voice fading to a series of soft whimpers as Luke slowed Tanner to a walk, continuing to rock in and out of the slippery channel.

Shifting his weight backwards, Luke drew the horse to a stop, pulling Jamison's quivering body up into his arms and holding him tight. Resting his lips close to Jamison's ear, he whispered soothing words as he petted the dark, damp curls.

Eventually he pulled back and dropped a chaste kiss on Jamison's forehead. "Let's get you cleaned up or grandmother will have my hide sewn into her tipi."

Jamison chuckled softly, but shifted out of Luke's lap. By the time they reached the village, they were ready to face their family.

ADAM arrived back in town six days after he'd left so suddenly. He was tired and dirty, but his mood lightened as he rode past the Justice sign, his lips actually curving into a smile. It felt good to be back even if he hadn't resolved anything while he'd been away. This town was beginning to feel like home, which was equal parts exciting and scary.

He missed his brothers. From time to time over the years, they had split up to follow different leads, but for the most part they were consistently at his side. If he chose to admit it, he missed Dale, too, but that thought was safely tucked away beneath layers of denial.

Adam considered the stable briefly before riding his horse directly to the hotel. He had no desire to confront Randy tonight. Tomorrow would be soon enough to feel out the prickly stable owner and see if his horse would be welcomed back.

After settling Sampson into the barn for the night, Adam headed upstairs to his room. Hannah was at the desk and promised to send up hot water immediately. She also informed him that his brothers had already headed over to the saloon for dinner and that Dale was at the library.

Adam started to say, "What do I care where Dale is?" but decided he didn't really want an answer to that question, and Hannah was likely to give him an honest one. With a tip of his hat, he thanked her and climbed the stairs wearily.

An hour later, freshly washed and in clean clothes, he arrived at the saloon. He had no appetite, but wanted to see his brothers. Spotting Noah and Simon immediately, he strode in their direction.

Noah jumped to his feet as Adam approached and pulled his brother into a big bear hug. Adam started to pull away but decided it felt pretty good and leaned into it instead.

"'Bout time you got back. Where in the hell did you go? New York?" Noah asked, sitting back down on his chair and resting his hand on Simon's thigh.

Adam laughed. "No, and to answer your next question, I didn't find out one fucking thing. Where's Nate?"

Noah nodded towards the piano. "Pouting."

Adam looked. Nathaniel was indeed pouting. The young man looked miserable, in fact, and more than a little drunk. He was sitting next to Charlie on the piano bench, his lanky body draped over the piano player, making it difficult for him to play. "What's up with him?" Adam asked.

"Luke and Jamison have been gone for three days. They headed up to the Lakota village for a visit. They do that every so often, spend time with their family, see what they need. Luke orders supplies for them through the saloon, so they don't get taken advantage of," Simon supplied.

"Nate had been spending pretty much every night with them until they left. Without them to entertain him, he's been useless." Noah snorted.

"Did you two find anything?" Adam asked.

Noah shook his head, taking a drink of his whiskey. Simon leaned close and kissed him.

Adam watched as the blond licked the whiskey off of Noah's lips. He shifted in his chair, his pants becoming uncomfortably tight. Trying to find somewhere for his eyes other than the two men sharing one mouthful of whiskey, he noticed the door opening.

Jamison stepped through the door with a flourish. "We're home. Anyone miss us?" he called with a grin. Various lewd comments rang out from around the room. Luke entered silently behind him with an indulgent look on his face.

Nathaniel was on his feet immediately, if a little unsteadily. He made a beeline for Jamison who hugged and kissed him passionately until catcalls filled the room. Luke shook his head and pulled Nathaniel away from Jamison for a quick kiss before pushing him back at the brunette. He leaned close to Jamison's ear and whispered something that made the young man smile.

Jamison tugged Nathaniel towards the stairs while Luke made the rounds from table to table, chatting, squeezing shoulders and signaling for fresh drinks. He approached Adam, Noah and Simon last.

"Hey Adam, welcome home," Luke greeted.

Adam smiled at the use of the word home. "I think you're the one that just arrived home."

Luke laughed and pulled up a chair. "I guess so. How'd your trip go?"

"Unproductive," Adam summed up.

"Let me buy you a drink," Luke offered. He turned to offer the same to Noah and Simon but decided not to interrupt.

"Don't you need to... urhm, well... won't Jamison...?" Adam searched for the right words, pointing towards the stairs.

Luke chuckled. "No, I've had Jamison all to myself for three days and two nights. I'll let the young ones tire each other out and slip in between them later. Morning is soon enough for me." Luke winked.

The barkeep's expression grew serious. "Our relationship with your brother doesn't bother you, does it?" he asked. "We can't offer him anything permanent, but we really do care about him."

Adam rushed to reassure Luke. "No, I think you guys are probably good for him. He has a tendency to be a little flighty and you seem to ground him. Actually I'd say he's damn lucky to have found you two."

"You're pretty lucky yourself."

"Oh?"

"Dale is a special man."

Adam looked down, uneasy about meeting Luke's eyes. "Uhm... Dale and I aren't together."

Luke smiled at Adam ruefully. "You can think that if you'd like, but I've known Dale since he was a kid, and I've yet to see him fail to get something he wants... and he wants you."

Luke rose, patting Adam's shoulder. "I probably should go up and make sure that they haven't broken the bed or anything else that would prevent me from getting a good night's sleep. Night, Adam."

Adam looked over, unsurprised to find Simon and Noah gone. Tossing some coins on the table and waving to Phillip behind the bar, he headed back to the hotel, thinking about Luke's words and trying desperately not to think about sparkling blue eyes and copper hair. Staying in Justice was dangerous. The longer he was here, the more he wanted to stay. Maybe it was time to move on.

THE next morning, Adam went out to take care of Sampson. The big horse was not happy with his cramped quarters and quickly let his owner know that they were not acceptable. After having his toes stepped on, his fingers nipped and a solid shove into the wall, Adam decided maybe it was time to face Randy.

He threw the saddle over Sampson's back but didn't bother to cinch it. With the mood his horse was in, he'd be thrown before his ass ever settled. He led the horse the short distance to the stables, berating himself the entire way for being a pushover.

Sampson nickered loudly the second they entered the barn. Randy's surprised voice came out of the tack room. "Sampson?"

She appeared with a smile on her face until her eyes moved from the black horse to his owner. "Back, I see," she stated in a flat voice.

"Uhm... yes, ma'am. I was kind of hoping you'd still have room for Sampson here. He seems to be spoiled by your hospitality." Adam looked hopeful.

Randy looked back to the horse and smiled. "Of course, how could you doubt that Sampson would be welcome here? He's a very special guy. Aren't you, boy?" She scratched the horse's nose and ran her fingers through his mane, combing out the tangles.

"Well, I know I'm not one of your favorite people right now..."

"I don't judge horses by their owners," Randy interrupted coolly.

Adam swallowed, shifting awkwardly from foot to foot. What was it about this woman that made him feel like a misbehaving child? "Oh well, thank you. Being here will make him happy."

Adam handed her the reins and turned to leave. Her voice stopped him halfway to the door. "If you were as smart as Sampson, you'd go see him, Adam. He missed you."

Adam's head dropped forward, his eyes on his boots. With a deep breath, he straightened his shoulders and walked out.

Chapter Six

THREE weeks after their arrival in Justice, Adam was growing increasingly frustrated. Another day of searching had proved fruitless, making Luke's food taste like dust. Noah's and Nathaniel's love diversions kept them relatively happy, but Adam was stubbornly refusing to have any contact with Dale, which was only increasing his frustration at their lack of progress.

The lead that had brought them to Justice in the first place had proven false. The name had been one of Elias's frequent aliases, but in this case, it actually belonged to a retired school teacher from Philadelphia who had bought a small farm outside of town.

"So what now?" Nathaniel asked.

"We keep digging," Noah answered, using words he'd heard Adam spout a hundred times.

"Do we? I'm beginning to wonder." Adam tossed back the last of his whiskey and stood. Raising a hand to Luke behind the bar, he headed out the door.

"What do you suppose he meant by that?" Nathaniel turned to Noah.

Noah shook his head, looking puzzled. "I'm not sure."

"You think he's headed to the library?"

The corners of Noah's mouth turned up slightly. "I sure as fuck hope so. He's been about as pleasant as a mama bear that's lost a cub." Spotting Simon from across the room, Noah pushed back from the table. "I, however, know a good thing when I see it. I'm calling it a night."

Ruffling Nathaniel's hair, he warned teasingly, "Don't do anything I wouldn't do, little brother."

Nathaniel laughed and swatted Noah's hand away from his head. "And that would be what exactly?"

ADAM left the saloon intending to go to bed, but his feet turned right instead of left. 'I'll just check and make sure Dale's not still at the library.' People had pretty much given up 'Rose Duty' since the first night Adam did it. Probably because most people assumed Adam was still doing it.

'Do you suppose he's eating or spending all night at the library because he's forgotten to go home?' Adam worried. 'I'll just walk by and make sure the lights are out. That's a load of horse shit, and you know it. Is it so bad to admit you just want to see him?'

Adam paused, turning towards the hotel and back to the library several times in indecision. An unexpected, warm voice decided for him.

"I was just headed to the saloon for some dinner. You weren't perchance coming to find me, were you?"

Adam turned to face Dale, who had appeared from inside the dry goods store. "I was talking to Eliza about some books she's trying to get for her class," Dale added when Adam didn't say anything.

"Did you lose your voice while you were gone?" Dale asked, tilting his head and examining Adam's face.

Adam shook his head. "No, of course not."

"Hmmm… good. I like your voice."

Adam's gut clenched as desire spiraled in his belly. The simplest comments out of Dale's mouth seemed to have a profound effect on him.

"So you want to come home with me for dinner?" Dale asked, gesturing in the direction of his house.

"Well… I'm not sure Randy would like that," Adam stated.

"Good thing she's staying with Meg tonight then, huh?"

Adam found himself following the copper-haired man down the street without having consciously made a decision to do so.

Dale entered the house, holding the door for Adam to enter, which he did with trepidation. Without even bothering to light a lamp, Dale turned and kissed Adam until he was breathless.

"Dale," Adam protested as soon as their lips were forced apart for lack of oxygen.

"Missed you," Dale mumbled before sucking Adam's lower lip back into his mouth and continuing the kiss.

"I thought you were hungry," Adam tried when their mouths parted briefly.

Dale's mouth remained busy, moving across Adam's jaw to his ear and then down his neck. Unconsciously, Adam tilted his head to allow greater access.

"I *am* hungry… for this." Dale's mouth sank into the V of Adam's shirt. Nuzzling his lips and cheeks against the soft, curling hair, he started to undo the buttons, seeking more skin.

Adam grabbed Dale's wrists with his hands, stilling their movement. Dale moaned and shuddered involuntarily. Adam's power really turned him on and having those strong hands restraining his arms sent dangerous signals to his groin. He knew Adam was trying to defuse the situation, not enflame it, but the image of Adam, looming over him, pinning his hands to the mattress as he fucked him, flooded his mind. He struggled momentarily just to increase the illusion. Leaning towards his captor, he rubbed his throbbing erection against Adam's hip.

The waves of arousal flowing off Dale were intoxicating. Adam found himself moving Dale's trapped arms down to his sides and initiating the kiss himself this time. Dale tilted his head back against the onslaught and made soft humming noises of approval. Taking a step back, he hesitated to see if Adam would follow. When he did, Dale started moving them backward towards the couch. Even though he was heading for it, the edge of the couch bumping into the back of his knees took Dale by surprise, and he fell backwards onto the cushions. Grabbing the front of Adam's shirt, he pulled the other man down on top of him.

Adam groaned and arched into the hard evidence of Dale's desire. Dale opened his legs, wrapping them around Adam's hips to prevent his escape. He whimpered as Adam surged forward instead of trying to pull away.

'God, what would Adam be like as a lover if he ever tried to seduce me? I can barely handle him when he's reluctant,' Dale thought fleetingly. Raising his hands to Adam's chest, he resumed unfastening the buttons.

Adam's first realization that Dale was undressing him came when warm hands smoothed down his chest and wrapped around his sides to his back, pulling his shirt free from his pants. Dale's hands slipped inside the back of Adam's jeans, grasping his ass firmly and pulling him closer.

The persistent voice of self-preservation was screaming at Adam to run, but he slammed a mental door on it and reached for the fastening of Dale's pants. This time it was Dale's hands that intervened.

"Oh no you don't," he warned in a rusty growl.

Adam looked up at lust darkened blue eyes, puzzled.

"It's my turn." When Adam started to protest, Dale continued, "You owe me."

Dale pushed Adam back the other direction on the couch and crawled over him, biting and teasing the peaked nipples rising from the bed of thick hair. He moved lower down Adam's torso, blowing warm, moist air over the sensitive skin. Electricity ran over Adam's body, concentrating in his nipples and cock, hardening them until it was almost painful, and he cried out. "Fuck, Dale!"

"I don't think you're ready for that," Dale answered honestly. "Once I let you fuck me, I refuse to let you go."

Adam groaned as Dale's fingers tackled the buttons on his pants before dancing up and down his freed cock. He squeezed his eyes shut tightly, trying to put off the climax he could feel building.

Dale licked the veined length with the pleasure of a child with new lollipop. They both groaned as the talented tongue swept the rosy head. Closing his mouth over the tip, Dale sucked the salty fluid from the slit.

"Oh God," Adam moaned, his fingers slipping into the impossibly soft hair.

Dale opened his mouth wide and sunk down the length.

"Oh hell... Dale... argh...." Adam's back arched and his head hung back against the worn velvet.

Dale sucked strongly, moving up and down the swollen shaft. With two fingers, he massaged the curve right behind Adam's balls. Dropping them lower, he flicked them lightly over the puckered entrance.

Dale felt every muscle in Adam's body tense. Relaxing his throat, he swallowed Adam completely, gripping the hard ass to hold him close.

Adam peaked. The sensation was so strong, he wanted to run from it, but Dale's hands prevented him from pulling away. Unable to retreat, he surged into it instead, releasing burst after burst down the welcoming throat.

Dale was humming in pleasure again, the vibrations provoking strong aftershocks. The librarian held Adam in his mouth until he had completely softened and melted into the couch, boneless and sated. Allowing Adam to slip from his lips, Dale laid his head on the firm stomach just over the dark curls, enjoying the intimacy of the position.

Adam absently stroked his fingers through Dale's hair. "We can't keep doing this," he said seriously. "You deserve better. You deserve someone who'll love you and live here in Justice."

Dale didn't even open his eyes. He just smiled. "Don't want that person, unless it's you."

"I can't be that person."

"You can be anything you want to be," Dale murmured sleepily.

Adam listened as Dale's breath grew shallow and even. He lay on the couch for several hours, stroking his lover's hair and wishing that he could become the man Dale seemed to see. Before daylight, he managed to slip from beneath the dozing man. Pulling the quilt from the back of the sofa down to keep Dale warm, Adam left to go back to the hotel. He couldn't sleep at Dale's; he needed the impermanence of a hotel room to be comfortable.

EARLY the next morning, Noah found Adam sitting on the front porch at the hotel. Pulling another rocking chair close to his brother, he took a seat. "Nate heard something at the saloon last night after we left."

"Really," Adam asked, feigning interest.

"It's not much. There's a ranch just northwest of here that seems to have a lot of unexplained comings and goings. I thought I'd ride up there today and put my ear to the ground."

Adam nodded thoughtfully.

Noah propped his boot on the porch railing and lazily rocked back and forth. "Do you remember how Mom and Dad were always touching each other?" Noah asked, not looking away from the pink streaks climbing from the horizon.

Adam grinned. "Yeah, they couldn't keep their hands off each other. When I was a kid, it used to bug the hell out of me. Now it makes me smile. They were so in love. They did everything together. He helped her cook and clean, and she helped him dig. I don't think they were apart for even a day from the time they met."

"I used to wish that Mom had stayed at home the day Dad ran into Elias, but I finally realized that she would have died without him anyway." Noah's voice was soft and contemplative. "I understand how she felt."

Adam turned and looked at Noah. "Simon?"

Noah nodded slowly. "I love him, Adam, and I'm not willing to give up a life with him to chase ghosts. Mom and Dad wouldn't have wanted Elias to steal our lives, too."

Adam nodded slightly, unable to meet Noah's eyes, but didn't say anything. He, too, had been questioning his decision to drag his brothers around in search of vengeance. At first, he'd been so angry that revenge had been his only option. Then it just sort of became a habit.

"I'm going to ride out today to see if Elias has anything to do with this ranch, but then I quit. I'm willing to let him come to his own justice. All his evil will catch up with him eventually." Noah's voice was determined.

Adam knew Noah was expecting an argument. Reaching over, he clasped his brother's shoulder. Squeezing firmly, he whispered, "Tell him."

Noah looked puzzled.

"Make sure you tell Simon how you feel about him," Adam clarified. "Often."

Noah nodded and reached out to his brother, pulling their foreheads together. "I love you, too, you know."

Adam blinked rapidly, trying to stem the tears collecting in his eyes. He didn't do this sentimental stuff well. "Love you, too. Now go find your lover and fuck him through the floor before you get people wondering about us even more than they already do."

Noah stood and strode into the lobby. Adam turned back to the sunrise. Not telling his parents how much he loved them still haunted him. Like a typical teenager, all he had done was complain... about chasing after the next gold rumor... about watching his younger brothers.

"I love you," he whispered to the rising sun, hoping his words would find their way to heaven.

NOAH made a beeline for the front desk where his lover was bent over the registration book with Hannah. Smiling his most charming smile at the young girl and making her blush, Noah grabbed Simon's hand and started pulling him towards the stairs.

"But... Noah... I need...." Simon sputtered.

Noah leaned close to Simon's ear and whispered, "You need my mouth on your cock, and my cock up your ass until you come so hard you forget your name."

Simon quit pulling away from Noah and willingly let himself be led towards his room. "Yeah, if I didn't know I needed it a minute ago, I sure as hell need it now."

Noah threw Simon onto the bed, tearing at his own clothes, while Simon struggled with his. Naked, he threw himself on top of his lover. "Need to be inside you."

Simon moaned and arched up into Noah's body. "Do it. You were just there. I shouldn't need to be prepped."

Noah quickly slicked himself with the oil by the bed, positioned himself, and slid inside. He groaned loudly, his head falling forward onto Simon's chest. Now that he was where he needed to be, all the rush fled. He held perfectly still, enjoying the feeling of being joined with the man he loved. 'Tell him,' Adam's voice whispered in his head.

"Noah?" Simon asked, looking worried.

Noah smiled to let Simon know he was okay. "Do you know that when I do this..." Noah rocked into Simon, brushing directly over his prostate, "your eyes change color?"

Simon groaned, planting his feet on the bed and pressing his erection up into Noah's stomach. "Fuckin' hell, that's not the only thing that changes when you do that."

Noah snickered softly. "I want to spend forever discovering those things about you."

Simon's eyes lifted, meeting Noah's. "Suits me."

"I love you, Simon."

Simon gasped, grabbing Noah's head and pulling him close for a kiss. "I never thought I'd hear you say that. I've been trying so hard not to fall in love with you, but it wasn't working."

"Good." Noah nuzzled Simon's neck, placing a trail of kisses along his collarbone.

"Will you stay with me here in Justice?" Simon asked.

Noah stopped his exploration. "That depends...."

"On?"

"How you feel about me." It was hard for Noah to ask, but he had to know.

Simon's eyes sparkled. "If I tell you I love you, will you move?"

"Cocky bastard," Noah cursed, stabbing his cock deep into Simon.

"Fuck, yes, I love you."

Noah thrust forward. "Say it again."

"I love you."

Noah started slow. It felt different, joining hearts as well as bodies. He wanted it to last forever, but at the same time, he couldn't wait to see Simon's face as he gave in to the pleasure Noah was stirring within him.

Increasing his speed steadily, Noah pounded into Simon, reveling in the arousing moans and curses that were urging him on. Wrapping a shaking fist around Simon's cock, he rasped, "Come for me, lover."

Simon gripped Noah's hair, pulling his mouth down to smother his cries as he obeyed, his semen coating their chests and Noah's hand.

Noah's motion actually slowed with Simon's release until he was moving in long, deep, controlled strokes, keeping himself balanced on the precipice of his climax. "You feel so fucking good. I never want to leave you."

Simon's eyes softened. "So don't. Fuck me forever. We might die of starvation, but what a way to go." Noah smirked which caused Simon to laugh.

"Oh hell," Noah cried as Simon's laughter caused the muscles around him to clench, unraveling his control. Waves of orgasmic bliss washed over him, his forehead falling to Simon's chest as the blond's arms embraced him tightly.

Noah rested against Simon's chest as his breathing and heart rate slowed. He didn't want to move, but he needed to check out the ranch and get back before nightfall. "I've got something to check out today, but I'll meet you back here for dinner," he said, his voice laced with regret.

"Well, if you aren't around, I might actually get some work done. That could be good for business," Simon replied, running his fingers through Noah's hair.

"I don't want to leave."

"I'm certainly not going to push you out of bed," Simon replied.

"I promised Adam."

"Who are you trying to convince? Me or you?"

Noah shot Simon a dirty look, withdrawing from his body suddenly, causing him to gasp. Simon grumbled as both men reluctantly started the search for their clothes.

ADAM left the hotel at a quarter to seven, proud of himself for managing to stay away from the library all day. He hadn't seen hide nor hair of Nathaniel and assumed that his younger brother probably hadn't left Jamison's company. Noah should have been back by now, and Adam was hoping he might find both of his brothers at the saloon.

Nathaniel was sitting at the table the brothers normally claimed, talking to Jamison, but Noah was nowhere to be seen. Adam pulled up a chair and ordered some food while they waited. Simon joined them several minutes later.

Luke was pouring another round of drinks when the door slammed open suddenly and Randy fell into the room, breathless. Her eyes searching, they stopped when they fell on Adam. "Noah's horse... came back... blood on the saddle..."

A hush fell over the room. It was broken by Simon's glass slipping from his fingers and shattering on the floor. The crash released a tidal wave of noise.

Luke calmly and swiftly took charge. Looking at Randy, he asked, "Did you bring horses?"

She nodded. "I've got seven with me, and I told your stable boy to saddle Tanner and Ares when I rode them in."

"Good." Luke turned to Simon, taking in his shaking hands and pale face. He needed to give the other man something concrete to focus on. "Simon... Simon, go get Doc Hank. Have him pack a bag and meet us on the north road."

Simon turned and left without a word.

Adam felt rooted to the floor. Nathaniel stood at his side, pulling on his arm, but he couldn't take his eyes off the position Randy had been standing in when she'd said the words, 'blood on the saddle'.

Luke's voice finally broke through the fog. When he turned, he was surprised to see Luke in boots, a coat and hat. Jamison was coming down the stairs in denim and leather instead of velvet and silk. Luke turned at Jamison's arrival. "Ride fast and safe. We'll meet you at the bluff." He kissed his lover quickly before Jamison headed out the door.

At Adam's puzzled look, Luke explained, "It's harder to track at night. We'll need all the help we can get. Jamison's headed to the Indian village for men."

"I don't even have a solid idea of where he was headed," Adam worried.

Luke placed a reassuring hand on Adam's arm. "That's okay. We have Rascal. Noah's horse knows exactly where he took him. We just have to get him to tell us." Luke turned to greet a dark haired man who had just arrived.

Randy nodded. "Luke's got a way with horses, Adam. We'll find him."

"But what if...." Adam couldn't finish the sentence.

Nathaniel spoke up for the first time. "He's not dead. He may be hurt, but we'd know it if he was dead. Let's go find him."

Luke returned. "Adam, Nate, this is Walter Jeffries. He's our sheriff. He'll be separating the men into groups and organizing the search, but I'd like you to ride with me."

Adam grabbed his hat. "Let's go." Luke was glad to hear the familiar determination return to his voice.

NOAH'S eyes drifted open long enough to see that the sky was dark. That meant he'd been unconscious for hours. The last thing he remembered was staring at the ranch house through the brush and hearing the crack of a pistol behind him.

He looked around but didn't see anything that indicated where he was. He was definitely not where he'd been shot, which meant they had moved him. He could be anywhere.

The last thought that ran through his mind before the blackness claimed him was, 'At least I told Simon that I loved him.'

Chapter Seven

ADAM jumped at a loud shriek, aiming his gun into the night. Luke reached out, put a hand on the top of the pistol and lowered it. "It's Jamison with Laughing Elk."

"A human made that noise?" Adam whispered, alarmed.

Luke smiled and nodded. "Laughing Elk has been perfecting his mountain lion cry since we were kids," he explained. "Come on. This way. They've found something."

Luke had backtracked the path Noah's horse had taken into town. The search became harder when they hit a section of rock outcropping and scrub. The group had split up to search the myriad of crevices. Nathaniel had joined Hank and Simon, Randy was with Walter, and Adam stuck with Luke. There were four other pairs from Justice searching and an unknown number that had come with Jamison.

Luke and Adam rounded a large cluster of jagged rock, and Luke slipped from Tanner's back in a fluid motion, joining the two men already present in a crouch. Adam dismounted and looked over Luke's shoulder.

"Blood trail," the man Adam assumed to be Laughing Elk said seriously.

Luke agreed, "He was still on horseback at this point." Rising to their feet, the three men spread out and walked in the same direction examining the ground with Adam trailing behind them, trying to resist the urge to scream, "Can't you walk any faster?"

Adam was fully aware of his strengths and weaknesses, and he wasn't a tracker. Noah's best chance for survival was with these men, and he wasn't about to piss them off by telling them how to follow a trail.

Soon their pace did increase until they were almost running over the uneven terrain. Adam envied the moccasins Laughing Elk wore as his boots scrambled for purchase on the loose rock. Coming to a dry creek bed, they stopped suddenly. Luke turned right; Laughing Elk turned left; and Jamison gracefully jumped to the other side. Adam stood at the point of separation and wondered at their silent communication for a second before following Luke.

A sharp cry from Laughing Elk, that sounded suspiciously like a coyote bark, had them all running back towards the tall warrior. By the time they reached his side, he had Noah's shirt torn away from a nasty looking bullet hole and was turning him gently to examine him for more injuries.

Adam dropped to his knees at Noah's side, running his fingers down his cheek. He was pale and hot, but undeniably still alive. "Hold on, little brother. Simon will kill me if you die," he choked out around the lump in his throat.

Luke's strong hands were pulling him away slightly as Hank appeared. Within moments, the area was full of people. Walter was directing a group back to town to get a wagon. Randy was seeing to the horses. Jamison was talking with a group of leather-clad Lakotas.

Nathaniel appeared at his side, solemnly. "He's going to be all right."

Adam wasn't sure if it was a statement, a question or a prayer. Wrapping his arm around Nathaniel's shoulder, he pulled his youngest brother close to him.

Simon stood at the edge of the commotion... watching... his green eyes glowing with unshed tears.

NOAH was lifted into the wagon to be taken to Hank's. Nathaniel and Hank climbed in beside him. Adam turned to Simon, waiting.

Simon gestured him up. "That's okay. I'll ride behind."

Once Hank had Noah cleaned up and settled in a big wide bed in the spare room he used as a makeshift hospital ward, Adam began to feel like there might be hope. Hank had removed the bullet, cleaned and bandaged the wound. Noah had lost a lot of blood and there was always the risk of infection, but Hank assured him that the slight fever Noah was running now was just his body healing and nothing to be worried about.

Adam pulled up a chair and settled in.

Hank looked at the oldest brother. "He's just going to sleep. I can send someone to get you if anything changes."

"That's okay. I have no intention of going anywhere," Adam answered, stretching his legs out in front of him and pulling his hat over his eyes.

Two days later, Adam had abandoned the chair to lie next to Noah in the bed. He'd sent Nathaniel back to the hotel to try and get some sleep. Almost against his will, his eyes drifted closed.

Adam woke, stiff from his awkward position and holding himself tense while he slept. He probably wouldn't have slept at all if he hadn't been completely exhausted. It was dark outside, and the room was only dimly lit by a single candle. Adam assumed that Hank had been using it to check on Noah.

A shifting shadow caught his attention. Allowing his eyes to focus, Adam saw Simon sitting in a chair by the window. Simon had been a constant presence since they'd brought Noah back, but always on the periphery.

Sitting up on the bed beside Noah, he called out softly, "Simon."

Simon shot to his feet and moved silently to the bed. "Do you need something? Is he okay?"

Adam smiled. "He seems to be resting easily. But he does have two sides, you know, and I think he'd like you close by." Adam glanced meaningfully at the bed on the other side of Noah.

Simon's face softened as he looked down at the still form of his lover. Toeing off his boots, he stretched out on the bed. The next time Simon's eyes opened, the room was filled with light, and a steady pair of hazel eyes were looking at him.

"Noah," Simon whispered. "Am I dreaming?"

"If you are, your dreams hurt like hell," Noah voice was dry. He tried to laugh, but it ended up a cough. He cursed as pain shot through his body.

Simon jumped to his feet to go find Hank, colliding with Adam at the foot of the bed. Adam shot his brother a smile before pushing Simon back towards the bed. "You stay with him. I'll go find Hank."

Simon sat gingerly next to his lover, running his fingers through the dark hair. "You scared the shit out of me. I thought I'd lost you," he admitted.

"I'm harder to get rid of than that." Noah's eyes were already drifting shut from the small exertion.

"I love you," Simon whispered, brushing a kiss over Noah's dry lips.

NEWS of Noah's recovery spread like wildfire. Hank still steadfastly refused to let anyone into the room except Adam,

Nathaniel and Simon, but one afternoon, Luke managed to slip in while Jamison distracted the doctor with a make-believe malady.

"How's everybody doing?" Luke asked cheerfully, opening a basket of food. "Not that Meg's broth isn't nourishing, but I thought y'all might like a something a little more substantial." Luke had been trying to lure Adam and Simon out for a real meal for days, but they weren't budging from Noah's side.

Silence descended as the men ate. Even Noah managed a few bites before falling back on the pillows to rest. Luke shot him a concerned look.

"I've got to eat if I ever intend to get my strength back," Noah told him. "And I'll need my strength when we go after the bastard that shot me."

Adam looked at Noah, startled. It was the first time Noah had mentioned the attack. "Do you remember what happened?"

"Hell, yes! Not something I'm likely to forget. I found the ranch easy enough. I tied up Rascal and snuck up to a group of bushes just to watch for a while. I heard the snap of a twig just before the shot."

"You turning was probably what saved you from being shot in the back," Luke speculated.

"Was it Elias?" Adam asked.

Noah shook his head. "Nope. But when has he ever done his own dirty work?"

"You said you'd gotten off Rascal, but there was blood on his saddle, and his trail led us back to you."

Luke interjected, "From what we can piece together, they dragged him to his horse, threw him over the saddle and either slapped him off or led him away. When Noah fell off the saddle, Rascal did what came naturally and returned to the barn."

"So you know where Noah was shot?" Adam directed at Luke.

Luke nodded. "Jamison and Laughing Elk followed the blood trail back that night. Walter and his deputies have been keeping an eye on the place ever since. Plenty going on out there and none of it legal."

"I don't need the law to tell me that, and I'm not going to need their help to take care of it either," Adam declared.

"Adam," Luke warned, "don't fly off half-cocked. Walter will get these guys, and they'll swing from a rope. I promise. He's only been waiting for Noah to get a better because he assumed you'd want to ride out with him."

"We'll see," Adam murmured.

Luke and Simon shared a worried look.

ADAM woke that night to the unmistakable sounds of Noah and Simon kissing in the bed next to him. He held completely still and willed himself back to sleep, but it didn't work. The soft whisper of touches and declarations of love ended as the lovers drifted back to sleep, leaving Adam wide awake and decidedly uncomfortable. The next day, he announced that he was returning to the hotel for a bath and a good night's sleep.

The bath felt heavenly. Adam had intended to go over to the saloon for a full meal, but the heat of the bath had sapped all of the desire to go anywhere. Drying himself off, he fell into bed and was immediately asleep. A rush of cool air and the brush of sheets woke him in the middle of the night.

Adam tensed and started to turn, when Dale's voice stopped him, "Shhhh… go back to sleep, my love. Just let me hold you."

Adam started to protest, but Dale's voice soothed him. 'Just for a few minutes,' he thought as the warm body curled behind him, and strong arms encircled him.

A loud knock and Nathaniel's voice woke him the next morning. He turned over expecting to find a sleep-tousled Dale. A jolt of disappointment stabbed him when he encountered nothing but an empty bed. 'Did I imagine the whole thing? Was I that desperate for comfort?'

Adam buried his face in the empty pillow and inhaled. 'Dale.' He smiled before swinging his feet onto the floor.

"Adam, get your lazy ass out of bed," Nathaniel hollered. "Hank says Noah can come home..." Nathaniel broke off as Adam swung open the door.

"First of all, a hotel isn't a home. Secondly, is Hank sure Noah is ready for this?" Adam asked.

Nathaniel laughed. "Hank said, 'Anyone strong enough to be doing what he was doing last night was strong enough to go home.' I didn't ask for specifics, but Simon was blushing a beautiful shade of pink."

Adam couldn't help but grin. "I guess this hotel is liable to be Noah's home after all. Come on, let's go get him."

THE next morning, Adam quietly crept into Noah's room after Simon had left to start his day. He stood staring down at his sleeping brother for a long time. Noah's color was back to normal, and he was moving a lot easier. They had been lucky.

'It's time to end this.' Adam returned to his room, grabbed his hat and his shotgun, and pulled on his coat. When he opened his door, Noah was standing in the hall, pants and boots on, buttoning his shirt. Adam mouth tightened, but he didn't say anything. Nathaniel fell into step with them as they crossed the lobby. This was familiar. This was what they knew.

The brothers stepped outside into the sunlight. Luke, Jamison, Simon, Hank, Walter, and Randy were standing on the porch. Adam immediately held out his hand as if to push them away. "I appreciate you guys trying to stop us, but this has got to be done. We might have stayed on here and tried to put revenge behind us, but when he hurt Noah, he ended that option."

Simon smiled wryly. "You misunderstand. We aren't here to stop you. We're here to go with you."

Adam traded a confused look with Nathaniel.

"No one hurts one of our own," Luke explained.

Nathaniel's face flushed at Luke's possessive declaration. His eyes searched out Adam's. His own doubt and confusion was mirrored there along with something else...hope. Maybe they had finally found a place they belonged.

"Let's get going, then. The day isn't going to wait on us," Hank reminded them.

Adam looked at Randy and started to protest her presence. He stopped when he remembered her shooting skill.

THE group approached the ranch slowly, scanning the area for any signs of life. Walter had posted lookouts, so Elias and his men couldn't have cleared out after they ambushed Noah. Adam glanced at Walter who made several hand gestures. The group split apart to approach from different directions.

Whoever said that time slows down when something bad begins to happen has never been in a gun fight. One moment, Adam was scanning the abandoned looking buildings for signs of life and the next he was in the middle of a barrage of bullets. Simultaneously, close to twenty men appeared from around buildings and in windows.

The group from Justice scattered, each focusing on a different area. Men on both sides were screaming and calling warnings and instructions to each other. Adam shot a man off the roof of the barn. Before the body even hit the ground, he was distracted by the sight of an older, well-dressed man disappearing into the barn. Elias! Older than he remembered, but undeniably the same man.

Noah, Nathaniel and Luke were holding their own with a group of men holed up in the main house. Hank, Walter and Randy were circling in from the back of the property, causing Elias's men to retreat towards the house. Walter and Simon checked the out buildings one by one as the others kept the men in the house occupied. They found several dead men, a printing press with phony deeds and documents, and lots of guns.

There was a break in the shooting and then several shouts as the remaining men fled from the side of the house towards the horses tethered by the pump. Hank and Walter took off after the fleeing men. Walter had enough evidence to put them all in jail if not hang them.

Adam pushed Elias hard, knocking the older man to the ground. "Not so fucking tough now that you aren't picking on unarmed people in the wilderness, are you? Your cronies were really fucking loyal when the chips were down. Now what? Are your balls big enough to fight me fair? Pistols at 20 paces?"

Hearing their brother's voice, Noah and Nathaniel ran towards the barn. Luke, Simon and Randy followed, not knowing how many men Adam faced. Entering the barn yard from various directions, they froze, watching the drama playing out like a stage show.

Elias continued to scuttle backwards like a crab. Adam stopped him with a boot to his chest, dropping a gun in the dust by his hand. "Pick it up," he ordered.

Elias shook his head, his eyes wide with fear. "No... no, I won't fight you."

"Pick it up, you coward!" Adam yelled, cocking his gun and placing the barrel against Elias's forehead. "I'll shoot you where you lay."

Elias shook his head again. "No, you won't. You won't shoot an unarmed man. That would make you just like me."

Everyone held their breath at the insult. Adam's finger tightened on the trigger. He stared at the quivering man for a long minute, before turning on his boot heel and heading towards the rope on his saddle. "You aren't worth the bullet. The sheriff can waste his rope hanging you."

Everyone released a collective sigh. Time skewed violently as Luke watched Elias pull a gun from his boot. Nathaniel lunged towards him, but he was too far away to get there in time. Luke yelled, "Adam!"

Adam stiffened and started to turn when the gun went off.

Chapter Eight

TURNING completely around, Adam watched Elias fall forwards, a dark stain quickly saturating the ground under him. Dale stood at the edge of the trees with a smoking gun in his hand. Adam's eyes were glued to the man on the ground who had caused so much pain in his life. It was over… completely over. A part of him felt so empty.

Adam raised his eyes and started towards his lover, still not really sure what his eyes were seeing. "Dale?"

"You almost got yourself fucking killed. I should shoot you myself. Damn fool!" Dale stomped towards Adam and pulled him into a tight embrace.

The action released the invisible hold that had been keeping everyone still and silent. All of a sudden, everyone was rushing towards the pair and talking over each other.

Adam pulled back and looked at Dale with disbelief on his face. "You shot him."

"Hell yes, I shot him! He was about to shoot you in the back!" Randy hugged her brother tightly from behind. Dale looked over his shoulder, startled. "Randy! You let Randy come and not me!"

"Well..." Adam stuttered. "Have you ever seen her with a gun?"

"Who in the fuck do you think taught her?" Dale asked with incredulity.

Adam looked at Randy, and she nodded her head slightly. Cupping Dale's face in both hands, he stared straight into the blue eyes. "I'm sorry for underestimating you. I'll never do it again. You saved my life."

"Damn right, you won't. I'm not letting you out of my sight. Can't be trusted not to go off and get yourself shot. Then where would I be? Love of my life six feet under...oh no...."

Adam shut him up with a kiss.

Dale closed his eyes as he fit his body to the other man's firm contours. Adam forcefully attacked Dale's pliant lips, opening, tasting, teasing slightly with his tongue before forcing his way inside to plunder. His hands came up to hold the other man tight, even as Dale's knees buckled slightly, a low moan reverberating in his throat.

"Am I really the love of your life?" Adam asked when they came up for air.

"Huh?" Dale mumbled dazedly before pulling Adam's head down for another kiss.

Everyone discreetly turned away from the couple with sappy grins on their faces.

Jamison appeared from around the side of the barn leading eight horses on a makeshift lead-line. "'Bout time," he grinned, looking at Adam and Dale. "Guess our Rose still holds the title for 'Most Stubborn Man on Earth'."

Luke agreed while Simon helped him tie Elias over one of his own horses. "Any trouble?" Luke asked his lover, pulling him close for a kiss.

"Nope. I rounded them up and kept them just inside the tree line. You should have seen the looks on the faces of the men who came looking for them. It's hard to outrun the law on foot," he laughed.

Luke mounted Tanner and held out his hand to help his lover up behind him. Jamison quickly wrapped his arms tightly around Luke's middle and pressed his face against the broad back. Stretching up, he feathered soft kisses just above Luke's collar, making the older man shiver.

"Hey, no fair! You guys are fooling around without me again," Nathaniel complained.

"Get used to it," Luke shot back with a smile. "I may be generous enough to share occasionally, but he'll always be mine." Jamison laughed and squeezed Luke harder, dropping one of his hands discreetly into Luke's lap to squeeze the bulge between his legs.

"And this will always be just mine," he whispered. Luke growled, placed his hand over Jamie's and pushed it harder into his growing erection.

Nathaniel pretended to be thinking very hard about something. "Well, I guess if that this best offer I'm going to get..."

Luke laughed and kicked Tanner into a gallop. "And it's considerably better than you deserve," he shouted over his shoulder. "Last one to the saloon, buys!"

Nathaniel swore as Noah, Simon and Randy raced by him already on their horses. Turning, he saw Adam and Dale devouring each other's mouths and realized that they weren't moving anytime soon, and then only to find the nearest bed. "God damnit! Last again!" Opening Adam's saddle bag, he grabbed a handful of coins before mounting his own horse and following the dust trail back to town.

ADAM pulled back from the kiss, framing Dale's face with his hands and caressing the soft skin. "You never give up, do you?"

Dale shook his head silently.

"Thank God," Adam murmured against Dale's lips before claiming them in another kiss.

Dale surrendered himself to the kiss, pressing himself as close to the taller man as he could, eventually winding his leg around one of Adam's and throwing them off balance.

Adam broke the kiss to keep them from falling and laughed as he clutched his lover to him. "You can't climb me like a tree. I don't have any roots to keep us anchored."

Dale gaped at him. "I've never heard you laugh."

Adam grinned at him and chuckled again. "I guess I don't laugh much. We better work on that." He bent to nuzzle Dale's neck eliciting a sigh.

"We?"

Adam looked seriously into Dale's eyes. If he hadn't seen how tenaciously Dale pursued him, he might have been worried. "Yeah, we. As in you and me... lots of laughter... lots of lovin'... for a really long time. Maybe if I put down some roots, you won't be able to knock me over so easily."

This time, Dale laughed. "I kind of like you off balance. You're cute when you're flustered." Head thrown back, sunlight glinting in the copper strands, blue eyes sparkling, Adam thought he was the most gorgeous sight on earth.

Adam scowled, but couldn't hold it past a few seconds. "So fluster me," he challenged.

"Gladly." Dale wound his arms around Adam's neck and placed a tender kiss on his chin. "Take me home, Adam. I want you to make love to me in a bed."

Adam growled and swung Dale up off the ground in a fierce embrace. "Where's your horse?"

Dale nodded to a big bay tethered to the fence. They retrieved Dale's horse and then moved towards Sampson, not wanting to lose contact even for a moment. As soon as both men were mounted, Dale reached over and grabbed Adam's hand again. They headed towards Justice at a slow walk, hands joined and legs brushing as their mounts moved.

"I'm beginning to see why Jamison and Luke ride together," Dale mused, impatient with the pace.

Reading his mind, Adam suggested, "You could come ride behind me. Sampson could carry us both." Sampson nickered and threw his head either in agreement or protest, but the desire of the two men to be closer made it a moot point.

Dale swung from his saddle to settle behind Adam, immediately imitating Jamison by wrapping his arms around Adam's middle and laying his cheek against the muscled back. Adam wrapped the reins of Dale's horse around his saddle horn and rested his free hand on Dale's thigh.

Glancing over his shoulder, he instructed. "Hang on." Quickly, he urged the horse up to a smooth canter.

In no time, they were entering Justice. Adam slowed Sampson to a walk and tensed when he saw Randy waiting for them in front of the house.

"Relax," Dale whispered next to his ear, stroking his chest soothingly. "She's just here for the horses." Sure enough, Randy grabbed the reins as they were dismounting and left without a word.

"I didn't know she could be so quiet," Adam stated, staring after the blonde as she swung up on the bay's back.

Dale smiled warmly at the retreating woman. "She has her moments, but I really am not in the mood to discuss my sister, no matter how wonderful she may be." Sliding his hand down Adam's back, he grabbed a handful of firm ass and squeezed.

Adam turned towards him and growled, the look in his eyes matching the predatory noise.

Dale's eyes grew wide, and he headed for the house at a run, Adam on his heels. The chase continued into the house, up the stairs and into Dale's bedroom. Dale stopped, but Adam's momentum carried them onto the bed with Adam on top, pinning Dale to the quilt.

Dale moaned as Adam's weight settled between his legs. Grasping the brim of Adam's hat, he sent it sailing toward a chair. "You have too many clothes on, cowboy."

"So do you." Adam's lips tasted the skin of Dale's neck as he unbuttoned his shirt. Boots were tugged off and clothes flew in every direction until both men were bare.

"You're beautiful," Adam whispered reverently, unable to drag his eyes away.

Dale pulled his lover to him. "I'm the lucky one." He brushed a hand through the thick hair on Adam's chest, his thumb grazing a nipple.

Adam gasped and arched into the touch. "God, what you do to me!"

"Tell me," Dale requested, his mouth replacing his hand on Adam's chest.

"Whenever you're close, my heart threatens to beat itself out of my chest. I can't think straight, and all I want to do is pin you to the closest wall and sink so deep into your body we'll never be separate again."

"Mmmm... sounds good to me," Dale murmured, teeth clamping down on the raised nub.

"Fuck!" Adam ground his pelvis hard into the valley of Dale's thighs.

"Oh yes... do that again," Dale ordered, winding his fingers into Adam's dark hair and pulling his face lower for a kiss.

Adam held back, only allow brief teasing brushes of their lips. "What? This?" he asked coyly as he ground again and again into the sensitive organs trapped between their bodies.

"Oh fuck… yeah… just… like… that…." Dale panted, his eyes squeezed shut and his face contorted with ecstasy.

"I want more," Adam whispered. "I want to be inside you."

Dale opened his eyes, focusing his clear blue gaze on his lover. "I told you my requirements for sharing my body. Are you ready for that?"

Adam put all of his love in his eyes as he looked down at the tousled man beneath him. "I've never been so sure of anything in my life. I don't do much well, but I know how to love. I've just never done it with anyone outside my family. I want to try with you."

Dale's eyes filled with tears as Adam spoke. "You'll do just fine," he promised. "And if you mess up, I'll whoop your ass." Dale's beatific smile canceled out his threat.

"You could try."

Dale pushed at Adam's shoulder only to find his hands firmly captured and held above his head by one strong hand. His body reacted instinctively, arching up his lover with a whimper. "Oh fuck, Adam. Need you to fuck me… *now!*"

Adam groaned at the wanton request. "We need…" Before he could even finish the request, Dale was nodding towards the table beside the bed.

"A boy can hope." He blushed a beautiful shade of red as Adam quirked an eyebrow at him.

Releasing the captured hands, he gave Dale a stern look. "Keep them there or I'll get some rope."

Dale moaned and wriggled against the hard body pinning him. Adam eased back and moved a slick finger between the creamy white cheeks of Dale's ass. As soon as he pushed against the tight opening, he felt it relax to receive him. Slowly, he entered the volcanic heat, twisting and stroking the smooth walls until Dale's curses and pleading turned to incoherent mewls.

"Ready for me, baby?" Adam asked.

Dale pushed into Adam's hand, sinking the fingers deeper. "Since the night I met you."

Adam smirked. 'A smartass to the end. I'm never going to be bored.' Coating his cock with oil, he positioned himself against the glistening opening, watching as the broad head pressed against the pink flesh.

"You've got three seconds before I flip you over and ride you," Dale growled.

Adam plunged deep in one long, sure stroke. Dale cried out, wrapping his legs around the thrusting hips and tilting his hips to pull him deeper.

Adam's pace was frantic. He couldn't get deep enough... close enough. His hands clutched desperately.

"So close..." Dale panted. "Touch me."

Adam complied, closing a rough hand around Dale's cock and stroking the slippery fluid leaking from the tip to the base.

"Oh yeah... more... Adam!" Dale screamed as his climax covered Adam's chest, wayward drops clinging to his cheek.

Dale moved his hands, hooking Adam's neck and pulling him down for a kiss, licking his seed from the stubbled chin before plunging his tongue into his lover's mouth.

Adam's body stiffened and shuddered as he pumped his come into Dale's body. "Dale! I... oh...." Boneless, he collapsed onto his partner.

Dale placed a kiss on the top of his head as he pulled him tight. "I know."

NATHANIEL sat at the bar staring into his glass of whiskey. It was over. It felt strangely anti-climatic. He had been very young when his parents were killed. He didn't have the good memories that had driven Adam and Noah, merely vague feelings. His anger had been based on their anger ... anger that in the last month had diminished as their love for their partners grew.

Adam and Dale had never even made an appearance at the saloon, not that Nathaniel had actually expected to see them. The look in Adam's eyes had left little doubt about what they were doing. Noah and Simon had drunk, laughed and even danced a little before Noah had grabbed Simon and playfully dragged him off towards the hotel.

Nathaniel swirled the amber liquid in the bottom of his glass. Where did he fit in now? He glanced over at Jamison sitting on Luke's lap, unconsciously running his fingers through the blond's hair while they talked to Walter and Hank. He was welcome there, but he wasn't fooling himself that they belonged to him. The sex was great, but it didn't feel like enough anymore.

Nathaniel looked over as a tall man claimed the seat beside him. He was turned away, signaling for a drink. Incredibly broad shoulders stretched the cotton of his shirt tight as his arms moved. Nathaniel's eyes skimmed down to narrow hips and a mouthwatering ass.

The stranger turned suddenly, and Nathaniel was caught staring directly at his crotch, his tongue in the process of wetting his lips. 'Damn!' Not one non-embarrassing option came to mind, so Nathaniel raised his eyes with a sheepish grin. "Sorry," he shrugged.

Laughter danced in the large dark eyes looking down at him. "Maybe you better buy me a drink before you look at me like that?"

Nathaniel smiled. He liked a man with a little attitude. He flipped a coin to Phillip to pay for the man's whiskey. "Be happy to. Probably should know your name, too." Deciding to push his luck, he added, "Give me a chance to practice it before I scream it out in bed tonight."

The dark eyes narrowed in consideration. "Eric."

"Well, Eric, I'm Nate. Welcome to Justice."

"Thanks. A welcome like that makes a man feel like he's found a home."

Rhianne Aile lives with her husband and four children on forty acres of long leaf pine forest in North Florida, writing, playing with her kids and taking long walks with her four dogs while working out story ideas. She has an unhealthy relationship with her computer, iced tea and chocolate.

Growing up, she split her time between Oklahoma and Chicago, making her equally fond of horses, skyscrapers, cowboys and men in well tailored suits. Facilitating retreats for women and authors keeps her traveling enough to stay happy.

Visit Rhianne's website for regularly posted free fiction.

www.rhianneaile.com

Printed in the United Kingdom
by Lightning Source UK Ltd.
131746UK00001B/169/A